MMP

MICAH MEMORY
○ PUBLISHING ○

The First

a story by Nathan Grushon

THE FIRST is a work of fiction. None of this really happened. All names, characters, places and stories were made up by the author or are used fictitiously. Any resemblance to actual events or locales or persons, living or dead, is entirely coincidental.

For information address Micah Memory Publishing, 321 Biltmore Road, Louisville, KY, 40207.

For information about purchases contact 502-724-3642 or visit www.micahmemorypublishing.com.

Cover Designed by Joel Ward

Edited by Kimberly Crum

Printed in the United States of America

9 8 7 6 5 4 3 2 1

ISBN: 0091444604
ISBN-13: 978-0-9914446-0-1
Library of Congress Control Number: 2014901351

There are always a lot of firsts when a child leaves home . . .

CONTENTS

Chapter 1

Our History

The elect had voted and the scientist Dafur had won the debate. A lottery would decide which citizens would survive and which citizens would be left behind on their dying planet.

When Dafur originally came up with the idea of a lottery, some of the elite opposed his strategy. But theirs had always been a fair society. For Dafur, the lottery was the *only* way.

Certain standards were required for a citizen to be eligible for the lottery. A citizen needed to be between the stages of 700 and 5000 trutons. They had to be fit, with no history of the black, and they had to have a replication factor of at least plus nine. Most citizens were eligible for the lottery. The student was not one of them.

Of those opposing the lottery, Wickem was the most powerful. Having greater influence than Dafur, Wickem was adored by both the privileged and the challenged. He was a great citizen, with great pedigree. Committing his life to the citizens of Cythera, Wickem felt it was his *calling* to serve society (like his father before him) and he believed citizens with the most influence would have the best chance of survival. Only a limited number of citizens would be able to complete the journey to their new home. Every one agreed survival would be difficult for the first few generations. Wickem believed survival would require healthy citizens able to influence their new surroundings. He felt only those with the highest probability for success should be selected.

Dafur believed the randomness of selection would assure all classes of citizens would be represented on the new home. Dafur hoped the new Cythera would rise as a reflection of their current society.

Wickem was less concerned about representation, and more concerned with how fast they could adapt to their new home. He believed their ability to advance society would be the key to their survival. Yes, some classes and races would become extinct, and Wickem agreed this was unfortunate. But he felt this was the only way to assure the future survival of the whole.

Early in the debate Wickem's plan for survival was better received than Dafur's. Then he was asked to name an ideal candidate for rebuilding civilization and everything changed. It was the one question Wickem had not prepared for, and naming his son Tatalc would be his greatest mistake.

From a young age Tatalc was destined to follow in his father's footsteps, to be a *great one*. By his fifteenth cycle Wickem's son had the social influence, measured in Trutons, of an average adult. Trutons were created by the ancient prophet Steffer to award citizens for good deeds. Trutons also represent the amount of influence a citizen has within society. Although one can never lose their trutons, if their actions are deemed

2

unacceptable, this can still negatively impact their influence. Tatalc learned this the hard way.

During his seventeenth cycle, Tatalc revealed his personal interests. While there were mixed feelings from those who knew him, it was Tatalc's future actions that society deemed unacceptable. Tatalc's mistake was not that he openly displayed his interests. His mistake was that he tried to persuade a boy. Even though the boy was near maturity, this was not acceptable.

Tatalc's mistake was only part of the reason the elect opposed Wickem's recommendation. In the end, many citizens believed if Wickem had not named Tatalc, Wickem would have won the debate.

How this would have changed the course of our history, one can only guess.

Chapter 2

The Discovery

The Rugal was found during an early age by a band of Transients. A man named Rual led the Transient group. Rual was a muscular man with a bald head and bushy eyebrows. He would have been a *great one* under different circumstances; unfortunately Rual had been born a Transient.

Due to their isolation from the elite, the Transients had created their own culture and traditions. One hundred and fifty families, inclusive of several generations, made up Rual's followers. A large band was difficult to manage, but the privileges made it worthwhile. One of those privileges was teaching the young boys how to become men. Rual was leading a small group of boys, many of whom were on their first great adventure. The purpose of their voyage was nothing more than knowledge and exploration, but the eventual outcome would change the way *all* citizens viewed Cythera's existence.

They were moving through a series of caves that had a reputation for danger. The darkness was damp and frightening. Barrie, already with 500 trutons, was a leader among the boys. He was the tallest of the boys. His curly hair was long, and light stubble peppered his face. His youthful features were fading as he neared manhood. Rual respected Barrie and encouraged the adventure Barrie sought. Rual let Barrie lead, and fearing no challenge, Barrie led the small group towards the Feber.

The Feber was a known site all wished to see, but few had the courage to visit. No citizen knew how the Feber captured its light, but this is exactly what it did. Deep within the darkness of the caves was a small pool of water about the size of a trunk hold. In the depth of the pool was a great light. Shining and reflecting throughout the cavern, the light was grand.

As was the tradition for any who viewed the Feber, the boys prepared to etch their name on the wall of the cavern as proof they had seen the light. It was by error that Barrie made the great discovery.

After carving his name in the wall of the cavern, Barrie started to belt his etch. Snagging on its sheath, the etch slipped out of his hands and dropped to the ground. As Barrie reached to pick up his etch, he stepped forward onto a wet rock, his foot slid on the slick surface, and he fell. Barrie looked across the cavern and noticed a subtle difference in the rock formations on the other side of the pool. Something stood out, something he had never noticed before.

Barrie was one of the few in the group who had been to see the Feber; yet he had never noticed this rock. There was something about the angle of where he fell that brought the image of the rock into view. Barrie started to get up, and the rock began to blur. He moved back to his original spot and he could see it again. Sitting still for a moment he studied the location of the rock in relation to the cavern.

Camouflaged by its surroundings, the rock's color and texture matched the cavern wall. Because of its large size, it blended into the environment. The shape of the rock was different than any he had ever seen. It was perfectly shaped. It was a perfect sphere.

Thinking he had the sphere's position, Barrie started to raise himself off the ground. His view of the rock began to blur. Lowering himself, the rock came back into view. Doing this several times, Barrie wondered how much he trusted himself to relocate the sphere if he left his position. Becoming less and less confident he would be able to find it again he yelled to Rual.

"I need your help." Barrie asked Rual to walk over to the side of the cavern next to where the rock sphere was. "Trust me, I'll explain in a moment." Barrie guided Rual, "Move a little to the left, more, more, there. Do you see it Rual?"

"See what?" Rual responded.

"Reach out. You're right next to it." Rual extended his hand and touched the sphere. "There, you have it. You have it. Stay right there." Barrie began to get up. Realizing he would lose his view if he left his position, Barrie paused, "Rual, wait and don't move. Shotum come here." Shotum was an ordinary boy; there was nothing special about him other than he was the closest boy to Barrie.

"Shotum, lay down next to me," instructed Barrie. "Come down to my level," Barrie pointed towards the sphere, "Can you see it?" Shotum nodded. "Shotum stay here and don't lose view of the sphere until I find it with Rual, understand?"

"Yes."

Feeling safe enough to leave his spot, Barrie reached over and picked up his etch. Lifting himself off the ground, he stood and ran around the glowing pool to join Rual by the rock sphere. As Barrie ran towards the sphere he was amazed by how it was no longer visible. From the moment he left his spot on the other side of the pool he had been staring at Rual, but had yet to see the sphere. He knew it was there, but he couldn't see it. He reached Rual and put his hand on the rock next to his mentor's hand.

"Shotum is this it?" Barrie yelled across the cavern.

"That's it Barrie."

Rual still didn't know what Barrie was doing, "What's *it* Barrie? What's going on?" Rual was an even-tempered man. His tone was soft, but he was starting to get impatient with Barrie's behavior. It was not unlike Barrie to be curious when they were on an adventure, but Rual didn't know what Barrie was up to and his antics were starting to gain the attention of some of the other Transient boys.

There were eleven boys in the group, most on their first visit to see the Feber. The caves often created fear in a first time visitor, and Rual was becoming concerned Barrie's odd behavior might frighten the other boys. Even worse, Rual had suspicions Barrie might be trying to scare the boys on purpose.

Barrie started feeling around the rock, from side-to-side, and then from top to bottom. Watching his hand move across the surface of the rock, Barrie said, "I can feel it start to curve in about here, but it doesn't look like my hand is curving in." Barrie looked at Rual. "From there, where Shotum is, this rock looks like a perfect sphere, but here it feels flat."

"Shotum," Rual yelled. "Shotum, what do you see from over there? What shape is the rock my hand's on?"

Shotum shouted back, "Circle, a sphere. It's round like a ball."

"Stay there. I want to see." Rual looked back at Barrie. "Barrie stay here. I need to see what you're talking about." Rual walked around the glowing pool towards Shotum. By now every young boy was focusing on the conversation between Rual, Barrie, and Shotum.

Rual lay down next to Shotum and asked, "How do I see it?"

"Come down a little lower and look towards Barrie. It's a perfectly shaped sphere, you can't miss it." Shotum pointed towards Barrie. "Do you see it?" Shotum asked Rual.

"Rual!" Barrie yelled from across the cavern. "Do you see it? Do you see what I'm talking about now?"

"I see it!"

Chapter 3

Wickem's Story - Part I

When Wickem had been nominated to chair the Federal Safety Commission, he proudly accepted. Now in his third term, his responsibilities had changed a lot since the post began. As a career politician Wickem had faced many challenges, challenges he always overcame while creating a strong legacy for himself. Throughout his career Wickem resolved many important issues and achieved the highest standing in Cytheran politics, other than Chief of State.

Wickem's contributions to Cytheran society were unmatched by any politician in recent history, including his own father. After a long career of service and sacrifice, Wickem desired a position where he could stay involved without the intense pressure of the highly visible offices he had previously been appointed to lead. His nomination to chair the Federal Safety Commission was the perfect position. It was an honorable acknowledgement for his lifetime of dedicated service and a gracious opportunity for him to stay involved.

Cythera was a peaceful civilization with few internal conflicts. Cytherans were safe and happy, making the work simple for the Federal Safety Commissioner. Even though the role was easily manageable for Wickem, *and* below his abilities, the position did have its advantages. Most notably, the position reported directly to The Chief of State. This assured Wickem a place at the table for all critical matters and discussions. At this stage in his career, that was enough.

But all of this changed when Wickem learned about the Rugal.

Many generations had passed since the Rugal had been found and decoded. Over time, most citizens had lost interest in it's message. Life was good for most Cytherans and it had become unpopular to believe in ancient religions and prophecies. But when Wickem learned of the Rugal, he took it upon himself to publicize it's warning. He was the first of the modern era to fully understand the impact of the prophecy.

Where there had never been a need for a strong leader

to head the Federal Safety Commission, all of Cythera was fortunate to have someone of Wickem's ability, during what would be the direst time in the history of their civilization. Even though Wickem had not anticipated such a challenge when he accepted the position as chair of the Federal Safety Commission, he responded to his calling.

But bringing attention to the Rugal prophecy was another challenge Wickem would have to overcome. The Chief of State's initial reaction was to avoid telling citizens the *complete* truth. The Chief feared the public would panic and turn their backs on him. His official statement was that the situation was not as bad as it sounded and a solution would be found. After The Chief of State made his announcement, the general lack of confidence in his overall abilities, combined with the reality Cythera faced, did nothing to ease the concerns of the citizens.

Citizens wanted answers, honest answers that The Chief of State deemed too devastating to share. Wickem disagreed with this strategy and against direct orders he went public with the *full* truth. Cythera was going to die and if they did not find a solution they would all die too. Maybe it was Wickem's approach to the topic, or the fact he was respected by so many, but citizens didn't respond with widespread panic as The Chief of State had expected.

Wickem's message was simple and direct. Their sun was growing; it had been growing since the beginning of time. And as their sun grew, it created more energy and heat. The size of their sun would soon reach a point where the energy and heat would become too dangerous for life to exist on Cythera. Wickem could not tell citizens when this would happen, but it would happen soon, and the irreversible damage had already begun. Wickem could not tell them their ultimate fate. Most likely, Cythera would become uninhabitable. What Wickem could tell them was there was still time to find a solution, not much, but maybe enough.

They were a strong and intelligent civilization. Wickem knew, if they worked together, they could come up with alternatives that might protect their civilization from extinction. Wickem wasn't sure what those alternatives were, but there was hope, and there always would be hope until the last Cytheran took their final breath.

After Wickem shared the news of the Rugal, the response from citizens was what he expected. Citizens were scared and shocked but understood the truth. They understood their only chance at survival was to work in unison. The Chief of State backed down from his stance that citizens couldn't deal with the harsh truth and allowed Wickem full autonomy in leading a coalition addressing Cythera's survival.

The greatest minds across Cythera began working on solutions. The civil engineers wanted to take advantage of cities' vast underground networks and move citizens beneath the surface. Terraforming engineers proposed the rerouting of rivers and other water masses to cool the planet. It was structural designers who submitted the idea to build biodomes over all major cities. Even citizens without formal educations were submitting ideas.

Wickem's office was overwhelmed, but he remained steadfast and focused on his great responsibility. For the first several cycles, Wickem felt confident about the resolve of his citizens. They would find a solution to the Rugal crisis; he was sure of it.

But this high level of collaboration would only last for so long. Even the most advanced societies become caught up in the here and now. They lose focus on what should be most important to them. They fragment and begin taking sides. Cooperation fades and the power struggle begins.

Chapter 4

Dafur's Story

Dafur's plan for saving Cythera had been accepted; he had won the debate. He knew his *was* the best way to save civilization. The *only* way to save civilization.

As he walked home from the debate, Dafur reminisced about everything that had led up to this moment. He felt sorry for Wickem. Not because he had lost the debate, but because of the *way* he lost the debate. Wickem was a good man. They were not adversaries. If Dafur had an adversary, it would be Cythera's sun.

Dafur's way home led him through the campus of the university where he was a professor. He passed the science building where his office and laboratory were located. He felt the urge to go into his lab and work, there was so much more work to be done, but he resisted the temptation and continued towards home.

Turning a corner, Dafur came upon the auditorium where he had given so many lectures. Dafur stopped and looked at the regal entrance, recalling how nervous he was the first time he spoke about his theories on flare surfing. So much had happened since that first lecture. So much had changed.

Continuing down the street, Dafur thought about everyone who had helped get to this point. His loyal assistant

Rigby, Tatalc, and even Wickem; they all contributed to the effort. But the most important contribution came from the one who gave him the confidence and courage to keep moving forward - his wife Lij.

Ahead, Dafur could see the white columns that made up the façade of the home he lived in across the street from the university. He was exhausted and glad to be home.

Meeting him at the door, Lij kissed him. "I've already heard. I'm so proud of you!"

Dafur returned a soft grin and embraced her. Her body was warm and comfortable. Dafur loved to hug his wife. When he put his arms around her, she fit into his body. She belonged next to him.

"You smell nice, did you take a bath?" Dafur asked Lij.

"I did. It was the only way I could relax." Lij looked up into Dafur's eyes. "I was so nervous for you. But you did it. You won the debate." She grabbed his hand and looked into his eyes. "Come with me."

"Lij. Lij. I'm so tired." Lij grabbed Dafur by the hand and led him. His desire for her drowned his exhaustion, and he followed.

When they entered the bedroom Lij let her robe slide off her body. She reached over to Dafur and touched him. They kissed and then Lij lay down on the bed. Her head fell backwards. Her auburn hair exploded into a soft padded pillow for her perfectly shaped head to rest on. "Dafur I'm so proud of you. You did what was right. No matter what happens to *us* you've secured the future of Cythera. I couldn't be prouder or more in love with you than I am right now."

***

"I'm going to go outside and get some fresh air." Lij stood up from the bed, put her robe back on and walked out to their private balcony braced by the large white columns at the front of their home.

Dafur followed Lij outside. "It's nice out. Hot, but nice." He wrapped one hand around Lij's waist, and with his other hand he pointed to the sky, "It's out there, in that direction. On a clearer night we could see it. Cythera's next home."

"How did Wickem react to the vote?"

***

The debate was a public story and Lij was as curious as every other citizen. Too nervous to attend, Lij wanted to know the details. She felt her closeness to Dafur granted her the right to a first hand account of the event. Husbands and wives were to share their deepest thoughts and secrets with each other. This was a privilege of marriage.

Dafur and Lij had only been married for a few telths, but the depth of their love was that of a mature marriage. Dafur had always been a traditional romantic. He had loved once before, but tragedy had stolen her from him. Dafur's hope for love had never died. He always remained optimistic that a soul existed out there somewhere, patiently waiting for their paths to cross.

Dafur and Lij met while he was giving his first lecture about his theories on the mechanics needed for flare surfing. Lij had known of Dafur's work from her own studies, and she was anticipating the opportunity to hear him speak. Ever since Wickem had brought attention to the crisis, the educated and common alike were anxious to attach themselves to a solution that might save Cythera. A large crowd had attended the event. It was by chance Lij and Dafur met.

Dafur was not a good orator. He knew his facts but struggled to inspire others with his words: ". . . data concerning random propulsions has proven difficult to align. But this is purely the fault of our own limitations and the limitations of our various states of measurements and mathematics. Herein lies the problem. The challenge is not in discovering the pattern and rhythm of solar flares. The challenge is in discovering an accurate and consistent way to measure and predict future frequency. I'll need a volunteer for this." Dafur moved from his podium to the front of the stage where he could better see his audience. His eyes moved across the crowd. Captured by her glow, Dafur asked, "You. Young lady. Would you mind joining me on the stage?"

Lij blushed. Everyone was looking at her.

"Don't be scared. I won't hurt you." Everyone laughed.

Standing up, Lij walked towards the stage. There was a delicateness to her nature. She was a petite woman with broad shoulders and long auburn hair. Her beauty was natural, a gift. As she approached the stage Dafur looked into her eyes and immediately felt desire. It was a moment and feeling he was uncomfortable with, especially while trying to lecture.

Dafur asked her, "What's your name?"

"Lij."

"Lij." Dafur looked back to the audience, "Lij. Thank you for helping with this demonstration. Everyone, thank Lij." The audience applauded.

Dafur reached out and took Lij's hand. He had not intended to hold the hand of his subject, but he wanted to touch her and find out if the warmth from her eyes also radiated from her flesh. "Tell the audience what cycle you're in."

Lij blushed again. Then with an elegant confidence and a sweet smile she replied, "Don't you know it's impolite to ask a lady her cycle?"

Now it was Dafur who blushed. "But this is in the name of science," he replied.

Lij found the professor to be sweet, not handsome, but sweet. "In that case, I will tell you I'm in my twenty seventh cycle."

"Twenty seven cycles." Dafur was a little lost for words. Based on her appearance he would have guessed a lower number. "Twenty seven cycles then. How many trutons have you acquired?"

"Nine-hundred and fifty. But my goal is to be over 1000 by my next cycle. If I have one."

"And what's your replication factor?"

"My replication factor? That's also rather personal, don't you think?" The audience laughed again. It *was* a personal question, but citizens generally knew the replication factor of others. "I'm a plus twelve."

"Thank you Lij. You can be seated if you like. You are a *perfect* subject."

Still holding her hand, Dafur embraced her (which he never did with his volunteers). From the view of the audience it was nothing more than a friendly gesture, a light hug. Turning to his board, Dafur wrote the numbers 27, 950 and 12. Resuming his lecture, "As we learned from our kind subject she is in her twenty-seventh cycle, she has earned 950 trutons and her replication factor is plus 12. That *is* a lot of numbers!" Dafur expected a laugh from the audience. He didn't get one. "So I ask, how mature is she?" It was a simple question that did not have a real answer.

"Herein lies the problem with the way we measure things. We have too many variables. All of these measurements tell us something, but what do they tell us? How many unique mathematical principles does it take to reach the same conclusion?

"This problem not only exists in simple measurements, like a citizen's maturity. These same *messy* rules apply to our physics. If we wanted to measure the distance from Cythera to the next planet, the results vary based on the math used. While some have strongly argued that multiple disciplines allow for broader solutions, I disagree. I think it's *messy*."

Messy was an informal word that Dafur intentionally chose to convey his point on the fragmented state of Cytheran mathematics.

"Messy math. This is our problem and our limitation, when it comes to measuring solar activity. This lack of consistency prevents us from making accurate predictions on projecting the timing and mass of solar flares. It is imperative that we unify mathematical models to create a new standard form of measurement."

Dafur walked to his board and erased the numbers. The light in the room dimmed, and a close up image of the surface of their sun was projected on the board. "Here is a view of the corona of our sun. In this picture you can see the trails of energy moving over our sun's surface. Solar flares are caused when the stored up magnetic energy erupts from the corona. This energy is massive, and travels well into the depths of our solar system. If we could better understand this energy, there's the potential we could harness the magnetism and ride its wave to the next planet. I call this *flare surfing*."

Dafur continued lecturing on the power of solar flares

and the importance of more unified mathematical standards. Despite Dafur's monotone voice and lack of natural presentation skills, the audience remained engaged. While the science was compelling enough to hold their attention, the audience was interested for a different reason. The man who stood before them may have found a way for them to leave Cythera before it was consumed by their sun.

Dafur was pleased with his reception, but he couldn't get Lij out of his mind.

Chapter 5

The Discovery

Staring across at the glowing Feber, Rual examined the strange sphere on the other side of the cavern. Only a few moments ago, he had been next to the sphere with his hand on its surface, denying its existence. Barrie stood by the sphere waiting for Rual's direction. *All* the young boys were waiting for Rual's direction. Finally, he spoke, "Barrie do you have your etch?"

"I do."

"Take your etch and try to mark on it."

Around Barrie's waste he wore a thick leather belt. All of the boys wore the belt; it was an important part of the Transient uniform. Hanging from the belt was Barrie's etch. A Transient's etch was always by his side and easily accessible for any immediate need. Serving many purposes, the etch was made of several metals and hardened ash. Barrie removed his etch from its sheath and raised it to the sphere. When he scratched the surface, the etch left a mark.

Barrie said, "I think it's working. I can see where I'm marking."

"Good. Keep doing it. I think I can start to see your markings. Tabor. Mistel. All of you go help Barrie. See if you can darken the whole sphere." The other boys ran over to the sphere and began marking the sphere with their etches.

From the ground Rual could no longer see the sphere; the boys were blocking his view. One by one, the boys began to back away from the sphere. As his view cleared, Rual began to see the marked sphere.

Lifting himself off the moist dirt floor of the cave, Rual could see the darkened sphere. As he stood, his leg cramped, reminding him of how long he had been lying on the ground in a fixed position. Approaching the sphere, Rual now had a clear view; it was easy to distinguish the round shape.

The sphere was bigger than it looked when viewed from the ground on the other side of the cavern. It was a taller than a full grown man and as wide as a stretchscape. Noticing that many of the boys had left their etches lying on the ground in front of the sphere Rual had another idea. "Barrie when you were marking on the sphere did you feel it move at all?"

Barrie reached over and pressed against the sphere to see if it would move, "I wasn't paying much attention. I don't think it did. Why?"

"I was thinking that since it's round we might be able to move it. Or somehow roll it."

"I hadn't thought of that but we might be able to, "said Barrie. "I don't know how we would."

Rual looked down at all the etches on the floor of the

cavern. "Why don't you take your etches and see if you can wedge them under the sphere. Let's see if it will give any."

Barrie was the first to start to force his etch under the sphere, the other boys followed. Within a few moments all eleven of them were working their etches beneath the sphere. "I think it's working. I can feel it start to move." Mistel shouted.

Shotum confirmed, "I can feel it moving too."

Barrie was pulling down on his etch as hard as he could. "Keep working it. See if we can get it to roll. I think we are moving it." The force of the entire weight of his body was beginning to bend his etch. All of the boys were working hard. Pushing, pulling and forcing their etches deeper and deeper under the bottom of the sphere. Several steps away Rual watched the sphere, keeping an eye out for any movement.

"Wait! I mean don't wait, keep pushing. It's starting to move some." Rual said. The sphere had begun to wobble.

"Rual come here and see if you can push it from the side."

Rual went to the side of the sphere and forced all his weight into the rock. It was working, the sphere was breaking loose. Taking a deep breath, Rual gave the sphere a massive push. It broke free and started to roll. Not wanting to be smashed by the rolling rock, the boys dropped their etches and got out of the way. Backing away they all stared in amazement that they were able to pry the rock sphere from its grounding.

The giant sphere was now rolling down towards the center of the cavern towards the pool of water and the Feber. They all stood with quiet interest watching the sphere turn over itself again and again. Anticipating what would happen next, time seemed to slow. With a loud splash, the sphere rolled into the shallow pool of water and towards the center where the great light of the Feber originated. Barrie was the first to realize what was about to happen. "It's going to hit the Feber! What have we done? It will . . ." Before Barrie finished his sentence the cavern began to darken. The light of the Feber was fading.

Rual yelled, "Everyone stay calm."

The cavern became darker and darker. Then with one more turn of the sphere, all went dark as the rock completely covered the Feber.

Chapter 6

Tatalc's Story

The morning following the debate Wickem woke up tired, like he had never slept. His plan had failed and he was disappointed and angry. He should have known better than to include his son Tatalc as one of the select. Wickem thought citizens would be more open-minded. He was wrong.

He honestly felt his son would be an asset on the new Cythera. Wickem did not understand why everyone reacted the way they did when he brought up Tatalc's name. It was true Tatalc was not interested in having relations with a woman, but not every citizen needed to procreate. There would be enough citizens to procreate. Growing the population on the new home was only one objective. The new Cythera needed leaders, visionaries who could appraise the new environment and successfully navigate through the obstacles and opportunities. Tatalc was such a visionary.

It would have been difficult for any citizen to doubt Tatalc's ability to lead. Even before the scandal, Tatalc had made a name for himself as a prominent social organizer, serving as chief advocate for several popular cultural assimilation movements. Tatalc's innate ability to stir the masses helped establish his reputation.

Tatalc was a gifted orator. With the rare ability to articulate his intricate thoughts in a way any citizen could understand. Special in a lot of ways, he masterfully understood multiple subjects at their most intense complexities; there was no subject beyond his level of comprehension. His ability to inspire an audience was unmatched; both the young and the old found themselves moved by his words.

Tatalc's most notable achievement occurred during his fifteenth cycle when he led a group of students in a revolt against the cost of higher education. Traditionally, higher education had been reserved for the elite. Wanting to provide more opportunity for the lesser classes, political leaders, including Wickem, pushed for a wider system of higher education. This was a noble proposition that most agreed could lead to a more advanced society. Implementing this plan would require financial assistance from the government to support both the students and the institutions of higher learning.

For a while, the plan achieved the goal of greater educational opportunities for the masses. As a result, more citizens participated in higher education and more institutions were being established.

But as the higher education framework matured, its value was diluted by schools more interested in financial gain than academic pursuits. Over time, institutions began increasing tuitions at higher and higher rates. The expense had become unreasonably high, and many citizens were beginning to question the value of higher education. When Tatalc started his own higher education, (this was before his father announced the Rugal crisis) it didn't take him long to recognize the disparity.

***

Tatalc walked into the cafeteria and was approached by another student. The student asked a simple question that would deeply impact Tatalc.

"Friend, do you have anything to spare so I can eat today?"

Tatalc noticed the young man wearing a satchel weighed down with books. "Are you a student here?" Tatalc asked.

"This is my third term. But it's my last . . . I won't need four terms. I've doubled my course load so I can graduate early." He extended his hand. "My name is Etan." Etan was a scrappy looking fellow, obviously a Transient.

"My name is Tatalc. This is my first term."

"So this is your first time leaving home?"

"Yes. The first time leaving home." Tatalc reached into his pocket and pulled out some coins. He placed them in Etan's extended hand.

"Thanks. Maybe I'll see you around again." Etan turned to walk into the cafeteria.

"Wait. Etan. Wait." Tatalc yelled out. Etan turned around. "Can I ask you a question?"

"Sure."

"I don't understand. How are you going to survive the term if you can't even eat now? The term has just started." Etan looked embarrassed. Tatalc soothed him, "I'm sorry, I didn't mean to offend you."

"It'll be better soon. I'm on the *program*. The start of the term is always rough. With books and supplies there's nothing really left for food. Especially with the double course load. More books, more supplies, less food. But I can't afford to come back next term. I have to finish now or I never will. To be honest, I never should have started. Tuitions have almost doubled in the three terms I've been here. I have a little sister, she's smart as can be, but she'd be better off waiting tables for the rest of her life than dealing with the debt I've piled up. I have to go, but thanks for this," Etan held up the coins Tatalc had given him, "I appreciate it."

***

Tatalc had come from an elite family where resources were never a concern, but meeting Etan gave him a new perspective. He knew if average citizens were no longer able to afford education, they would begin to devalue it, which would negatively impact Cytheran society. He foresaw a time not too far into the future where citizens would start to forego the opportunity for an education and society would regress. In an attempt to understand what was taking place Tatalc decided to focus his mind on the issue and what he found was alarming.

Since institutions knew the government was subsidizing a portion of tuitions and no citizen would dare suggest cutting those programs, the institutions had figured out they could continually increase their fees, and the government would keep subsidizing them. The real problem wasn't the increased government spending; government resources were always available for the right projects. The problem was the increased portion the student had to borrow.

Feeling he needed to do something about it, Tatalc went to his father. While his father believed his theory and wanted to help, Wickem suggested Tatalc uncover proof before making public accusations. Tatalc knew he would never find tangible proof that institutional leaders were conspiring to inflate their revenues at the cost of the government and their own students; his only choice was to rally the students who were being taken advantage of, and lead them in a social revolt.

Tatalc's theories were correct. His revolt not only empowered the students, it also empowered those within the system who also felt tuitions had become too high. Once the government understood the issue and realized they had been manipulated, they stepped in and created new regulatory restrictions that would keep tuitions low for the students while still allowing the higher education system to flourish. All of this was credited to Tatalc.

Extremely proud of his son, Wickem began to realize Tatalc's potential. From that point forward Wickem began to seek Tatalc's advice on many critical matters. Even after Tatalc's shameful conduct, when most citizens lost faith in his wisdom, his father stood by his side. Wickem agreed Tatalc's actions were wrong and Tatalc suffered the social consequences, but Tatalc was still his first and only son, and he deserved another chance.

While creating his solution for the Rugal crisis, Wickem consulted with Tatalc. Tatalc was aware of most of his father's thoughts, though it would be the one he was not aware of that would have the most impact. Tatalc never would have considered including himself with those selected to travel to the new planet; Wickem came up with that idea on his own. And even though wanting to send Tatalc to the new planet had caused Wickem to lose the debate, his mind was made up, Wickem had to find a way for Tatalc to go.

Chapter 7

Before the Debate – Dafur

As Dafur walked off the stage of the university auditorium he felt he had accomplished his goal. He needed the scientific community to understand his idea for flare surfing and how this could save Cythera. This was the first step.

Dafur had been well received by the audience. The audience was primarily made up of academics, Dafur's type of citizens. Dafur was more comfortable speaking to other educators, especially scientists. His comfort with scientific language and data gave him enough confidence to successfully convey his message (at least to this audience).

In the coming times, both he and Rigby knew they would need to find a simpler way to explain flare surfing. Ordinary citizens would be confused by the details. Ordinary citizens didn't care how flare surfing worked. They wanted to know it *would* work.

Stepping from the stage, Dafur was greeted and congratulated by top scientists in attendance. Besides the actual *speaking*, the handshakes and pats on the back were Dafur's least favorite part of public speaking. Trying to appreciate their gestures, he was polite. But he could never believe others were being completely honest with him. No citizen had ever come up to him after a lecture and said *"Dafur, that was horrible, I can't believe how stupid you are and that I wasted my time listening to your babbling nonsense!"* After respecting and accepting their compliments, Dafur was always eager to wrap up the ceremonial congratulations and talk to the one citizen that *would* be honest with him - Rigby.

Rigby had been waiting outside for Dafur. He didn't like large crowds or the stuffiness of a lecture hall. Rigby preferred to be outside in the heat. He knew that as the heat on Cythera became more intense, citizens would avoid the outdoors, but he believed citizens should do the exact opposite. Spending as much time outside as he could, Rigby rationalized *the heat was coming, why run from it? Possibly if one were to grow accustomed to the heat they might be able to survive longer.*

"Rigby, there you are. I've been looking for you." Dafur found Rigby outside.

"Here the whole time sir. Have you noticed the horizon at dusk?" Rigby pointed to the sky where light was transforming to dark. "The color is changing. It's subtle, but it's changing."

"I don't spend enough time outside at dusk to notice these things, but I believe you. Let's go somewhere and have a drink."

Dafur and Rigby walked down the road and around the corner to a small diner that had a patio. The diner was nearly full inside. But since no citizen wanted to be outside in the heat, they were able to find a quiet table on the patio.

"What did you think of the lecture?" Dafur asked Rigby.

"Honestly, I was somewhat bored. But then again none of it was a revelation to me."

Dafur didn't take offense. "So were *you* bored, or was the lecture boring?"

"From my perspective isn't that the same thing?" Rigby laughed at his own witty reply.

"Let me ask the question this way. Do you think the audience was bored?"

"You lack confidence in yourself, Dafur. Of course they

weren't bored. They gave you a loud ovation didn't they?"

"True."

Dafur was feeling better until Rigby said, "But these were also your peers, maybe they were only being nice."

Their drinks arrived. They were cold and refreshing. Dafur took a large gulp then asked, "Do you think they really understood it all?"

"I think so. Your context was technically sound and those were intelligent citizens in the room. Though I'm a little worried about how we, or should I say *you,* would present this in a way that *any citizen* would understand."

Dafur agreed, "We'll need to work on that, or should I say *I'll* need to work on that."

"Yes. You need to be more dynamic in your delivery. The common citizen will have trouble engaging in the science."

Dafur took another drink, "I'm worried about that too. Dynamic speaking is not my forte. I could learn some lessons from Tatalc. Have you ever heard him speak?"

"Who hasn't? That's what he's famous for. He could give a lecture on baking bread and a thousand citizens would show up to hear it." Rigby finally took his first drink, "He was there tonight."

Dafur was surprised, "Tatalc was at my lecture? I wonder what he was doing there."

"I don't know. His interests are typically more social than scientific. But then again I suppose the end of Cythera would have some social implications."

"Maybe we should recruit Tatalc to be our voice?"

Thinking about this for a moment, Rigby answered, "He could be a powerful advocate. Do you know him at all?"

"I've never met him. But I'm sure we could find out why he was there. He may be interested in helping us. And I guess it wouldn't hurt anything to explore the opportunity. Could you look into this for me Rigby?"

"That's what I'm here for sir."

The server came to their table and asked if they would like another drink. They both said no. "Can I ask you one more question," Dafur said to Rigby. "It might seem a little strange."

"You ask strange questions all the time." Rigby chuckled at his own wit, again.

"The subject. The one I brought on stage. I think her name was Lij?"

Rigby smiled, "You know her name was Lij. It was obvious you were enamored." Rigby lifted his glass, and in one large gulp, finished his drink, "I'm actually surprised you were able to continue on with your lecture after she sat down."

"Was I that obvious?"

"I don't know if it was obvious to everyone else, but I know you well and it was obvious to me that you were *stricken*."

"*Stricken* is an understatement. I don't know what it was. Something in her eyes, her walk, the way she carried herself. She reminded me of Jiferen, but not in a way that made me sad. More in a way that had me wanting to love again."

The smile on Rigby's face grew wide and he started to laugh.

"Why are you laughing at me? I know I shouldn't have said anything to you. You wouldn't understand love unless you could quantify it in a theorem."

"I'm not laughing at you dear friend. There are few

things that would make me happier than to see you find a companion that would put up with you. Then maybe I could have some peace from time to time."

"Then why are you laughing?" Dafur asked Rigby.

"I know Lij. I actually know her pretty well."

Chapter 8

The Discovery

Barrie held his hand in front of his face and tried to gauge the darkness. "I can't even see my hand. Rual, what are we going to do?"

Knowing he needed to say something before the boys began to panic, Rual asked, "Does anyone have a . . ." A loud cracking sound interrupted Rual, coming from the center of the cavern where the sphere had blocked the great light of the Feber.

"What was that?" One of the boys asked.

"I'm not sure, "Shotum answered. "It almost sounds like the sphere is doing something. Does anyone else hear that hissing sound?" The cracking and hissing noises grew louder and louder. Even Rual was beginning to scare.

Mistel screeched, "Ouch! The water is getting hot!"

"Mistel, get away from the water. Everyone get away from the water and the sphere. Try to move to the back of the cavern, against the wall," ordered Rual.

One of the boys shouted, "The hissing sound, it's the water. It's, it's, I think it's beginning to boil!"

"Back up," Rual yelled to get the boy's attention. "Everyone back up as far as you can. Now!"

"Rual, I'm scared." Cried a boy. "I can't see anything!"

"I'm scared too. Everyone listen to my voice and try to find me," Rual said. "Keep one hand on the wall of the cave. Don't go near the center! Let's all try to get together."

Using only their senses of touch, each boy navigated the absolute darkness. The pool of water hissed and boiled, creating a heavy steam that was beginning to fill the cavern. Rual had to raise his voice to be heard over the hissing and cracking noise coming from the pool of water.

"Is everyone here?" Rual hoped they were all together, "Barrie, where are you?"

"Over here. And is it me or is it starting to get really hot in here?"

"I feel the heat too. Shotum where are you?"

"Right here."

"Mistel?"

"Yes, here."

Continuing to call each boy's name until they were all accounted for, Rual was relieved the boys were safe. "Ok, everyone's here."

Even though no one could see the cloud forming, the cavern was filling with steam from the boiling pool.

"The ground. Do you feel that? And the walls. Everything keeps getting hotter," Barrie said.

Panic was setting in. All the boys were terrified. Rual was scared too, but he knew he had to remain composed. "Everyone *has* to try and stay calm."

"But I'm getting so hot. I can't breathe."

"What do we do now?" One of the boys asked.

"We have to get out of here before we all boil to death."

At the exact instant the word *death* came off of Rual's lips the whole cavern began to quake. The floor below their feet began to shift and the walls beside them began to tremor. Small pieces of rock started breaking off the ceiling of the cave. The sheer loudness was painful and the heat was sucking the life out of them. Everyone gathered together, holding each other, hoping the boy next to them knew what to do.

"We have to get out now!" Rual shouted. "We have to move together against the wall until we find the exit." It was so loud in the cavern that Shotum, who was the closest to Rual, could barely hear Rual's commands. Wondering if any of the boys could hear him, Rual reached into the darkness with both his hands and grabbed as many boys as he could. Rual wasn't sure how many of the boys were following him; he knew it wasn't all of them. But they had to start moving *now* if any of them had a chance to survive.

The walls were falling in. Rocks were dropping from the ceiling and hitting the boys. No one could see anything. A large rock broke from the ceiling, falling on Barrie's head. He dropped to the ground unconscious. It was so loud and dark and violent that the others didn't notice Barrie was knocked out and kept moving on without him.

Trying to find the exit, the boys kept moving forward with their hands against the wall. Rual was pulling a boy; he didn't know which one. Exhausted from the heat, the boy dropped to the ground. Rual tried to drag him along, but he was too heavy; they were running out of time.

Shotum lost track of Rual and they were all losing track of each other. It was so dark and loud, even Rual was worn down. His mind started to cloud. *What if I'm going the wrong way? What is the right way? Where am I supposed to be going?* Rual wasn't sure if any of the boys were still with him. He was getting weaker. He tried to take a deep breath but choked. The air was thick and heavy and impossible to breathe. He was suffocating and he knew his mind was dying.

"Steffer, can you hear me? Steffer, can you help me? Steffer, can you hold my hand while I cross to the other side?" Rual fell to the ground. Reaching out for the hand of Steffer, Rual saw the light of his ancestors. It was peaceful and welcoming. He felt his body begin to cool. He was at peace, and ready

***

"Rual! Rual! Wake up! Please Rual!" Hearing the voice of Shotum, Rual realized he was not dead. "Rual. Wake up. It's over. The quaking stopped. The Feber is shining again. Rual! Please wake up!"

Rual began to regain his mind. "I can see you Shotum. It's not dark anymore."

"I know. And the Feber light is back."

"And it's cool. What happened to the heat?" Rual asked Shotum.

"I don't know. I passed out. When I woke up everything was back to normal."

"The others? What about the others?"

Shotum leaned down to help Rual off the floor of the cavern, "Everyone's okay. We have some cuts and bruises and Barrie's head is bleeding, but we're all alive." Shotum pointed over to Barrie who was sitting on the ground holding a cloth against his bloody head.

Rual began to regain his sense of life, "I thought I was dead. What happened?"

A voice called from across the cavern, "Shotum. Rual. Come here. You have to see this!"

Rual walked to the center of the cavern where some of the boys had congregated. "What is it?"

"The sphere. It's gone. It broke apart."

"I guess that's why the light of the Feber came back on," Rual said.

"Yes. And look where the sphere was. What *is* that?"

Rual looked where the rock had broken apart in the pool of water and he saw something shining. Not knowing what it was, he was nervous to touch it; but something inside him pushed away his fear and he reached out and picked up the object. Rual held it in the air and the grand light of the Feber reflected off of it. "I don't know what it is. But it's beautiful."

Chapter 9

After the Debate - Wickem's Story - Part II

Wide-awake, Wickem laid in his bed staring at the ceiling. He had lost the debate and he was depressed. His mind raced back and forth. The depth of his failure paralyzed his body. This was a new emotion for Wickem, one he was not familiar with.

His entire life had been a series of successes, one

closely followed by another. Successes he created though his own desire to be a *great one*. Wickem's lineage gifted him with a comfortable life, but that wasn't enough for him. He wasn't motivated by the simple comforts of life. All of his life he had masterfully applied his intellect, his character, and his will to every challenge. As a result, his range of influence was wide and well deserved.

But this morning he could not pull himself from bed. He thought about losing the debate and about his son Tatalc. He wondered how many more times he would see his son before Cythera was consumed by the heat.

It was unlike Wickem to lie in bed all morning. On a typical morning he would wake early with a fresh spirit. Today, he was sluggish. After mustering the strength to pry himself off his bed, he walked towards the wide doors that opened to his master balcony. On his way to the balcony, he paused next to a mirror and looked at his reflection. *When did I get so old*, he thought to himself. He combed his hand through his thick silver hair, *When did I get so old?* His was still strong in stature: he had always been tall and broad, but he was no longer fit, and he hadn't been fit for a long time.

He turned to the left so he could view his paunch. *So big, what happened? I was an athlete once.* As a young man, Wickem had participated and excelled in many Cytheran games. Especially accomplished at racket sports, he earned several professional awards. Those times were long in the past. He couldn't remember the last time he exercised.

Wickem's life was busy and he preferred it that way. This was the only way to keep his attention diverted from the *angers of life*. Throughout his life he had faced several debilitating angers. As a child, Wickem idolized his father and would travel with him during his political campaigns. Wickem's father had served in multiple high offices within Cytheran government and was positioned to be elected to the highest office, Chief of State.

Wickem recalled the last time he was with his dad at a successful rally in the large city of Clocktic. The election was approaching and polls were predicting a landslide victory for his father. His father would become the youngest Cytheran elected Chief of State. They were walking off stage when a skinny man wearing a yellow vest emerged from the crowd with a pistol. The man shot three times. All three projectiles hit Wickem's father in the chest. Wickem held his father in his arms and watched him quickly die.

Anger

The assassination of Wickem's father impacted all of Cythera. Every citizen was saddened by this unnecessary act committed without meaning. The man in the yellow vest was a lunatic. His only motive was to make a name for himself as a disrupter of history.

Because of the attention surrounding the episode, mourning was difficult for Wickem and his family. Sick with depression, his mother struggled to carry on. As time passed she grew weaker and weaker. Wickem's responsibility shifted from mourner to caretaker. His mother would not leave her bed. Assuming she would eventually come to the realization that there was nothing she could do, that she must accept the death of her husband and begin to heal, Wickem provided her with the comfort she required. As her weakness lingered, Wickem arranged for a medic to analyze her condition. Her prognosis was shocking.

Wickem's mother had contracted the black, which had

been building in her system long before the death of her husband. There was no cure for her strand of the black and Wickem watched his mother slowly die.

Anger.

***

Standing in front of his bedroom mirror Wickem examined himself (both physically and mentally). Pondering the failure of his plan for survival, Wickem wished his father and mother were there to guide him. He didn't know what to do next.

To Wickem, Dafur's plan was too simple and conservative. Dafur was correct in believing the key to long-term survival would be the ability to repopulate, but in Wickem's eyes there was much more to be considered.

The primary difference between their two plans was Dafur wanted accurate representation of Cytheran civilization and Wickem wanted to select citizens with the highest probability of success, regardless of their class or race.

Dafur's idea to include citizens from all classes was illogical to Wickem, but it was not because he feared the mixing of classes and race. Instead he knew there would only be a limited number of citizens traveling to the new planet and they would have no choice but to breed with one another. Within a few generations the bloodlines would be mixed, therefore any effort to reflect an accurate representation of the current Cythera was a lost cause.

There were additional risks as well. Wickem could foresee a class struggle in the new world. He was not convinced every citizen would work together for the overall betterment of society. He was concerned certain groups might see this as an opportunity to gain influence and control over the new civilization. Dafur disagreed.

Dafur's optimism seemed unrealistic to Wickem. The new civilization would populate itself quickly, this didn't concern Wickem. Wickem was mostly concerned with how the travelers would adapt and advance in their new surroundings. He felt the most important trait any traveler should have was the *influence* to lead. In Wickem's mind this was the only way to assure survival.

***

Wickem walked to the doors of his great balcony and opened them. He moved outside into the glaring heat of the morning; the heat that was growing stronger and more deadly with each revolution. Wickem placed his hands on the railing of his balcony. From this vantage he could view most of Cythera's capital city, Regiowide. He could see tall buildings, he could see parks, he could see rivers and the great lake, and he could see citizens. *His* citizens.

These were his citizens and his father's citizens. He had a responsibility towards them. His family had always been responsible for the citizens of Cythera. But now that he had lost the debate, Wickem wasn't sure if the citizens of Cythera still needed him.

In his mind, he had let the citizens down. He had let himself down. He had let the spirit of his father down. He didn't know what to do next. He only knew that he would not let his son down.

Chapter 10

After the Debate - Tienneis's Story

While the view from Wickem's porch was a picturesque sight of tall, intricately architected buildings, below the sounds and the heat of the Cytheran capital city were the ancient structures of past civilizations. Like most modern cities, Regiowide had built upon itself over the generations.

Regiowide was thought to be the oldest city on Cythera. Earliest records indicate the area was a center point along a popular trade route. It was located in the highlands and safe from the floods caused by the end of the Brumulage era. This location was an ideal place for civilization to grow and prosper.

The oldest structures, now subterranean, were a series of connected buildings. These buildings were designed for a dual purpose, to defend against raids and protect citizens from what was then a colder climate. The buildings were maintained by the government, which used the space for low level officials and administrators. Many government employees started their career in the subterranean offices nicknamed, The *Vault*.

***

Tienneis, a quiet man from a middle class family, had been working for the government since completing his higher curriculum. His assigned workspace was in the records building, a particularly moist section of the vault. His job was important, but it was not the career he had envisioned. He was bright, the son of a physicist, but his poor social skills and slight speech impediment disrupted his path to higher influence.

Being part of a large team, Tienneis's job was not

unique. There were thousands of other truton clerks in other large cities around Cythera.

The forecast for this season's workload had been low. Many assumed with the looming death of Cythera, recommendations for trutons would be less than normal, but the exact opposite was happening. Citizens were submitting endorsements at a record high. It was as if citizens wanted to collect a few more trutons to carry with them into the spirit world.

Tienneis was annoyed by all the incongruous applications; he didn't have time for this nonsense. Final approvals for truton allotment were due soon, and in the long history of truton ceremonies this could be the most important one, ever. It could be the last truton ceremony before Cythera would be destroyed by it's sun.

The recommendation Tienneis was currently reading had been submitted by a middle aged widow who wanted the young boy next door to receive 500 trutons for watering her plants while she was on holiday. *Really! 500 trutons!* The request made Tienneis sick to his stomach; he couldn't believe the audacity of some citizens. The great war hero, Numitor received 500 trutons for successfully leading the recapture of Regiowide from a rogue band of dissidents. Granted, that was many generations ago and the value of trutons had adjusted with the times. But to equate the salvation of a peaceful civilization to the survival of a houseplant was absurd.

It was nearing mealtime and Tienneis needed a break from the painful task of filtering through nonsensical truton recommendations. Leaving his office, he locked the door behind him. It was one of his quirks. He was paranoid that a coworker would enter his office while he was gone. Tienneis knew this was silly and there was nothing in his office another citizen would want, but he still double checked to make sure the door was locked.

Instead of riding the lift, Tienneis elected to walk up the three flights of stairs that led to the street level. He wasn't in the mood for a chance encounter—an awkward, empty conversation with someone in the lift. Unless there was something in it for him, he was rarely in the mood for conversation.

It was a short walk to his favorite diner and he was happy his favorite table was available. Sitting down he began to read over the menu, a meaningless ritual he performed every time he dined here. Ultimately, he would order the strafultap with a glass of ice water.

"How are you today? Is this the first light you've seen today? It's getting hotter and hotter, isn't it? I don't know why I still come to work. I should be enjoying my last revolutions on a float in the lake. Let me guess strafultap, water with ice?" Konja was a nice lady. Her short hair didn't match her pear shaped frame but she had no one to tell her that. Thinking she was building rapport with her customers, she talked a lot. Tienneis mostly ignored her. It didn't bother him because he realized she was only doing her job.

"That sounds g-good, thanks K-Konja."

The strafultap arrived and Konja kept his water glass full, which was important to Tienneis. It was a good meal that briefly took his mind off spending the rest of the afternoon reading truton applications.

"Here's your bill. Thanks for coming in today. Take care of yourself. Stay out of the heat. I hear some citizens are already starting to get sick. I'm trying to stay positive myself. Who knows, maybe I'll get lucky and be selected as one of the travelers. Or maybe you will. It would be nice to know at least one citizen who wins the lottery."

Tienneis had been so busy with truton recommendations that he had not been keeping up with any news stories or much of anything happening outside of the vault. "Lottery? What lottery?" He asked her.

"The lottery. You don't know about the lottery?"

"I d-don't." Tienneis stuttered.

"A scientist named Dafoo, or Dafrer, something like that, thinks he's found a way for citizens to travel though space to the next planet. No one knows what will be there, or if we would survive. But we won't survive here so it's worth the chance. Obviously we all can't go, so The Chief of State asked Dafron who should go. He said there should be a random lottery so everyone would have the same chance of being selected. But then Wickem, you know who Wickem is, right?"

"Of c-course I know Wickem," Tienneis said. "Well, I know of him."

"Wickem stepped in, like he always does, and said we shouldn't do a lottery. We should send our best and brightest."

"That sounds reasonable."

"Except he wanted to send Tatalc."

"What's wrong with T-Tatalc? Everything I've read about him has always been g-good."

Konja extended her hands out as she asked, "Don't you remember . . ."

"Yes, b-but I always thought that was b-bl-blown out of p-pr-proportion."

"Even so, we'll need to repopulate if we are to survive

on the new planet. And I don't want to sound crude, especially to a good customer like you, but Tatalc, you know, really isn't, you know, *willing*."

"I'm sure the others would b-be more than *willing*. I d-don't think p-populating will b-be a p-problem."

"You're probably right but it really doesn't matter any more. They had a debate and it went to a vote, Wickem's plan versus Dafur's. Dafur, that's his name, the scientist. And Dafur's plan won. So there's going to be a lottery."

"When is it t-taking p-place?" Tienneis asked.

"I think it will be after the truton ceremony."

"And how d-does D-Da-Dafur think he'll b-be able to move t-travelers through space?"

"The papers explained how, but I didn't understand it. You seem to be a smart man. You should look into it. And when you figure it out come back and explain it to me."

"I will."

Chapter 11

Before the Debate – Dafur

It was hot outside, another sweltering morning. Dafur was already working inside his lab. Still energized from his lecture on flare surfing, Dafur was eager to get to work and had walked to campus before sunrise.

Contemplating the structural integrity of solar flares, Dafur was convinced the energy created during a solar flare had enough force to propel an object through space, but he was challenged by the flares lack of propensity. If he were unable to predict the timing of a solar flare, it would be impossible to ride the wave of energy it created.

Dafur had always been curious about the possibilities of space travel. This was a rare interest for a Cytheran. The ancients had raised questions and documented histories defining the stellar system they inhabited, but those histories were infrequently visited by modern minds. Dafur had been an exception, and had made a life's hobby out of calculating opportunities to travel into space. It was a hobby without urgency, a riddle without the demands of a solution, until Dafur learned about the Rugal.

***

The Rugal had been found during the early era by a band of Transients who were exploring a dangerous cave housing a mysterious light called the Feber. The legend tells how the Transients removed the Rugal from the cave and then something terrifying happened convincing them to rid themselves of the artifact.

The man who took the Rugal was a devious artist name Lairnam. Lairnam was enamored by the unique shape and design of the object. It was unlike anything he had ever seen before. It would be his new masterpiece.

Lairnam went on to claim the Rugal as his own artistic creation and soon garnered acclaim for his new work. Upon his death, Lairnam's meager estate was donated to the museum in Regiowide, Cythera's capital city. This is how the Rugal ended up on a shelf in the basement of the Regiowide museum where it sat untouched for many generations until it was found by a student. According to the museum's curator, the student gave the artifact to him and was never heard from again. The curator went on to write a popular book proclaiming the Rugal as a mysterious piece of ancient art that foretold the end of Cythera.

Many citizens considered the story of the Transient boys finding the Rugal in a cave to be folklore. Citizens really didn't care how the Rugal ended up at the museum. It wasn't important how the Rugal was found or even when it was found. What *was* important was the prophecy the Rugal told.

***

Dafur was deep in thought and didn't hear the door to his lab open. It was his assistant Rigby. "Good morning sir, sorry to interrupt you." Rigby was more mature than a typical student. His sloppy hair, beard and rough features gave him an appearance well fitting his character.

"Rigby. Good morning. Come in." Despite the struggles with his theories, Dafur was in a good mood. "How was class this morning? Assuming you went." Recently Rigby had developed a habit of working late into the night, then over sleeping and missing his early class.

"Sorry but I . . ."

Rigby was about to explain why he missed his morning class but Dafur interrupted him, "Stayed up all night working and overslept again?"

"Actually I didn't sleep at all."

"Rigby, I know it's not a core course but it's a required course. You'll need it to complete your curriculum. Sometimes I think you are trying to get kicked out of the class so you can remain a student forever." Dafur wasn't scolding Rigby; their friendship was beyond a normal mentor/mentee relationship, but being the professor Dafur felt he had an obligation to remind Rigby of the importance of attending every class.

"Then I could work for you forever. At least until our sun destroys us." Rigby had a dry sense of humor. "You should consider it a compliment I would want to delay my graduation and continue to be your assistant."

"I would consider it a complement if *one* of my best assistants actually graduated."

Rigby sat down in the plush chair across from Dafur's desk. "*One* of your best? That's offensive. Name another *one* of your assistants who could have developed an antidesultory empyreal fulmination theory?"

Dafur jumped out of his chair. "You did what? Why didn't you tell me right away?"

"You were busy lecturing me about the importance of finishing my degree, which is pointless considering our circumstances."

Dafur was thrilled. He was also curious to know how Rigby had developed the theory. "Well, explain it to me. Let's find out if you're as smart as you think you are."

Rigby began, "To start, you've been correct all along about Cytheran mathematics. The different fundamentals of measurements and calculations that work on Cythera don't reconcile on the subatomic plane."

"Can you prove this?" Dafur asked Rigby.

"No, I can't prove something isn't true. That's like trying to prove you're not a woman. That's impossible. I can only prove you're a man."

"I get it, but try to come up with a better example than that."

Rigby continued, "Our math doesn't work because it's infinite. As you know, all Cytheran math applies infinity

45

principles. This is why our mathematical theories, either independently or combined, can't solve to the extreme probabilities we need to solve to. Simply put, the physicists are wrong. Take 1/0, what does that equal?"

"Infinity."

"And why?"

Dafur looked at Rigby, "We both know the answer."

"Indulge me."

"Ok. When you take the function 1/x, as x nears ∞ you get closer and closer to 0. Therefore, $1/\infty = 0$, transversely $1/0 = \infty$. Where are you going with all this Rigby? You know this as well as I do."

"I do," Rigby confirmed, "but I no longer believe any of it."

"Why not?"

"Simple logic. Not everything can be explained on an X/Y axis. Mathematics is not the perfect box we think it is. There's integrity in math at its simplest forms. 1 + 1 will always = 2. I'm not arguing that. But the more complex our math becomes the more theoretical it becomes."

Dafur was enjoying Rigby's rant. Dafur always found it interesting when Rigby let his thoughts flow freely.

"When we begin to treat theory as fact, we allow these *theoretical facts* to trump simple logic. If you take 1/0 the result is not ∞. 0 = nothing, therefore 1/0 is the same as 1/nothing and 1/nothing would leave you with 1. So actually 1/0 = 1."

Dafur was intrigued, "How have you applied this in your theory?"

"As I mentioned, Cytheran math doesn't work because it's infinite. If you replace $1/0 = \infty$ with the absolute of 1/0 = 1, instead of being confronted with an infinite number of probabilities, I now only have one."

Rigby stood from his chair and walked over to a clean board. He drew a big circle with a smaller circle inside of it. Pointing to the large circle, Rigby explained, "Here's the corona of our sun." He pointed at the smaller circle, "Here's its solar interior." Drawing wavy lines from the inner circle to the outer circle, he continued, "The solar interior and corona are held together by extreme magnetism. As atomic particles accelerate they form a magnetic loop where electrons violently expand and cause a coronal mass ejection."

"A solar flare."

"Yes, and thousands of solar flares occur on a regular basis, but most don't release the energy needed to accomplish our objective. With that said, I have been able to locate several hundred areas on the surface of our sun with hot spots regularly producing high enough levels of magnetic energy to meet our needs. Therefore, I know *where* the flares are occurring, so now I only need to know *when* they are going to occur.

"But that's only one problem solved. The other problem is that the conversion of magnetic to kinetic energy is unpredictable." Rigby drew four more circles and shaded them with different colors. "These circles represent areas of the sun where enough magnetic energy exists to create a wave of kinetic energy powerful enough to move an object through space."

"I thought you determined there are several hundred hot spots?"

"I have, I just don't feel like drawing several hundred little circles." Rigby drew another smaller circle. "Here is Cythera. Let's hypothetically say we know exactly when the hot

47

spots would erupt."

"*Hypothetically*? I thought you solved this last night?"

"I'm getting there," Rigby said, "The point I'm trying to make is, we've always believed that even if we knew exactly when a sun spot would erupt it would have to align with Cytheran's orbit. In other words," Rigby pointed to one of the circles on his drawing, "if this hot spot over here erupts," Rigby pointed to the smaller circle that represented Cythera, "and Cythera is orbiting on the other side of our sun, we wouldn't be able to surf that flare, right?"

"That's not the only issue regarding orbits," said Dafur. "Don't forget about our destination. Its orbit would need to be somewhat aligned with ours, we won't have enough energy to circumnavigate our sun."

Rigby replied, "Not necessarily, and this is another area where we've been wrong. We don't need to predict one big solar flare. We need to predict multiple, smaller solar flares."

Dafur was beginning to grasp Rigby's theorem.

"If we can predict when solar flares are going to happen, we could potentially plot a course that allows us to *bounce* from one flare to the next. As long as the series of flares leads us to our destination, we wouldn't need our orbits to be aligned."

"So you can predict the eruption of multiple solar flares?"

"Yes, by removing the infinity principles from our equations and applying the singularity of one, we can eliminate the vast majority of scenarios. The number of remaining variables would be manageable for testing and evaluation."

Impressed, Dafur asked, "And you think we can find a

solution within one of these variables?"

"It's our only hope."

Chapter 12

The Discovery

Rual wasn't sure what he was holding in his hands. It was shiny but not as dense as yellow rock. Its surface was smooth but not polished.

"What is it?" asked Barrie, whose bloodied head was wrapped with cloth.

"I have no idea." Rual handed the artifact to Barrie.

"It's lighter than it looks." Barrie moved his hands over the surface of the object. The base was wide and thick. Underneath the base it was hollow with strange markings inside the concave. Protruding from the base was a cylindrical neck, about half an arms length. The neck narrowed and formed a perfect sphere at its top.

"What should we do with it?" Barrie asked Rual.

Rual turned and began to walk away from the Feber. "Bring it with us. We'll take a better look at it when we get outside."

As they walked out of the cave Rual was having difficulty processing everything that had happened. None of this made any sense to him. Since childhood Rual had been drawn to beauty of the Feber. To view the awesome light within the darkness of the caves was as ritualistic as it was inspiring.

He recalled his first trip to the Feber. Rual was with his

father. It was a fond memory he had always kept close to his heart. Flashing through his mind were the countless other times he had been to the Feber. He could remember all the boys he had led here. There were so many. The enchanted looks on their faces when they would first witness the light always filled him with warm joy. This is why he liked to visit the Feber. Rual wanted to see the looks on their faces. That first look of awe and disbelief all expressed when Transient boys viewed the Feber for the first time. Rual saw himself in their eyes, as a small boy, holding hands with his father. This image always made him happy.

But that's not what he would remember from this visit. Instead of the childish joy and amazement, instead of the fond memories of his father, he would recall the fear, the terror, and the sounds of a child wondering if they were going to live or if they were going to die. Rual took one last look back at the Feber. He knew it would be his last.

Chapter 13

After the Debate – Tienneis

When Tienneis opened the front door and left the diner, he was already loathing the pile of truton applications waiting for him on his desk. Although curious about the lottery, he would have to wait until later to learn more about the process. With the truton ceremony approaching, he needed to focus his energy on reviewing as many applications as he could.

Hoping to yield at least one or two worthy recipients, Tienneis wanted to review several more files that afternoon.

There was not an official quota. *If a citizen is worthy they're worthy, if they're not they're not.* But it had been a while since he had found a deserving candidate, and he was optimistic this would soon change.

As Tienneis walked from the diner back to his office the heat was grueling. The heat seemed to *pour* from the sky. Citizens were spending more time indoors and it was quiet outside, especially for lunchtime. While the heat was uncomfortable; he enjoyed the quiet. Tienneis never liked crowds, he was *at home* in the quiet; it helped him think. *Space travel,* he thought to himself, *it's definitely possible,* at least he had always presumed it was.

Tienneis had learned physics from his father. He considered space travel simple but pointless. *Why would any citizen ever want to travel to space? Where would you go once you were there?* No Cytheran had ever traveled to space. There never had been a reason to, until now.

Tienneis was almost back to his building when he heard a loud thud from behind. It wasn't a crash or a bang, just a thud, as if someone dropped a heavy object on the ground. Turning to look, Tienneis was shocked to see a collapsed man lying face down on the sidewalk. Tienneis ran towards the man, as did a few others. A stranger shouted, "Medic. Someone call a medic." The man was still alive.

Tienneis noticed how the man was shivering and breathing heavy so he rolled the man over on to his back. When Tienneis saw the man's face he was terrified by the condition of his skin, it was dry and tinted a bright orange and pink. Dark red spots covered his body. Attempting to calm the man, Tienneis reached down and touched him. When his fingertips touched the man's arm, Tienneis felt the heat radiating from the man's quivering body. "Someone g-get some ice or water, he's b-burning up."

A stranger spoke, "But he's not even sweating. I don't think he's hot."

From the distance Tienneis heard the sound of an emergency medical unit approaching and looked up to see how far away they were. Tienneis wanted to comfort the man, but he wasn't sure what to do, suddenly the man pulled on Tienneis's arm. Tienneis looked down at the man and made eye contact with him. The man's lips were pulsing. He was trying to tell Tienneis something.

Tienneis leaned down closer to the man's face so he could hear him. In a slow, quiet voice the man said. "I'm sorry I never believed in you. But here you are. Will you forgive me and hold my hand to the other side." The man grabbed Tienneis's hand and squeezed it tightly. "I'm sorry Steffer." The man's body quivered one more time and then stopped. Still holding his hand, Tienneis felt the man's flesh begin to cool.

"Move out of the way. I'm a medic."

"He's already d-dead." Tienneis told the medic.

Wanting to make his own assessment, the medic reached down and checked for vital signs and then looked back to Tienneis and the crowd of citizens congregating around the dead man's body. "Everyone back up," the medic ordered. "He's dead. Does anyone know him?"

The crowd looked around at each other but no one spoke.

The second medic arrived with a stretcher. "Are we too late? That's a shame. What was the cause?"

The first medic replied, "Cardiac arrest. Severe. He

never had a chance."

Tienneis looked over at the medic, "C-Cardiac arrest? A heart attack? He d-didn't d-die from a heart attack, he d-died from the *heat!*"

The medic looked at Tienneis; he looked around at all the citizens then back at Tienneis. "This was a heart attack. It's hot, but not hot enough to kill a citizen. This was definitely a heart attack."

Tienneis argued, "I was the first one on the scene. I saw the m-man's eyes and felt his skin. He d-died from the heat."

"Sir, are you a professional medic?" Tienneis shook his head. "Precisely, then all you are doing is frightening citizens. This man died from cardiac arrest, nothing more. Are we clear?" The medic didn't seem comfortable being this direct.

Tienneis turned around and walked away.

Tienneis was not a fool. He knew this man died from severe heat. But why wouldn't the medic admit it? Something was odd. This was all peculiar to Tienneis. Since he left his office a short time ago, he learned of a lottery to transport citizens off Cythera, and now a man died in his arms from heat stroke. Something was happening and he needed to know more.

Chapter 14

Before the Debate – Dafur & Lij

Since explaining his antidesultory empyreal fulmination theory to Dafur, Rigby had been working on the algorithms needed to test the model. Dafur was convinced Rigby's theory would work, but they wouldn't know for sure until they could run some trials.

While Rigby's discovery was an important milestone, it was the first in a series of problems they needed to solve. With so much to do, Dafur rarely left his lab. The goal they were trying to achieve, moving citizens to another planet, was abstruse, yet Dafur was calm as he stood alone in his lab reviewing the different steps needed for a successful mission. Some he felt good about, others he didn't.

In addition to plotting a course to the next planet, they needed to build a vessel strong enough to support life and survive space travel. They also needed a way to launch the vessel off the surface of Cythera. The vessel needed to be propelled towards its destination and land on the new planet. They *needed* a lot.

Dafur also wanted to maximize the number of citizens they would be able to save. Standing at his board, he contemplated this question. Dafur had settled on two possible scenarios that might increase the number of citizens travelling to the next planet. After plotting both on his board, neither one seemed likely to succeed.

The first option was complex. Originally thinking he could build a vessel capable of landing, then relaunching to return for more citizens, this equation was becoming more and more of a challenge. He wasn't even sure how he would launch the first vessel off Cythera, and Cythera was a known variable. He was familiar with Cytheran's terrain, winds and atmosphere but he knew nothing about the terrain, winds and atmosphere of the other planet.

Also, the vessel would travel to the new planet by riding flares caused by their sun. Solar flares travel outward, away from their sun. Travelling back towards Cythera, the vessels would be moving against the natural forces of solar flares. Rigby had discovered several flares that bounced off of other planets creating reverse energy, but the energy was unpredictable and Dafur was convinced there would not be enough sustainable force to direct a vessel back home.

The second option was to build multiple vessels. While in theory this seemed the better solution, the reality of time and resources stood in their way. They had barely started the design of the first vessel. It needed to be engineered, prototyped and tested; and they still didn't know how they would acquire the resources to do that. Dafur struggled with both options, worrying if he would even have enough time and resources to build one vessel, let alone multiple vessels,

"Sorry to interrupt you."

Dafur had his back to the door. Recognizing the voice of his assistant, Dafur remained focused on the work on his board. "Yes, Rigby?"

"I have someone with me who'd like to meet you."

Dafur set his pen on the tray at the bottom of the board and turned around. His heart began to pound as he felt the nervous energy in the pit of his stomach start to spread throughout his body.

"Sir, do you remember Lij?"

"I do. I do." Dafur said. "Come in. Welcome." Dafur moved behind his desk and sat down. He knew it was rude not to greet her with a handshake, but his palms had started sweating and he would have been embarrassed to extend his hand. Rigby and Lij sat down in the two chairs opposite of Dafur's desk. Not knowing what to say, Dafur began to shift papers around. His desk was a mess. Typically he didn't care. Now he did.

Lij started the conversation with a compliment. "I wanted to let you know how much I enjoyed your lecture. It's interesting and important work you're doing."

Dafur was not expecting such a sincere compliment from Lij and he felt the heat rush to his face and was worried he was blushing. After a brief moment he was able to compose himself. "I appreciate that and thank *you* for being a good sport. You'd be surprised how many subjects have taken offense when I have analyzed them in a public setting." Dafur said with a smile.

Lij smiled too. "I was happy to help." She pointed to Rigby, "Rigby's told me more about your work. I know you realize this, but what you're doing is by far the most important work ever done by a Cytheran."

"I'm sure there are other scientists working as hard as we are to find a solution to the Rugal crisis." Dafur replied.

"Yes. But you've made the most progress. Actually, the only notable progress."

"You're kind, Lij. Rigby, how did you two meet again?" Dafur knew Rigby was bored with their dialogue and he felt a need to draw him back in. And Dafur was afraid he couldn't carry the conversation by himself.

"I've had the pleasure of taking a few classes with Lij," said Rigby. "And how many times have we been in a study group together Lij? Four or Five?"

"Probably more than that. I think since we're both older students that started later in life, we gravitated towards one another. I don't think either one of us were interested in the late night study groups the younger students prefer."

Directing his response towards Rigby, Dafur asked, "That's surprising Rigby, I've always thought you preferred nighttime?"

"I don't mind the late nights. But I don't have much in common with the younger students. They tend to spend as much time socializing as studying." Rigby answered.

"That makes more sense. You've never been fond of social interaction." Dafur turned his attention back to Lij. "So Lij, what did you do before you came back to school?"

"I was a performer. A dancer."

"So you're a Transient?" Dafur asked.

Lij was set back by the boldness of Dafur's question. Gathering herself, she replied, "I *am* a Transient and I'm not ashamed of it."

Realizing he might have offended her, Dafur felt bad. It was unintentional and he was embarrassed. "I'm sorry. I didn't mean it like that. I'm actually an appreciator of the Transient arts." He lied. He wasn't hateful towards the Transient lifestyle, just indifferent.

"Really," Lij knew he was lying. "What was the last performance you saw?"

"Well." Dafur stammered. "Well, it's been a while since I've been able to see a performance. I've been so busy with my work. It's hard to find the time. Rigby, tell Lij how busy we've been." Dafur was looking to Rigby for *help*.

"Terribly busy sir. I'm not sure how we find time to eat." Rigby was enjoying Dafur's struggle to remain poised. "And since I know how much you love the arts, I'd be happy to do some extra work if it would free up more time for you to catch up on your interests."

Dafur did not appreciate Rigby's sarcasm. "That is kind of you, Rigby."

Deciding to let Dafur off the hook, Lij interjected. "I realize you probably don't like Transient performances, and as long as you don't look down on our traditions it's all right and I understand."

"Honestly Lij, I don't *dislike* them. I simply don't know anything about Transient traditions and performances," Dafur admitted. "I've never been to a show."

"That's easy to fix. If I were to get passes for a show, would you go with an open mind?"

Dafur thought about this for a moment. He *was* busy. The future of civilization was relying on his focus and determination to complete his work. But she was so beautiful.

"Yes, I would go."

Chapter 15

After the Debate – Tienneis

Stepping into the cool dampness of the vault was a relief to Tienneis. The extreme heat during his break had worn him down. But his own discomfort was nothing compared to another citizen dying in his arms from heat stroke. And he did *die* from heat stroke. Tienneis was convinced of this. There were so many questions swirling in Tienneis's mind, but now was not the time. Those questions would have to wait. He had a job to do.

The first several files he reviewed were a waste of time. More nonsense. *These citizens should be ashamed of themselves for wasting the government's time*, Tienneis thought.

Picking up a new file, he started to read. The submitter was requesting the allotment of 200 trutons for a man who risked his life to enter a burning home. There was no one there at the time, no lives were saved, but this was still a noble feat and worthy of acknowledgement. *Two hundred trutons seems fair, maybe even conservative.* Finally, Tienneis felt he had found a worthy file.

Reading down further, he searched for who had submitted the application. It was a land grower from outside Regiowide's city limits. *Unbelievable. I finally find a worthy application and it's outside of my jurisdiction.* Angry and frustrated, Tienneis leaped out of his chair. *Stupid. Who are these stupid citizens in the file center? This should have never been in my queue.*

He exploded out of his office, not stopping to lock his door. Tienneis charged down the hall towards the tunnel that led to the file center where truton applications were sorted and assigned. The office was in a different building connected by an underground tunnel. Tienneis walked into the office and up to the counter where a large woman wearing a monocle said, "How can I help you?"

"C-Clerk ID-D 18790314. This file's not mine. I c-cover city matters." Tienneis tossed the file onto the counter. "This is out of my j-jurisdiction and it's a g-good application. You know how many g-good applications I g-get? Not many."

The woman was polite. "I'm sorry for the mistake. We're extremely busy. Let me take that from you."

"Thank you." Responding with a tinge of anger, Tienneis told her, "Try to g-get it right next time."

The woman wanted to help. "I can give you a replacement file. One in the city limits. We have plenty." She adjusted her monocle. "We recently received a file submitted by Wickem that might be interesting." The woman held up a file and offered it to Tienneis.

"I d-don't want another file. I already have a stack of files, p-pr-probably all j-junk, waiting for me b-back in my office." Tienneis started to walk away, and then realized the opportunity. Turning around he asked, "D-Did you say you have a file submitted b-by Wickem? Wickem the p-politician?"

"Yes. Do you want it? I promise it's in your jurisdiction."

Tienneis walked back to the counter with a smile on his face. "Yes, I'll t-take it."

Chapter 16

The Discovery

The small group of Transients joyfully shouted at the first light of their sun. Barrie was the first to start running; the other boys followed after him. Even Rual, the strong and stoic leader of the bunch shouted in celebration and ran towards their sun's light at the opening of the cave. When they crossed the threshold to the outside they all jumped in the air and hugged one another.

"We made it out!" One of the boys shouted, adding, "I don't want to ever go into a cave again."

"Me neither." Another agreed.

"I don't think any of us wants to go into a cave again, ever" said Rual. "We're safe now. Let's sit for a moment and rest. Then we'll go home."

"Good idea." Barrie pointed to an area with several large trees. "There's some shade over there."

Rual and the boys walked over to the area and sat down, they were exhausted. Dirt cloaked their faces. Their arms and legs were grimy from the combination of dried sweat and dust. Their bodies were covered with bruises and cuts. Their clothes were tattered and torn. They all looked roughed up, but Barrie was the worst. His curly hair was covered in dried blood from the rock that had fallen onto him from the ceiling of the cave.

"How's your head, Barrie?" Rual asked.

"It hurts, but I'll be ok." Barrie was a strong boy.

Looking around at the other boys, Rual asked, "How's everyone else?"

"I'm all right."

"Ok."

"Tired, but I'll live."

Everyone seemed to be fine. Rual was relieved. They all felt lucky to have come out alive. One of the boys pulled out a sleeve of water and passed it around. Another boy passed around some bread he had packed in his satchel. One of the boys asked, "Rual, what happened back there?"

Rual had a bite of bread in his mouth and paused to swallow before answering, "Honestly, I don't know. But whatever it was, it had to do with the sphere we moved. When it fell on the Feber it blocked the light and something happened, but I don't know what."

"It was like a groundquake, but then everything stopped when the sphere fell apart." Shotum said.

"Yes. I'm not sure what caused that either," replied

Rual.

Barrie held up the artifact they had recovered. "Do you think it has anything to do with *this*?" Still wrapped in cloth, he placed the artifact on the ground where they all could see it.

"I think it has everything to do with *that*." Rual started to stand. "Is everyone rested? We should probably be moving on."

The boys stood up and stretched. It was a long walk back to their village. If they left now they might be home before dark.

***

Considering their variety of injuries, they were making good time. Their sun was not to its peak yet and a cool wind aided their comfort. Since leaving the shaded area none of the boys had spoken a word. They just walked. Barrie was leading the march with Rual at the rear. Barrie interrupted the quiet. He stopped and turned around. "The artifact! I left the artifact back where we were resting. I'm going to go back and get it."

"Wait." Rual interrupted. "Shotum, why don't you go back and get it. I'm still a little worried about Barrie's head injury. We'll take a rest here and wait for you."

"I'll be quick." Shotum turned around and started running back to retrieve the artifact. Shotum was fleet footed and moved swiftly over the terrain. In less than half the time it had taken the group to cover the distance, he was already at the caves.

He went to the area under the trees where they had been resting and found the wrapped artifact. Looking around, he noticed a figure walking out of the cave. He couldn't tell what type of animal it was, but it was big.

Shotum reached down and picked up the artifact. He turned and started to run back to meet the others. Glimpsing back over his shoulder, he was relieved when he didn't see the animal again. As he swiveled his head forward, he tripped over a large limb he had not seen. As he was falling, he lost grip of the artifact and it flew forward through the air.

Shotum stood up and brushed himself off. He picked up the cloth and started to walk towards the artifact. Hearing a noise from behind, he froze. He pulled out his etch and turned around, fearing the noise was from the animal he had seen at the cave's entrance.

It wasn't an animal. It was a man. A long haired man with a beard.

**

Rual was wondering what was taking Shotum so long. He wasn't overly worried, but Shotum should have been back by now. A few of the smaller boys had fallen asleep on the ground and everyone else was resting.

Barrie knew Rual well and was beginning to sense Rual's concern. They looked at each other and Rual finally spoke up. "What do you think?"

"He should've been back by now."

"I think so too. Let's wake everyone up and go see if we can find him."

Rousing all the boys to their feet, Barrie told them Shotum wasn't back yet. "Everything's probably fine. But instead of waiting around, it might be best to go back and look for him." They gathered their belongings and started walking back towards the caves. When they arrived at the caves and the large trees shading the area where they had rested, they didn't see Shotum anywhere.

"Where could he be? We should have passed him along the way," one of the boys stated.

"What's that?" Rual pointed over to an area close to the trees. They could all see it now. Someone was lying on the ground.

They all ran over. *Hopefully he only fell and hit his head,* Rual hoped to himself. Reaching the body they turned it over. It was Shotum, and he was dead.

Chapter 17

Before the Debate – Dafur & Lij

Dafur and Rigby had been working through the night. The calculations they were working with were intense, and both men were exhausted. As worn out as they were, great progress had been made, and they would rest well knowing how much they had accomplished.

Predicting a solar flare was no problem. This had become simple for them. The quandary was in predicting and aligning multiple solar flares in a purposeful pattern: a pattern forming an elongated wave of energy capable of moving a vessel through space towards a specific desired location. This was much more challenging.

It had been Rigby's idea to work during the night. The sophisticated instruments they used were powered by hydroelectrics, the same source of energy powering the cooling systems at the university. With the brutal heat overworking their cooling systems, the university had to start rationing electricity. Occasionally, if the university's power grid maxed, the electricity would be shut down without warning.

Rigby didn't want to risk being deep into a calculation when the power shut down, and the likelihood of a shut down at night was much lower. Even though Dafur didn't want to work through the night, he had no choice but to agree with Rigby. Certain critical experiments, the ones highly reliant on electricity, would have to be done at night. This was the only way to guarantee completion.

Dafur and Rigby were almost finished packing away their equipment when there was a knock at the door of the lab. "Come in." Dafur was too tired for a guest *and* too tired to ignore one.

"Good morning." It was Lij. "You two look busy. Did you get an early start this morning?"

"Actually," Rigby said, "we had an early start last night."

"Good morning Lij." After staying up all night Dafur realized he probably didn't look his best. Knowing he was making it worse, he still brushed through his hair with his hand. "What brings you to the lab this morning?"

"Well, I stopped by your classroom and no one was there. So I thought I'd check here, and sure enough here's where I found *you*."

Dafur could tell she was talking about both him *and* Rigby. Wishing she was only talking about him, Dafur asked her "Why were you looking for us?"

"Do you remember how you said if I were able to get tickets you'd be willing to go to a Transient show?"

"Yes. I remember that," replied Dafur.

"You're in luck; I was able to get tickets for *us*."

Who did she mean by us? Dafur again wished she was

only talking about him, but she probably wasn't. "That's wonderful."

"I think you'll like this show. It's called *Pepper.* You still want to go, right? I hope so because it was sold out and the tickets weren't easy to get."

"Certainly. I can't wait." Dafur said.

Lij turned to Rigby who was still packing equipment. "Rigby, what about you? I have three tickets."

Dafur's hope that Lij would invite him alone came to an abrupt end.

"I'm sorry Lij, I don't think I'll be able to go," Rigby said. "Dafur has been working me too hard. There's so much work to do. Plus, I've already seen *Pepper* numerous times. Why don't you two go? Dafur could really use a night off *and* a good dose of culture."

Dafur tried not to look as happy as he felt inside.

Lij turned towards Dafur, "Is that ok with you, if it is only us two? I can probably sell the other ticket at the gate."

Hoping he was not giving away his excitement, Dafur said, "I suppose that would be fine."

"Then it's settled. I think you'll really enjoy the show." Lij was looking directly at Dafur. Gazing back into her eyes, he smiled. For the briefest of moments Dafur felt the *spark,* but he wasn't sure if Lij felt it. Matter of fact, he was certain she didn't, but she did pause for a moment. *It was something.*

Breaking the eye contact Lij turned back towards Rigby. "I guess I should let you get back to whatever you were doing. I'm sure you're both tired and I need to get to class." She looked back at Dafur, "I'll call you later about the details."

She again made direct eye contact with Dafur, but this

time he didn't feel the *spark*. He must have been imagining things before. "Sounds good. I look forward to it. Thanks again for inviting me, I mean us." Lij responded with a smile and walked out of the lab leaving Dafur and Rigby to finish packing away their instruments.

For the next few moments the lab was quiet. Finishing the last bit of work they were both eager to leave the lab and go home to rest. Dafur finally interrupted the silence. "So you've seen *Pepper*. Is it any good?"

"I've never seen *Pepper*," Rigby said.

"Then why did you say that?"

"I didn't want to go."

"Why not?" Dafur asked.

"I think she likes you and I know you are smitten with her. I would be in the way."

"Not at all. This is purely social. I don't think she sees me as anything more than an old professor."

"You're really not that much older than she is."

"I know, but it would've been nice if you came, and she did invite us both."

"You're a bad liar, sir. I saw your face when I said I wasn't going to come. This will be good for you. Take advantage of the opportunity. Charm her with your unmatched wit and companionship."

"Now you're making fun of me." Dafur didn't care. He was thrilled Rigby wasn't going. "I am a little worried about what kind of impression I'll make. It's been a long time since I've been on a date."

"I wouldn't call it a date sir. I'd call it an opportunity."

"Right, it's not a date."

"I wouldn't worry too much about it. You'll spend most of the evening watching the show. As long as the show is good, the night will be a success."

"I'm over analyzing this, aren't I?" Dafur asked Rigby.

"You over analyze everything. Why would this be any different?" Rigby stacked the last case of equipment on the shelf in the back corner of the lab. "I think we're done here. I'm going home. You should too. You need to rest up for your big *date.*"

Chapter 18

After the Debate – Tienneis

Returning to his office much happier than when he left, Tienneis's frustration over countless truton applications for unworthy citizens had begun to subside. In his hands he held an application from Wickem, the man who probably knew more about the lottery and the fate of Cythera than any other citizen. It really didn't matter whom Wickem's truton application was for. Protocol required direct confirmation with the submitter if trutons were to be distributed. This gave Tienneis the perfect opportunity to speak with Wickem.

Tienneis sat down at his desk and opened the file. Wickem was asking for 2000 trutons. *That's a lot,* Tienneis though. The recommendation was for a woman named Dekayb. Tienneis read on.

Dekayb was Wickem's assistant. In the application, Wickem stated he would like 2000 trutons issued to Dekayb for her long time service. Wickem said he realized 2000 was a lot of trutons. He had never recommended Dekayb before, which he regretted, but her service and contribution to his work warranted the large sum.

Throughout the application Wickem detailed the specific contributions Dekayb had made to his efforts. She was much more than an assistant. She was an intelligent woman who helped draft many of the decisions he'd made over his career. She had been especially instrumental and courageous during the most challenging times, including Wickem's leadership during the revelation of the Rugal. Wickem submitted nearly twenty pages of specific examples, concluding his recommendation by acknowledging he wouldn't have accomplished anything without the loyal commitment of Dekayb.

Tienneis was impressed with the care and time Wickem had put into the application. Even if he didn't have an ulterior motive he would have approved it. Picking up his receiver, Tienneis dialed the number Wickem listed. After a few tones a man with strong voice answered.

"Hello."

"May I leave a message for Wickem?"

"This is Wickem. Who's calling?"

This must be Wickem's private line. "My name is T-Tienneis. I am from the t-truton office and my c-call is regarding the application you submitted for your assistant D-Dekayb. Is now a g-good time to d-discuss this?"

Wickem was patient with Tienneis's impediment, "Yes, now's a good time. I'll have to admit I wasn't expecting a call so soon. Hopefully your office didn't give me preferential treatment."

"That's a c-considerate thought on your b-behalf. B-But

we d-did not." Stretching the truth somewhat, Tienneis said, "There was a filing error and b-by simple luck your application was expedited."

"Good. I would not expect or want any special favors. I imagine your office is busy right now."

Tienneis was surprised by how conversational Wickem was. Tienneis was expecting someone of Wickem's influence to be more stilted. "We're b-busy as I'm sure you are. C-Could I ask you some qu-qu-qu-questions about your application?" Tienneis asked.

"Of course."

"You mentioned D-Dekayb has been your assistant for many cycles, yet you have never recommended her for t-trutons b-before. Why not?"

"I feel terrible that I haven't. It never occurred to me."

"Have you recommended others for t-trutons?"

"I have on occasion. But Dekayb is not one to covet accolades and I simply never *really* considered how deserving she is."

"As you know 2-2-2000 t-trutons is a lot, even c-considering her c-contributions. Explain to me why you think this is fair allotment." Tienneis was not challenging Wickem. This was a question Wickem was prepared to answer.

"I realize it's a lot. I consider this to be more for a life's work versus an isolated event. I know the system is not designed to work this way, but due to Cythera's fate, I believe this to be a reasonable request."

Satisfied with the answer, Tienneis continued, "In your application you mention D-Dekayb's assistance in helping you lead through the c-current c-crisis. I apologize for my ignorance.

I'm not one who c-cl-closely follows the news. Would you be willing to g-give me more d-detail so I can assess her c-contribution?" Tienneis was cleverly steering the conversation to the topic that most interested him.

"Sure. I would assume you know of the decoding of the Rugal and how Cythera is slowly dying from the heat of our sun?" Wickem didn't wait for Tienneis to answer the question. "When the prophecy was discovered, there was a lot of controversy within the highest levels of government. Some felt that we shouldn't reveal the full truth; that citizens wouldn't be able to cope with the reality. Originally, I agreed with that assessment, but Dekayb disagreed with me. She felt we should hold nothing back from the public. She believed in full disclosure. She told me this was a problem the government could not solve behind closed doors. We needed every available resource working towards a solution."

"V-Very b-brave of her." Tienneis said.

"Yes. It was." Wickem continued, "Her bravery has always been beyond compare."

"G-Go on." Tienneis urged Wickem.

"After she convinced me that we needed to broadcast the full truth, she coordinated the effort to find a solution. By the time I made the announcement to the public, she had already composed the details of the challenge before us. She also removed many of the bureaucratic hurdles that organizations face when partnering with the government. This allowed for the approval of non-government researchers to access government data if it would help them find a solution. All of this is more difficult than I'm making it sound. You'd be amazed how many ideas have been submitted. Filtering through all of them to find the ones that might work is tedious, but

Dekayb has been relentless with every detail."

Because of his own experience with the tediousness of truton applications, Tienneis sympathized with Dekayb's effort. "She sounds like a remarkable asset. You're lucky to have her b-by your side."

"Should I go on?" Wickem asked. "Or do you have enough information to make your decision?"

"I think I've made my d-decision." Tienneis said in a positive tone. "But if you would allow me to ask a few more questions so I c-can c-complete my file it would b-be helpful."

"Whatever I can do to help." Wickem replied.

"I'd like to ask you about the d-debate."

Chapter 19

Before the Debate – Dafur & Lij

Dafur never considered himself to be a handsome man. He didn't think of himself as ugly either, just ordinary. His appearance was plain, with no distinguishing characteristics that would instinctively attract the opposite gender. He was of average height and size and had always blended in with others. Typically, none of this bothered Dafur. Usually personal appearances were not that important to him. Tonight was different. He worried if Lij would find him attractive.

He had spoken to Lij several times about their plans for the show. They were casual conversations regarding the start time, the meeting place, and if they would eat before or after the show. During the conversations, Dafur was so focused on the details of their night together he forgot to ask one simple question: What does one wear to a Transient show? He tried to reach Rigby (Rigby would know, Rigby seemed to know *everything*); Dafur could not get a hold of him. Dafur would have to figure this out on his own.

His logic, one distinguishing characteristic he did possess, finally rescued him from his anxiety. *Transients dress like everyone else. Therefore, they probably dress the same for their shows. But what if they don't? What if they wear traditional garments? If they do, I don't have any and I wouldn't even know where to get any. Therefore, I have no other choice than to pick something out of my closet.* Concluding this was his only option, Dafur started to get ready.

His wardrobe was mostly limited to casual attire fit for an academic environment. Not wanting to look *academic*, he did not have many choices. *I should have at least bought a new pullover, something fresh and modern,* he thought. *There isn't enough time now.* Then he noticed a bright red vest in the back of his closet.

The vest had been a gift given to him so long ago, Dafur could not remember who it was from and if he had ever worn it. The vest still looked new and was brighter than anything else in his closet. *This might work.* He decided to wear casual khaki pants and a clean white shirt. He put the vest on and looked at himself in the mirror. *Not too bad. She won't be awed, but she shouldn't be embarrassed to be seen with me either.*

The plan was for Dafur to meet Lij at her apartment; then they would take a carriage to the show. The carriage ride was Lij's idea. She said she liked to be outside at night when the climate was more comfortable than when their sun was out.

They would go to the show first and eat after. This was Dafur's idea. Reasoning if they ate first then went to the show, the end of the show would also be the end of the night, and the end of his time with Lij. By going to the show first, then to eat, the evening did not have a definitive end. Dafur thought of *everything*.

***

Dafur arrived at Lij's apartment and rang for her. When she answered the door, Dafur stared. Lij's auburn hair was pulled back tight accentuating the flawless structure of her face. Her wide smile and full lips sat perfectly under her thin nose and bright eyes. Frozen by her pure beauty, Dafur was speechless. He realized he was staring and Lij was becoming uncomfortable.

"Why are you staring at me like that?" Lij questioned him.

"I'm sorry, how rude of me. I've never seen with your hair pulled back."

"Does it look that bad?"

"No. No. Not at all." Dafur stammered.

Lij smiled and then pointed at Dafur's vest. "Nice shirt and vest."

Lij was laughing now. Dafur was embarrassed. *The vest was a bad idea*. Dafur, who to this point had only been looking at Lij's face, looked down and realized why she was laughing. She also had on a white shirt and red vest. Dafur began laughing too.

"Do you think I should go change?" Lij asked.

"That's up to you. Though we do make a cute couple." Dafur wished he had not said that. *We are not a couple and this is not a date* he reminded himself. He was relieved when Lij laughed at his statement.

"I think I'll leave it on. They'll be plenty of oddly dressed citizens at the show. We'll probably fit right in."

Together they walked down the street in their red vests until a carriage came by to take them to the show.

Based on Transient folklore, *Pepper* ended up being better than Dafur had anticipated. Not knowing much about Transient history and their struggles as a class, Dafur found the show not only entertaining, but educational. A lot of Transient history had been omitted from the academia of his upbringing, and it was a fascinating history.

After the show they found a small quiet diner where they could get something to eat. They sat and talked. Neither of them realized how late it was until the diner began to close.

Deciding to walk back to Lij's apartment, they left the diner. It was a long walk and they were enjoying each other's company. When they reached her apartment Dafur hoped she would invite him in. She didn't.

"I can't believe how late it is. The night seemed to move right by without us." Lij said as she was opening the door.

"Thanks for inviting me. I had a wonderful time. Stop by the lab sometime and say hi." Dafur began to turn around to walk home.

"Dafur, wait."

"Yes." Dafur turned back around.

"Would you want to do this again sometime? Maybe not another Transient show, but, I don't know, maybe something else."

"Do you mean a date?"

"Yes, a *date*." Lij said.

"On one condition." Dafur smiled. "Let's make sure

we're both not wearing red vests."

Lij smiled then walked into her apartment building.

Chapter 20

Before the Debate – Tatalc

Rigby didn't realize until later Dafur had been attempting to contact him. There was an important reason for this. After the night of Dafur's breakthrough lecture on solar flares, Dafur and Rigby had agreed they needed a more influential voice to add support to their cause.

Tatalc had attended Dafur's lecture and there had to be a reason why. Ever since that night Rigby had been pursuing a face-to-face meeting with Tatalc. Hoping Tatalc had been moved by their discovery, Rigby needed to find out if he would be willing to help them.

Tracking down Tatalc and getting an appointment with him had proven more difficult than Rigby ever imagined. After multiple attempts, Rigby finally reached Tatalc. He was willing to meet with Rigby on one condition: they would meet in a secluded area far outside the city limits of Regiowide. Though confused at the need for a secret meeting, Rigby agreed. The importance of having Tatalc on their side far outweighed his peculiar request.

It was a long journey to the rural estate where they were meeting. When Rigby arrived, Tatalc was outside waiting for him. "You must be Rigby?" Tatalc extended his hand.

"I am. It's a pleasure to meet you Tatalc. This is an exquisite landscape. I really enjoyed my trip in."

"Thank you. It's peaceful here. Follow me. I have a meal prepared for us in the garden." Tatalc led the way around the side of the estate and down a path that led though a sprawling grove full of bright colorful flowers and short bushy trees. "The estate has been owned by our family for generations. When I was young we spent a lot of time here. But as my father became more and more involved in politics, the trips became less frequent. I couldn't tell you the last time he was here. I still come as often as I can though. I find this place to be the perfect escape from the *chaos* I often find myself engaged in."

Tatalc had been involved in many public causes where he always seemed to be in full control of both his audience and his adversaries. Rigby found Tatalc's choice of the word "chaos" interesting and hoped his request would not add to the *chaos*.

In the center of the garden was a large gazebo covering a stone porch. Under the gazebo was a table prepared with their meal.

"Have a seat Rigby. Hopefully it's not too hot for you to eat outside?"

"I don't mind the heat."

"The estate has a live-in staff of three." Tatalc pointed to a man in the distance. "The man over there is Olmsted. He maintains the land and the buildings. My grandfather hired him long before I was born. If you have any question about this area he would know the answers. A while ago his sister and her husband also moved in. She's a retired chef and would be offended if you didn't try her urdle."

"Urdle is a favorite of mine and I'm sure I'll like her interpretation of the recipe."

Enjoying the comfortable surroundings and the delectable offerings, the two men ate. "This is delicious, Tatalc.

You're lucky to have such a talented chef at your disposal."

"That I am." Tatalc placed his fork upside down on his plate. A servant appeared from nowhere and cleaned off their table. "So tell me Rigby, what can I do to help?"

Knowing this wasn't a true offering to assist in their cause but more a polite way of opening the dialogue, Rigby replied, "I suppose a good place to start would be Dafur's lecture you attended. To be truthful, I was surprised to see you there. How did you find out about it?"

"I have a friend at the school who told me about it. But I want to make sure I understood everything Dafur was saying. Could you summarize it for me?" Tatalc asked.

"Of course. As we all know from your father's announcement, Cythera will soon be uninhabitable. You've probably heard about other scientists' ideas to move citizens underground or build biodomes. Those are all short-term solutions. The only *real* way our civilization can survive is to move to another planet. We believe the closest planet to Cythera has an atmosphere similar to ours and could sustain life. The challenge will be getting there."

"No citizen has ever attempted space travel," Tatalc said. "Dafur mentioned solar flares in his lecture. Tell me more about them."

Rigby began to explain, "The sun is nothing more than a large mass of energy created by the collision and explosion of atomic particles. These interactions become intense, causing areas on our sun's surface to overheat and burst. When these spots burst they release an enormous amount of magnetic energy that travels away from our sun and into the darkness of space. Our hypothesis is that if we could launch some type of vessel into space, we could align it with the waves of energy and let that energy propel the vessel through space towards the next planet."

Tatalc summarized, "It sounds like the same principles used in sailing a boat. Except, instead of being powered by wind, you are being powered by the energy, or the flares, of the sun."

"That's a fair analogy, simple, but fair." Rigby responded.

"How confident are you that it would really work?" Tatalc asked.

"Very confident. The energy produced by solar flares is more than enough to propel us towards our destination, but we have other concerns."

"Like what?"

"Our two major concerns are how to launch a vessel far enough into space to align with a solar flare and how to design a vessel that can withstand the rigors of space."

"Have you made any progress with either of these?"

"We've made a little progress, but our resources are limited. We're still calculating the variable paths we could take based on when and where solar flares occur. We need to chart the course, actually several courses in case something unpredictable happens." Rigby paused to take a drink. "As far as the vessels, I feel with enough time and resources we could build an adequate vessel. The vessel would need to be able to sustain life, store supplies, and most importantly, protect the occupants from the dangerous radiation they'll encounter."

"What about the launch?"

"We don't have an answer for that yet, and *all of this* is why we need your help."

"I'm not sure I understand how I could help. I'm not a scientist."

"It's not the science we need help with. We need help with resources. To this point we've only been working with formulas and algorithms, calculations we are equipped to study and develop on our own. But *really* building a vessel and figuring out how to launch it will take resources, lots of them."

"So you're asking for resources?"

"Not specifically from you. We're asking that you support our cause, that you become our voice to the citizens." Rigby leaned in closer to Tatalc. "Tatalc, you carry great influence and no one rivals your ability to motivate citizens into action. If you were to speak of what we are doing, of the possibilities of our discoveries, that this might be the only chance of survival, citizens would listen and they would act. The government would support us and we would have all the resources we would ever need." Rigby continued, "This is the most important thing you could ever do."

Tatalc sat back in his chair, pondering Rigby's request. This *was* the most important crisis to face Cythera and he felt an obligation to do whatever he could. But was this the right place for him to dedicate his energy? He wasn't sure. "Rigby, I'm going to have to think about this. I'm hoping you weren't expecting an answer right away."

"I understand. This is a lot to weigh." Rigby asked, "Is there anything else I could answer for you? Anything to help you have a better picture of what we are attempting to do?"

"No, you've done a good job explaining your objectives." Tatalc paused, and then continued. "I'll have to admit that when my father asked me to go listen to Dafur's lecture I really didn't want to go, but that was only because I didn't understand the possibilities. If I decide to partner with you, you'll need to further educate me and bring me to a point of full clarity. I can't stir the citizens to support your plan if I don't believe it myself, and I can't with a clean conscience give them hope and then have something go wrong."

"Of course." Rigby agreed. "I wouldn't want to create false hope either."

"I'll let you know soon, Rigby." Standing up from the table, Tatalc walked Rigby back to the front of the estate. "Thank you for contacting me and taking the time to come here and meet me."

"It was my pleasure, Tatalc. I look forward to hearing back from you."

As Rigby left the estate he felt positive about the conversation with Tatalc. *At least he didn't say 'no'.*

But one thought puzzled Rigby. Tatalc said he attended Dafur's lecture because a friend told him about it, then later he said his father had sent him. He wondered if this was a misunderstanding or an innocent miscommunication by Tatalc, *or* was Tatalc hiding something.

Rigby reasoned it did not matter why Tatalc attended the lecture. Tatalc had nothing to hide, but what was of crucial importance was whether or not Tatalc would help. Rigby would have to wait for that answer.

Chapter 21

The Discovery

The bearded man stood over Shotum's body. He had

not intended nor wanted to kill the boy, but when the boy drew his weapon he had no choice. Needing to look like an accident, no one could know he had been here. The bearded man moved the boy's body next to the limb the boy had tripped over.

Nearby he found a large rock and moved the rock next to the boy's head. After crouching to the ground he lifted Shotum's head. Wiping his fingers through the warm blood that still ran from the fatal wound he had caused, he rubbed the blood on to the rock. Standing up, he evaluated his work. Pleased with the staged scene, he turned towards the artifact which had been propelled a long distance when the boy *really* tripped and fell.

Moving toward the area to retrieve the artifact the bearded man stopped. In the distance a group was approaching. They had come back for the boy.

Assessing his distance from the artifact and the distance of the approaching group, the bearded man calculated he wouldn't have enough time to reach the artifact without being seen, and he couldn't take that risk. He turned and ran back into the shadows of the cave where he could hide from their view. As he reached the entrance to the cave, he heard the shout, "What's that?" Feeling safe, since the group had not seen him, he watched and waited.

***

Rual had been the first to notice the body lying on the ground.

Before the words were out of Rual's mouth the entire group of young boys began to sprint toward the body. When they reached Shotum they turned him over. "Oh no, Shotum. What happened?" Rual sat down on the ground and rolled Shotum's body into his lap. Wiping the hair from his bloody forehead, Rual whispered, "Poor boy, poor boy. I'm sorry I wasn't here for you. I'm sorry I sent you back."

Shotum was like a son to Rual. All the boys were. The fear Rual had experienced in the caves when he *thought* the boys were going to die did not compare to the pain he was feeling now that one of his boys *had* died. Rual held his hands over the dead boy's eyes and closed his eyelids.

"What happened Rual?" one of the smaller boys asked.

"I think he fell. You can see where he tripped." Barrie pointed to the large limb and then to the rock with blood on it, "There's where he hit his head. Shotum I'm sorry. I'm the one who should've come back." Barrie began to cry. When Barrie began to show his emotions, the other boys cried too. They had all lost a brother.

With all his fortitude Rual remained composed. Trying to calm them he said, "I know everyone is shocked and sad. I too am devastated. But it was an accident, an awful accident. It could've happened to any of us."

Everyone sat quietly for a long time, each afraid to break the silence. They all knew what would happen when the silence stopped. As their leader, Rual knew it was his responsibility to lead the transition for Shotum. He was the first to speak. Rual's voice was shaking but direct, "Everyone go gather wood. We have to do what's right so Shotum's spirit can move forward."

One by one the boys stood up and scattered around the area collecting small pieces of wood. After carrying the wood back they began to build a large pile of sticks. The boys were thorough in gathering every available stick and branch they could find, except one. The one Shotum had tripped over they left alone. No one wanted to touch it.

Rual and Barrie lifted Shotum's body on to the pile of sticks and covered his face with a cloth. As Transient tradition dictated, they didn't search his body to remove any personal items. Whatever was with Transients when they died was to stay with them into the next life. Rual lit the fire, and then joined the boys who were forming a circle around the blaze. They all held hands while Rual spoke. "Steffer, our dear friend Shotum now walks with you. He's not afraid, only lost. Guide him and show him the path to the next world where he will find peace and happiness."

Everyone watched the flames burn larger and brighter. The fire grew and spread to the spiritless body of their friend. Shotum's lifeless flesh cracked and sparked as it was ignited and engulfed in flames. They did not need to stay until the body was burnt to ash, their role in Shotum's passage was complete, they would let the fire burn itself out.

"He has left us." Rual said. "And now we must leave him."

The boys broke hands. With sad faces they looked at each other knowing they had said their last goodbye to Shotum. Without words they began to collect their belongings to start their journey home. Out of the corner of his eye Barrie noticed the artifact Shotum was sent back to retrieve. *This is all my fault*, Barrie thought to himself. He walked over to the artifact, picked it up and placed it inside his satchel.

Led by Rual, the young clan of Transients *again* began their long walk home. Once they were on their way, the bearded man walked out of the darkness of the cave and from a safe distance he followed them.

Chapter 22

Before the Debate – Tatalc & Wickem

After leading Rigby to the front of the estate and bidding him farewell, Tatalc walked up the patio steps and went inside the house. Before closing the large wooden doors, he looked back to confirm Rigby had left. Like a museum, the home's foyer was decorated with crafted statues and timeless prints Tatalc's family had collected over the generations. The foyer transitioned into an atrium where there were four columns, each the thickness of a large tree. A circular flowing fountain served as a centerpiece to the exquisite entrance.

Tatalc was not impressed. He'd never been impressed with his family's lavish collections. In his mind these were worthless instruments his ancestors procured to awe their guests. Tatalc preferred substance and action versus mundane possessions. His father Wickem was the same way.

Paying little attention to the valuable art on display, Tatalc walked through the large foyer. Passing the fountain, he turned right down a long hallway leading to a sitting room where his father was waiting. Tatalc entered the room and sat in a chair across from his father. Wickem closed the book he was reading and placed it on a nearby stand. "How did the meeting go?" Wickem asked Tatalc.

"Were you listening?"

"I was. And I'm not sure why you were compelled to lie about me never visiting the estate. It's public knowledge I still vacation here at times." Wickem scolded his son.

"I got carried away, but I'm not worried about it.

They're the ones asking for *our* help."

"You're right, but if you're going to help them, don't you think it would be best to avoid trivial untruths? Whether I come here or not is irrelevant. There was no need to even bring it up. You have to be careful Tatalc; sometimes your tongue moves faster than your brain." Wickem paused, and then continued. "You're not as clever as you think you are." This was not the first time Tatalc had heard these words from his father. His father had lectured him many times on how to conduct oneself in conversation.

Tatalc had always been loose with his words. It wasn't that Tatalc had deceitful intentions, but sometimes he spoke without weighing the consequences of his words. This trait served him well when improvising a speech or motivating a crowd, but in face-to-face conversations his carelessness could put him in a precarious position.

Knowing better than to start an argument with his father over this issue, Tatalc waited until Wickem was ready to discus the meeting with Rigby. "So they want you to be their voice." Wickem's comment was more of a statement than a question.

"That's what I gathered. Have they even submitted their idea to your office yet?"

"I don't know. We have so many ideas coming in right now it's hard to keep up with them all. When I get back I'll ask Dekayb if she knows. It does seem like a plausible idea though."

"It almost seems too simple. It makes me wonder why no other citizen has proposed space travel," Tatalc added.

"The best ideas are sometimes the simplest," Wickem said.

Tatalc stood up and walked to the bar. He poured two

drinks. Returning to his chair he handed one to his father and took a small sip from his own glass.

"Their approach was unexpected," Tatalc stated as he sat down.

"How so?"

"I assumed they would first ask for financial support of some kind. Isn't this what every citizen with an idea is asking for? I'll admit I'm rather humbled that they believe my influence would be enough to stir the masses into supporting their idea."

"Don't sell yourself short Tatalc. I agree with them. If anyone could create a movement to back their cause it's you."

"I appreciate the compliment Father. But I'm not sure if this is the best use of my energy and time."

"Really? What else is more important than finding a way to save Cythera? All of your other projects might help make Cythera a better place to live, but if Cythera dies, do those other projects even matter?"

"I suppose that's true if you really believe Cythera is doomed." Tatalc's comments caught Wickem off guard. Wickem had no idea Tatalc had doubts about the decoding of the Rugal. Tatalc knew his words surprised his father. He wasn't ashamed. It was his father who had linked his entire reputation to the decoding of the Rugal, not him. But Wickem was still his father. "I'm sorry, Father. I think you misunderstood me. I believe you, and I'll believe *with* you. But I still have hope we're all wrong and Cythera will be fine. If I join these men I'll be sacrificing that hope. I'm not sure I'm prepared to do that yet."

"Tatalc, I understand. I have doubts and hopes myself. Nothing would please me more than to be wrong about this. But I can't take that chance. There's too much at stake and my responsibility is to assure our civilization survives."

Tatalc asked his father, "What do you think I should do?"

"I can't make that decision for you. You love the citizens as much as I do and I know you would do anything for them. But this is your decision and it's one you have to make on your own."

Chapter 23

Before the Debate – Dafur & Lij

The morning after the *Pepper* show, Dafur arrived at Lij's apartment with a picnic lunch. Lij was surprised and charmed he wanted to see her again so soon. "Dafur, this is unexpected." Lij said when she greeted him at the door.

Dafur grinned, "I know there's probably some unwritten rule about waiting a while to ask you out again, but I couldn't wait to see you. And it was your idea that we go on an official date." Dafur held up the picnic basket. "I've packed a lunch and was planning on catching a carriage down to the lake. It should be breezy on the water and comfortable enough to be outside for a little while. I was hoping you would join me?"

"Are you willing to wait outside while I get ready?"

"I'm in no hurry."

"Then I'd be happy to join you for a picnic," Lij said.

Lij closed the door and walked up the stairs to her apartment. Dafur found a nearby bench where he could sit and wait for her.

Lij was able to quickly prepare herself. She never was

one to wear a lot of make up and the comfort and confidence she had in her own appearance allowed for an easy transition from a *being at home look* to a *being in public* look.

When Lij emerged from the front door of her apartment building Dafur was impressed by how fast she had made herself ready. Most women could spend a revolution preparing themselves but would not glow in the way that Lij did. "Do I look all right? I decided to dress light since we're going to be outside." Lij asked.

"You look stunning."

"Stunning?" Lij laughed. "Are you trying to flatter me? I don't think anyone has ever been called *stunning* while wearing short pants and a pull over." Dafur stood up from the bench and Lij wrapped her arm in the crook of his elbow. "But I'll take the compliment." The two walked arm and arm down the street.

***

As time passed Dafur and Lij were together more and more. Lij was becoming a fixture at Dafur's lab; she was spending nearly as much time there as Rigby. Rigby didn't seem to be bothered by Lij's constant presence. In fact, he encouraged Lij to contribute to their work.

Dafur was ecstatic Rigby had been so welcoming. Initially, Dafur was concerned that Rigby might see Lij as a distraction, but this was not the case. Rigby was familiar with Lij's academic background and believed she could help them. Rigby was also happy Dafur had found someone to make him smile.

Currently, Dafur and Rigby's most difficult challenge was finding a material that could withstand the rigors of space travel. They'd been testing experimental metals and having the extra pair of hands was making the task more bearable. It was pure trial and error, and Lij's patience with the process was helping them stay on course. It was during the testing of a combination of two rare materials that they were interrupted, by a surprising guest.

Lij was the first to notice the man walking through the door. He seemed familiar, but she couldn't place him. Thinking he was probably another teacher, she returned to her work. The guest, not wanting to disrupt the experiment, waited on the other side of the lab observing the scientists at work.

Rigby, whose back was to the visitor, held a long metal spoon, which he used to mix two molten metals in a large basin. Standing next to Rigby was Dafur. In his left hand, Dafur held a hot air torch with a flame blowing from the end. With his right hand he was taking notes. "Are you ready Lij?" Dafur asked without raising his head from his notes.

"Ready when you are."

"Go ahead then."

Using a long set of tongs Lij reached into a thick container sitting on the lab table and pulled out a small chunk of steaming ice. "Now," Lij said as she dropped the ice into the basin.

Dafur released the trigger on the hot air torch and the flame extinguished. Rigby continued stirring the metals as the three scientists observed the reaction from extreme heat to extreme cold. As the metals bonded and hardened, they began to fracture. "Ziam and Gar, negative reaction to cold, unsuitable for any trial," Rigby stated.

"The Ziam froze too quickly. You can see that here, here and here." Dafur pointed out. "I'd like to test the Ziam by itself so we can eliminate it from consideration. Lij, can you get another sample?"

"I have one right here. By the way, did you know we have a visitor?" Lij pointed to the man standing on the other side of the room. Dafur and Rigby turned around to see who was there. They both recognized the guest.

"Tatalc, welcome to my lab." Dafur walked to greet him. "I don't believe we've formally met." They greeted each other with a handshake. "I'm sorry I didn't notice you come in. Have you been here long?"

"Only a few moments. I was enjoying watching you work." Tatalc followed Dafur to the back of the lab. "My apologies for the unannounced visit. I was in the area and was hoping I could speak with you."

"I'm glad you came." Dafur said. "I've been looking forward to meeting you for a while now."

"Rigby," Tatalc greeted Rigby, "it's a pleasure to see you again."

"Likewise," responded Rigby.

"And this is Lij. She's my . . ." Dafur paused, he was uncertain about how to introduce her. "She's one of our research assistants."

Lij accepted her introduction, "It's a pleasure to meet you Tatalc."

"Mine as well." Tatalc replied.

"Come. Let's sit down." Dafur led them to a cleared table. "So Tatalc, what brings you here today?"

"I've been giving strong consideration to your proposal. The one Rigby told me about."

"This is good news. You can't imagine how much your endorsement would help our cause." Dafur said.

Tatalc continued, "But first I need to learn more about

your idea and what your expectations for me would be. I have to feel confident in your plan before I could commit myself to it."

"Of course," Dafur replied. "What questions can we answer for you?"

"I suppose my first question is about the Rugal. Is there any evidence to validate the prediction? I also wonder if there are not alternative solutions that wouldn't require us to leave Cythera."

"Good questions, ones I've asked myself numerous times," answered Dafur. "But let's answer them one at a time. Your first question is 'how do we know the interpretation of the Rugal is accurate?' Rigby, you know the Rugal's history as well as anyone, I'll let you field this question."

"Certainly. For some time now, even before your father brought attention to the Rugal, scientists have theorized about the extensive warming of our planet. There's a massive amount of evidence illustrating Cytheran's core and surface temperatures have been rising. There's always been debate in the scientific community about what was causing this. Some felt it was being caused by too much terraforming, others felt it was because of our industrial progress. There has never been a hypothesis that gained full consensus. The facts are there though. Average temperatures have dramatically increased. We've seen a reduction in ice masses. Ocean water levels are continuously rising, yet lakes and rivers are drying up. I could go on."

"For example," Dafur chimed in, "Lij and I were recently at Lake Regiowide and it was obvious the water level had significantly dropped."

Rigby continued, "The evidence has always been right

here under our noses. But we, or should I say the scientific community, were misinterpreting it all."

Taking it all in, Tatalc asked, "How could that many citizens have been wrong?"

"I don't know. You have to understand how scientists think. It's not always about the science. Sometimes it's about personal interests; sometimes it's about saying the right thing so the resources continue to flow in. Sometimes it's about making a bold statement to try to get publicity. Unfortunately, this is the way it is."

Dafur added, "The bottom line is no scientist knew the real root cause of climate change until your father brought attention to the Rugal prophecy."

"How do we know the Rugal is true? Couldn't it be another *misinterpretation*?" Tatalc asked.

"We might not ever know for sure," Rigby answered, "at least until, or if, the prediction comes true. But the prophecy reconciles with what we know about how our sun produces energy."

"In what way?" Tatalc asked.

"Our sun's energy is created by the fusion of the two known lightest gasses. As the fusion occurs explosions transfer energy away from the core causing our sun to grow larger. Eventually our sun will be too large, too hot, and too close to Cythera. As I mentioned we're already seeing many signs of the environmental impact.

I believe your second question was 'why do we need to leave Cythera'?"

"It was."

Rigby continued, "The answer to that question is

simple. What's happening is inevitable. We can't prevent it. It's simply nature. I suppose we could take some measures to extend our existence on Cythera but eventually we'll have to leave. All of Cythera will become uninhabitable."

"What about moving underground as some engineers have suggested?" Tatalc asked.

"That would buy us some time. But most of the resources needed for survival like abundant fresh water and food are all above the surface. Once those resources run out we would have nothing left to sustain us." Rigby stated.

"Also," Dafur interjected, "There's no guarantee we could even live underground for very long. As Cythera grows hotter, oxygen burns out of our atmosphere. Underground temperatures will also rise. It's not a viable long-term solution. Our only option is to leave Cythera."

Tatalc stood from his chair. He put his hands in his pockets and paced back and forth. Dafur, Rigby and Lij allowed Tatalc to collect his thoughts. Tatalc imagined citizens suffering. This hurt his soul. He was still not convinced his influence would be enough to help them but he had no choice; he couldn't stand by and do nothing.

After several moments of silence Tatalc turned to Dafur, Rigby and Lij, "For generations my family has held a certain responsibility for the citizens of Cythera. If our system of famocracy has accomplished anything it's allowed families like ours to influence civilization from one generation to the next. In the same manner I have my father's eyes or my grandfather's frame, I inherited the compassion and caring my ancestors have had for Cythera.

"Our family has not always been the most intelligent or the most articulate public servants but we've always protected the concerns of the populous above any other interests. There have been other families entrusted to lead Cythera who have proven unworthy and have lost favor, but our family is different and the reason is simple."

Dafur, Rigby and Lij sat spellbound as Tatalc spoke. His words flowed so eloquently. The gravity of each word slowly pulled them closer and closer to what Tatalc said. This was their first up close encounter with the *great orator*. Tatalc's control over his delivery hypnotized them. *This* was the exact reason they needed his help.

"There is an entitlement that comes with political power. It's the most enticing temptation we encounter. All public servants strive to fulfill the needs of the citizens, to put the citizens first, at least initially. The nobility and virtue of service is what draws citizens to the political arena. But then the seduction of power and self-interest feed the weak ego. If you talk to a new politician they will all say the same thing, 'This will never happen to me.' Revisit them at a later date and you will find the truth. They no longer put the citizen first. Their own interests are all that matter.

"From times before I can remember my father warned me to be on guard against the greatest enemy of all, myself, and it's no secret I've lost a few of those battles. But at night when I lay down to sleep my thoughts are with the citizens of Cythera. Before closing my eyes I pray to Steffer to never let me lose sight of my destiny, to never let me be seduced by my own fear, to always put others above myself.

"And then I ask myself, what can I do at this moment to make their lives better, their lives safer, and in the instant right before I fall asleep I realize the privilege, the honor and most importantly the responsibility I have."

"So regarding your plan and your request for my help. If your plan will help save the citizens of Cythera, I have no choice but to help you."

Chapter 24

The Discovery

Rual knew there would not be enough time before sunset to travel all the way home, but the farther they could get away from the caves the better. The death of their companion Shotum had taken a toll on the boys. They were hollow. "I think this is about as far as we can go tonight." Rual turned and announced to the boys.

"I want to go home," pleaded one of the smaller boys.

Rual answered, "I know. We all want to go home. But it's not safe to travel at night, plus we need the rest. Tomorrow, we will get home tomorrow. I promise."

The boys laid down their satchels and began to gather wood for a fire. They didn't speak to each other. No one wanted to be reminded of the last fire they had built. After building their fire they set around and shared the food they had left. There was enough food for everyone to have a little, but not much more. After eating they began to fall asleep.

***

From a safe distance the bearded man watched them. He needed to retrieve the artifact, but he wasn't sure which boy had it. He had to get close enough to look around but feared if he came too close he would wake them. If he woke the boys up he would have to kill them and he didn't want more blood on his hands. Fortunately the night was dark. As the bearded man approached the boys' campsite the only noticeable light came from the fire that burned lower as the boys slept.

Making sure not to create any noise, he previewed where his foot would land before each step. After each step, he raised his eyes, surveying the boys to see if any of them had moved. It was laborious, but necessary if he were to remain unnoticed.

When he reached the campfire the flames had burned off and only a few embered logs and orange coals remained. The boys were still sleeping and he felt safe looking around. He made his way into their circle and stood next to the dying fire. Looking around for the artifact all he saw were the boys' satchels. It had to be in one of them, but which one?

Of all the satchels he could see, only four looked large enough to hold the artifact. He had to look inside all of them without waking any of the boys. Knowing it was better to steal than to murder, he realized it would be easier to take the satchels then when he was safely away he could review their contents. Moving around the fire he picked up the satchels. After grabbing all four satchels he was ready to return to the darkness. Now he had to leave the site as quietly as he had entered it.

He was soon standing outside their circle. He turned to take one final look at the boys; he had compassion for them. They had done *no* wrong. They didn't know what they had taken and had lost a friend because of their innocent mistake. He was sorry for their loss.

As he departed the camp he heard something move behind him. Looking back to make sure one of the boys wasn't waking up, he saw a log fall off the pile and roll out of the pit.

Relieved that none of the boys woke, he moved on into the darkness. When he was safely away from the campsite he sat down to review the contents of the satchels he had stolen.

He opened the first satchel. Reaching in he pulled out a canteen with some water and some small trinkets. That was all. The second satchel contained a book, probably a diary, and a pair of gloves. That was all. He opened the third satchel and reached inside. He felt something long and round. *This was it,* he thought to himself, *the neck of the artifact.* He pulled it out and was disappointed to find it was only a measuring rod. That was all.

It must be in the fourth satchel. It has to be. He opened the fourth satchel and reached inside. It wasn't there. He was going to have to go back to the campsite and look again. Standing up he gazed back at the campsite and noticed it was much brighter now. *One of the boys must have wakened and noticed the missing satchels. They were rekindling the fire and would come looking for him.*

Then he heard a scream, a painful scream coming from the campsite. Then another scream and another. The boys did not wake up and start the fire; the fire had started and awakened them. Recalling the embered log that fell from the fire the bearded man knew what had happened. The ignited log was burning their entire camp. He couldn't help the young boys. He could only watch them burn.

Chapter 25

After the Debate – Tienneis

Tienneis's curiosity about the lottery was fresh. *A lottery to determine who lives and who dies.* The magnitude of such a concept was still settling into his conscience. Yet here he was, by pure chance, speaking with the man who had lost the most important debate in the history of Cythera.

Wickem had been kind and cordial answering Tienneis's questions. Tienneis knew transitioning their conversation from the accomplishments of Wickem's loyal assistant Dekayb to a conversation about the lottery was risky, but this would be his one and only chance to learn more about the debate. "Wickem, is it safe to assume that D-Dekayb also helped you p-pr-prepare for the lottery d-debate?'

"Yes, of course. She was instrumental in the planning process. But allow me to correct you on one thing. The debate wasn't really about the *lottery*. The debate was about Cythera's future."

Tienneis wasn't sure he understood Wickem, "What d-do you mean?"

"When the prophecy of the Rugal comes true, Cythera will come to an end. But we think we know how to transfer some citizens to the next planet where they can rebuild Cytheran civilization. But *who do we send?* That's really what the debate was about," Wickem explained.

"And you lost the d-debate, c-correct?"

"I did, and it's unfortunate because I truly believe my plan has the higher probability for success. But I've long defended our famocracy and the matter was taken to a vote. The elect agreed with Dafur. Dafur is a good man. We simply disagreed."

"It sounds like you know D-Dafur personally? D-Do you know him well?" Tienneis knew he was probably taking the questioning too far but proceeded anyway.

"Yes, I know him well. We have worked together for a while, closely I might add, developing the plan to move citizens off Cythera."

Wickem didn't seem to mind Tienneis's probing. Tienneis continued, "I apologize but I'm not v-very familiar with the p-pl-plan. Is it c-complex?"

"Parts of it, yes, are extremely complex. But the fundamental plan is simple."

"How so?"

Pausing for a moment to determine the best way to explain, Wickem said, "Well, the simplest way I can state it is we are moving citizens from point A to point B. We need to supply them with the needed resources to start a new life on the next planet, and most of this we've figured out."

"Most?"

"Yes, most. There are three primary objectives. We need to be able to launch a vessel off of Cythera, we need to be able to propel it towards its destination, and we need to safely land the vessel." Wickem continued, "Dafur and his team are working on the vessel. They've also written the algorithms that will determine the patterns of solar flares, so we have our propulsion. Landing should be simple, but they are still working on a way to launch the vessel into space. They haven't solved that problem yet."

Tienneis' excitement came through in his tone, "Have you c-considered a *Thunderwell*?"

"A Thunderwell?" Wickem didn't know what that was, "I'm sorry. I'm not familiar with a Thunderwell. I don't believe I've ever heard Dafur mention it either."

Tienneis explained, "You would need a d-deep well, or shaft. It c-could b-be man made or natural as long as it is c-cl-closed in. You would seal the t-top and affix your p-pr-projectile, or in your c-case your v-vessel to the t-top. Then you would c-cr-create p-pr-pressure within the well. When the reaction from the p-pr-pressure builds up, it will p-produce enough energy to launch your v-vessel into space."

Wickem was intrigued, "Have you ever seen a Thunderwell work?"

"I've actually b-built one b-before, well, at least on a small scale."

"I don't mean to sound rude," Wickem was being sincere, "but aren't you only a truton clerk?"

"No offense t-taken. My father was a physicist and I've study physics myself. When I was a child we would go out t-to the rurals and launch t-toy rockets using natural Thunderwells. It's just a matter of having enough p-pressure to m-match the m-mass of the object."

"And you think something like this would work to launch a vessel into space?"

"It c-could. If you'd like, I'd b-be happy to meet with you and D-Dafur and show you how it w-works."

Wickem thought about this for a moment. This could be the breakthrough they'd been looking for, the missing piece that could save Cythera. He needed to learn more. "Yes. I definitely want to see how it works."

"I'd b-be happy to show you." Tienneis couldn't have imagined the conversation with Wickem to have gone better. He now had a full understanding of the Rugal crisis, the debate, the lottery, and he had provided a possible solution that would help save Cythera.

He thought back to what Konja had told him in the diner and about the man that died from heat stroke. If Cythera were really coming to an end and only a few citizens would survive, was there a way to make sure he survived? Was there a way to make sure he was on one of the vessels?

Tienneis realized he was lost in thought and knew it was time to conclude his conversation with Wickem. "Let me know when you and D-Dafur want to see how a Thunderwell works." Tienneis was about to end the call when he remembered the original reason they were talking to one another, "And one m-more thing, I would m-make reservations for the t-tr-truton ceremony. I think you'll want t-to b-be at The Muy when D-Dekayb receives her t-tr-trutons."

Chapter 26

The Discovery

Tired hands and homesick souls had built the campfire. Struggling to stay awake, none of the boys had noticed the log was rotten. With heavy eyes the boys started to drift before the first log began to burn. Heavy they slept, and heavy they dreamt. Deep into the night most of the flames of the fire were gone, but the embers still glowed.

A rotten, hollow log supported the fire. It was getting weaker. Burning through and collapsing, the piece of wood shifted the fire. The shift was subtle, but enough to disturb the fire's integrity. When the burning wood displaced and resettled, a small log rolled to the ground onto a patch of dry grass.

Aided by a breeze, the heat swiftly moved from the log to the grass. The grass absorbed the heat and ignited. Fire began to spread. The fire had encompassed the entire circle of their campsite before the first boy awakened.

***

In his dream he was the captain of a great ship on an unfamiliar sea, an explorer forging ahead toward the unknown. From atop the mast he could see land in front of them. They were getting closer. It was a land that promised a new life for him and his crew. This would be their new home.

His ship crawled ever closer to the dry land ahead. The crew began to scream and shout. They were almost there. Suddenly the view of the land faded and the pain of a lost dream began to feel real, the pain was so real. The boy woke up and realized the fire was consuming him, *his* pain was so real. Death swallowed the boy before he could react. The scream of another boy, one of his friends, was the last thing he heard.

***

Rual was deep in his own dreams when he began to hear the horror. At the moment he awoke, he felt intense heat surrounding him. Standing up, he looked around the campsite. Everything grew quiet for Rual, as the scene in unfolded in slow time. Boys were waking up and trying to stand only to be weighed down by the flames that engulfed them. Some boys were running, and some were rolling on the ground. Rual was paralyzed.

The screams and cries came into focus for Rual. He didn't know what to do but he could no longer stand and do nothing or he would burn to death too. "Run!!! Everyone, run as far as you can!" Rual screamed, "Roll on the ground! Put yourself out!!" Saving himself, he ran out of the fire.

Reaching a safe distance Rual examined himself. He was all right. He searched around for something, anything that might extinguish the fire, but there was nothing. Looking back towards the fire he noticed three boys trying to escape the flames. Running back to aide them he pulled them as far from the fire as he could. He went back to the fire to see if he could find any other boys. He was hoping to see movement, any movement from another boy that might indicate someone was still alive, but there was none.

What happened? What happened? What happened? Rual repeated in his head. The cadence of the words inside his head matched the beat of his heart. He was having trouble breathing as each breath was becoming more difficult than the last. *What happened? What happened? What . . .*

"Rual, is that you?"

The voice came from behind Rual. Turning around, he saw Barrie. "Barrie, you're all right." Rual ran and embraced the boy. "How did you get out?"

"I don't know. I woke up and heard you yell. I grabbed my satchel and ran. Where's everyone else?"

"I'm not sure. I pulled a few boys out," Rual pointed to where the boys were. Rual and Barrie ran to the three boys Rual pulled out of the fire. Two of them had already died and the third boy was badly burned and struggling to breathe. Rual leaned down and whispered in his ear, "Hold on. You'll be fine. Just hold on." The boy breathed his last.

"There has to be more, right? There has to be more. Others had to escape, right? Right?" Barrie pleaded.

Rual couldn't speak. What words could he say? He didn't know if any other boys had escaped the fire. He didn't know anything anymore.

Chapter 27

Lila's Story

One of the grandest structures in Regiowide was the office of *The Daily Word*. A showcase of modern architecture, the building was designed as an inverted pyramid with a curved roof made of shiny reflective glass. It was known as The Diamond.

As the most widely distributed and read publication on Cythera, *The Daily Word* had existed for many generations. To be employed by *The Word*, as most citizens referred to it, was prestigious. Even more prestigious was to be a writer for *The Word*. Journalists were highly regarded and admired by every class of citizen. It was a trade built on integrity and respect for all citizens regardless of their stature in society.

More than purveyors of information, journalists helped guide and direct the evolution of Cytheran society. At every tangent where civilization could have easily made the wrong choice between good and evil, between peace and war, between equality and injustice, it was the journalists who informed Cythera and guided society to choose the correct path. Without the influence of journalists, Cythera would have never evolved into the near utopian state of advanced sociological, economical and educational ideals that were the core of Cytheran culture.

Lila, a long time fixture at *The Word*, was one of the most celebrated journalists of the modern era. The sophistication and polish of her writing stood out as much as her long platinum hair and her tall thin stature. She began her career writing short social interest articles and rose to become one of the most respected journalists throughout Cythera.

Lila's first major series of articles focused on the education of infants and proved advanced mathematical theories could be absorbed by children. The series made her famous.

Exercises were developed based on a series of exposures to flash data. Correct choices were rewarded with small treats. Opposition argued the behavior was reflexive but Lila was able to prove tangible learning was taking place. Publishing over one hundred articles on the subject, most appearing in *The Word*, she gained instant notoriety. As the movement gained acceptance, and the evidence proving her model compounded, her prominence as a journalist increased by epic proportions.

It was by random chance that she discovered her next big story. As part of her research she would visit the homes of families who had exposed their infants to her educational model. Observing a child's development firsthand was always a joy for her.

Lila had grown particularly close to one family, the family of Inar. By most standards Inar's was a traditional family. Inar and his wife had two sons close together in age and both sons were being exposed to early development. Also living with the family was Inar's aging mother who suffered from the *Loss*.

The loss was a terrible disease afflicting many aged Cytherans. Symptoms included memory deprivation, severe confusion and the depletion of fine motor skills. There was no treatment for the loss. Families with loved ones suffering from the disease were burdened with the responsibilities and frustrations of care.

For some time, Inar's mother's condition had been growing worse. During the children's education she would sit quietly in a corner chair with an empty and expressionless look on her face. Then something remarkable happened, and Lila was there to see it.

"I remember." Inar's mother quietly said from her corner chair, "I remember."

Inar, who was sitting on the floor on the other side of the room, turned his head around. "Mother, did you say something?"

"I remember. I remember." With each utterance her words became louder.

Inar stood and walked over to his confused mother. He reached out and took a hold of her hand and held it between his hands. "Mother, what do you remember?"

"Everything."

Lila began to spend more and more time with Inar's mother trying to determine what caused her total recall. Her memories, which were lost, had been found, and there had to be a reason why.

Inar's mother's recovery was so full she was able to articulate to Lila what had happened to her. She remembered sitting in her corner chair while her grandchildren were being exposed to mathematical flash data. As she listened to the children's lessons her own brain began to change.

Lila knew memories are stored in the electrical chambers of the brain. She knew when a citizen aged, those parts of the brain began to degenerate and the degeneration was accelerated in those suffering from the loss. Researching as much as she could, Lila also learned most citizens store memories as visual images. As deterioration takes place these visual images overlap and become blurred. Lila believed a subject could slow degeneration, and possibly regenerate the brain, if the subject could find ways to mentally stimulate themselves.

Inar's mother agreed that the formulas she witnessed while her grandchildren played with the flash cards had rewired her brain. Her lost visual memories had been recalled. Her brain was building new bridges based on mathematical relationships. Initially, this only confused her, but as the new electrical bridges and roads took shape, her confidence in the authenticity of her experience grew. Realizing she could remember everything, she finally spoke up.

Lila went on to test the method on other subjects suffering from the loss. While it didn't work for everyone, a great majority experienced some form of recall. *The Word* dedicated an entire series on Lila's research, forever changing the lives of citizens suffering from the loss.

Lila's work with behavioral and educational concepts also exposed her to a different problem. Often she recruited students from schools of higher learning to help with her research. In addition to providing young learners a good experience, this helped Lila manage her sizable workload. Over time she developed close personal relationships with many of her volunteers. Since she couldn't pay the students for their efforts, she would look for other ways to help them.

One of the greatest burdens many of the students faced was the increasing cost of their tuition. Learning more about the issue, she became an advocate for the reform of higher education cost. It was during this time that she got to know a young leader with unbelievable promise, Tatalc, the son of Wickem.

Working together to lead the educational reform movement, Lila and Tatalc became close friends, and that friendship continued. So when Tatalc needed help raising awareness about Dafur's plan to leave Cythera, he first went to Lila.

Chapter 28

Before the Debate – Dafur & Lij

After getting out of bed, Dafur began his morning ritual. He showered, ate, and walked from his home to the school. Leaving early enough to avoid the heat, he arrived in his classroom with enough time to review his lectures. He would teach his morning courses and spend the afternoon and evening in his lab. It was an ordinary routine that some might consider dull, but Dafur didn't see things that way.

Throughout his career as a professor he'd been required to teach his share of requisite courses, some of them dull for both him and the students. Uninteresting classes were a part of academia and Dafur accepted this, but his life *was* more enjoyable when he was not teaching a boring class. His current classes were complex and interesting and his students seemed engaged. But teaching interesting classes was only one of the reasons Dafur's life was more enjoyable.

His work with Rigby and Lij was progressing well. After completing their solar flare prediction model, which would provide navigation for the travelers, they started the final testing on several polymetals that they hoped would be strong enough to build the vessels. Dafur was confident they would soon reach a final verdict on the most suitable polymetal; then, they could start building a prototype.

Dafur's real joy came every evening when Lij would arrive at the lab. Lij was currently enrolled in a full course load and not available to assist Dafur and Rigby during the afternoon. But after her last class concluded, she would always come to his lab.

Outside of the lab, Dafur and Lij were inseparable. Their young love was still fresh and growing stronger. Lij had never been in love before. For her, love was new. Dafur had loved before, but it was a long time ago. His love for Lij was invigorating; it energized him.

***

This morning the energy of Dafur's love for Lij carried him as he walked down the street towards school, it was a lightness that he had been feeling for some time. Whatever else was going on in Dafur's life, whatever weight he felt from the stress of the mission, whatever pressure squeezed on his soul, as long as Lij was there Dafur knew he could achieve anything. She was more than his energy, more than a muse, she was becoming a part of him and he was becoming a part of her. He loved her and he knew she loved him. Then, with no predisposition or prior considerations a random and profound thought came to him. Materializing in his head, the thought came from nowhere. *I want to marry her.*

Dafur was caught off guard by his own conscience. He loved Lij, but he'd never thought about marrying her before. *Would she even want to marry me? Do I really want to get married again? Especially now, with Cythera coming to an end?*

For the rest of his walk to school Dafur continued this internal conversation with himself. There was an argument taking place between different parts of his psyche, part of him desperately wanted to marry Lij. Even if they faced an uncertain future, they could at least face it together. Part of him was terrified. What if she said no?

When his first class started, Dafur was happy to have a distraction from the bustling in his head. He hadn't reached any conclusions; nor did he feel he needed to. Until this morning, the thought of marrying Lij had not occurred to him. No need to rush into any decision.

After his second class ended Dafur went to lunch, *another* part of his routine. There were several on-campus diners that Dafur frequented. Typically, he would purchase a copy of *The Daily Word* to read while he ate by himself. After receiving his food, he made an attempt to read four different articles but during each one he would lose track of the content and find his mind swirling back to the question that snuck into his mind earlier on his walk to work. He couldn't get the question out of his mind.

On his way back to the lab Dafur had to clear his head and made the abrupt decision that his earlier thoughts about asking Lij to marry him were premature. Even though their love was growing, they had only known each other for a short time and with everything going well it seemed best not to disturb things. This conclusion felt right to Dafur and now he would be able to focus his mind on the work of transferring citizens off of

Cythera.

***

Usually when Dafur returned to the lab after lunch, Rigby was already there working. Today the room was dark. No one was there. Turning on the lights, he walked across the room. He passed the two large work tables and sat down at his desk to begin reviewing yesterday's notes. Dafur had barely opened his notebook when there was a knock at the door. "Come in."

It was a clinician from the lab across the hall. "Hello. Dafur, I have a message for you."

"What is it?"

"Rigby came in a little while ago but said he wasn't feeling well and was going to go home and rest. He said he'd see you tomorrow."

"Thanks for letting me know."

The lab assistant closed the door leaving Dafur to his work. Dafur wasn't upset with Rigby. If Rigby wasn't feeling well, he wasn't feeling well.

For the rest of the afternoon Dafur analyzed their data on the different polymetals they had been testing. The vessel had to be light enough to be launched, but strong enough to reflect the radiation of solar flares. It had to be insulated enough to withstand the cold of space, while durable enough to successfully land on the next planet.

They had identified three different compounds that met their needs and now it was simply a matter of determining which one best matched all their different requirements. Dafur was deep in thought and did not hear the door to the lab open.

"Where's Rigby?" Her silvery voice warmed him.

"He wasn't feeling well today. How were your classes?" Dafur asked Lij.

"They were good. How are you?" Lij leaned over and gave Dafur a kiss on the cheek.

"I've had a lot on mind today, but I'm fine. And I'm even better now that you're here."

"You've had a lot on your mind?" Lij playfully said. "What's been on your *brilliant mind* today?"

Dafur contemplated telling her, but decided not to, "It really wasn't that important."

Lij walked over to a tall set of shelves and pulled down a box of equipment. "Ok, you don't have to tell me if you don't want to. It's not like I'm your wife or anything."

Dafur laughed out loud. The irony in her statement tickled him. Lij looked back at him and asked, "What was funny about that?"

Dafur looked at her. She *was* amazing. She was beautiful and smart. She was funny and kind. She was his friend. Dafur was hypnotized by *all* she was.

"Why are you staring at me? Do you always act this weird when Rigby isn't feeling well?"

"Will you marry me?" The words fell out of Dafur's mouth. "I'm sorry, I'm sorry." Dafur started to apologize. "What am I saying? Maybe I'm the one who should be at home in bed."

Lij wasn't as surprised as Dafur had thought she'd be. "Are you being serious?"

"I don't know." Dafur knew they only had a little time left, all of Cythera only had a little time left. But he was still nervous and wondered if Lij shared the same feeling, "I do love you. And you love me, right?"

"I do."

"I had this thought this morning on my walk to work. I know its crazy and I've been going back and forth about it. Sorry, I just . . ."

"Shh." Lij put her finger against Dafur's lips. "Don't feel like you have to apologize for loving me. I will never apologize for loving you. If you want to ask me to marry you, you can. If you don't, that's ok too. Follow your heart and say the first thing that comes to your mind."

Dafur pushed his chair back and stood up. "Lij, will you marry me?"

"Of course I will."

Chapter 29

Before the Debate – Tatalc & Lila

"How much do you know about the Rugal?"

"I *am* one of the most influential journalists on Cythera. What do you think?"

They both laughed. "I think you're old enough to have built the crazy thing!"

"I *am* not that old." Lila paused to take a sip of her drink. "It's great to see you again Tatalc. It's been too long."

It had been a while since Tatalc and Lila had spent any *real* time together. Occasionally they might see each other at an event and exchange an embrace and a pleasantry, but this was the first time they had formally met for as long as either could remember.

"You know Tatalc, you're not as young as you used to be either. Every time I see you, you look more and more like Wickem. You were such a childish looking boy when we first met."

Tatalc smiled, "Are either of those statements supposed to be compliments?"

Lila reached across the table and patted Tatalc's right hand, "Both, my dear." She continued, "I'll never forget the first time I heard you speak, it was actually near here, at one of the university auditoriums. You were talking about the injustice of high tuition."

Tatalc let her reminisce, "One of my research assistants told me I needed to come and hear Wickem's son talk. You'd started giving speeches on campus and students were beginning to rally behind your words. I showed up late and was stuck out in the auditorium lobby. I couldn't see inside, but I was able to hear most of your speech. The way you moved the audience, it was like nothing I'd ever heard before. After your speech I went backstage to see you. I'm not sure what I was expecting, but I wasn't expecting someone like you. You were so *young* looking."

"I'm still waiting for the compliment here," said Tatalc.

"Yes, this was supposed to be a compliment wasn't it? You know I get carried away with my story telling. Let's say I was surprised someone so young had such a *natural influence* with words. How's that for a compliment? But now you've outgrown your boyish looks and have the look of Wickem."

"I'm still waiting for the compliment *there* too," Tatalc joked.

"Wickem is a handsome man. You're lucky to have his features." Lila sincerely stated.

"That's kind of you, I'll be sure to tell my father you're still attracted to him. Do you want me to try to set you up on a date with him?"

Lila blushed and slapped Tatalc's hand, "You know that's not what I meant." Tatalc pulled his hand back and rubbed it, "And if I wanted Wickem again, I wouldn't need *your* help."

***

During the tuition reform movement Tatalc and Lila had become close. They were beyond friends. With her busy career, Lila had never found time to build a family. The children she advocated for, the elderly suffering from the loss and the students who were so willing to help her—they were her family.

Likewise, there was a certain element that had always been missing from Tatalc's own life. Wickem had been a good father, but a busy one. And Tatalc had never known his mother. During the tuition reform movement Lila formed a near maternal bond with Tatalc. And regardless of how much time passed between their visits with each other, that bond was always there.

***

"All joking aside Lila, I do need *your* help."

"Of course, whatever I can do."

"What have you been hearing about the Rugal?"

"Well, of course I remember Wickem's speech. That was courageous of him to go against The Chief of State. It was the right thing to do. I know passions were strong afterwards. A lot of citizens were concerned and scared. I also know a lot of scientists and engineers have been working on possible solutions. There are so many, it's impossible to keep up with

116

them all, and as far as I know no one has come up with anything substantial. There are other things I hear too."

"Like what?" Tatalc asked.

Lila paused for a moment and said, "There is some skepticism forming."

"Skepticism about what?"

"Everything." Lila adjusted herself in her chair and leaned in close to Tatalc. "Citizens are starting to stop believing in what Wickem told them."

"I can relate to that, but why do you think this is happening?"

"It's only my opinion, but I think it's because there's not a lot of information being provided to the public. And the information that is being provided isn't the right information. Sure, there's a story here and a story there, but they're all about scientific matters like core temperature change and some crazy idea to save the planet. I think after the initial shock, the whole issue has become less real to the average citizen, and as more time passes, it *all* becomes less real."

"What about you Lila, do you still believe?"

"Absolutely I do. More than you can even imagine."

"You have no idea how good it makes me feel to hear you say that. I won't be able to do this without you."

"Do what?"

Tatalc took a drink of his water and looked around the room. He took a deep breath and looked into Lila's eyes. "We think we have a solution."

"A solution?"

"A solution that could save Cythera."

Chapter 30

The Discovery

Sitting on the ground Rual and Barrie watched the large fire burn. As they waited and hoped that some of the boys were still alive, their exhaustion took over and they both feel asleep. Rual's last thought before falling asleep was *just one, please Steffer, even if it's just one boy that's still alive, have him find us.*

When the morning sun poured over the horizon Rual and Barrie awoke. No one had returned. They were the only ones who survived the fire. "What do we do now?" Barrie asked Rual.

Rual was barely able to speak. His mouth was dry. There had been so much pain and he was numb. Rual mumbled, "We gather them all for passage. We pray for them. And then we go home."

Rual and Barrie searched around the campsite. In addition to the three boys Rual had pulled from the fire, they found two more boys who escaped the campsite but still died from their burns. The other five boys had been consumed. The vicious fire that had attacked them while they slept was now a low burn. The burnt, unrecognizable bodies around the campsite were the hardest to move.

When they were done piling the bodies Rual reached over and held Barrie's hand. "Steffer I have no words for you and if I did I wouldn't expect you to listen." Rual's voice began to grow and he shouted, "Why? Why? Why have you taken them all? You should've taken me instead!" Rual released Barrie's hand and fell to his knees pounding both of his fists into the ground. Gathering himself, he whispered, "Steffer, take their souls and give them peace." Rual stood up off of the ground and he and Barrie started their long walk home.

***

Off in the distance the bearded man was waiting. The smoke from their fire had been blowing towards him, it was dark and thick and full of pain. He had watched the bald man and the young boy perform their ritual and wanted to comfort them, but he could not approach them. He never intended to hurt anyone, especially a small group of boys, but he had to protect the artifact. They were not ready for its message. It would be misinterpreted or abused and when the time was at hand, when the message of the artifact would be needed, they would have long lost faith and *every* child would die.

When the two Transients left the area, the bearded man stayed behind to wait for the fire to cool so he could search for the artifact. Once the fire cooled, the bearded man found a long and sturdy stick similar to a Transient etch. He poked around through the large pile of ash looking for the artifact. *It had to be in there somewhere.* The artifact would have no doubt survived the fire, what it was made of was not native to Cythera and it could not be damaged by *any* native element. The pile of ash was large and full of different burnt materials, including the bones of the dead. The bearded man used his long stick to poke and pull and turn objects. Eventually one of those objects would be the artifact.

***

Rual and Barrie were far from the campsite and far from the cave. Without uttering a single word to each other they walked all morning. Reaching the small village of Reechoed, they decided to stop for a brief rest. They found a place to sit down and eat, the rest helped to clear their heads. Soon the shock began to wear off and the reality started to set in.

Rual could remember the boys' enthusiasm when they left their village to see the Feber. This was a rite of passage for Transient boys that only a few of them had experienced. The boys' parents had entrusted Rual with the safety of their children. He had been to the Feber multiple times and had always returned with a group of boys whose lives had been positively impacted.

Starting like all his past trips, the most recent pilgrimage to the caves was full of excitement as the boys bonded with each other. When they camped the first night, they sat around the fire listening to Rual tell stories from generations past. They were important stories that taught the boys about the history of their ancestors and illustrated how Transient men should honorably act. These lessons would provide the foundation for the boys to transition into men.

But this was not like any of Raul's past trips. Everything that had happened raced through Rual's mind. Sometimes in the clarity of a specific expression of fear he witnessed on a boy's face and sometimes in the blur of everything that had happened too fast for him to react.

Rual searched his mind for an explanation. How would he explain this to the boy's families and to the rest of their village? It couldn't all have been bad luck, or could it have? Suddenly Rual realized something. He was superstitious and he was desperate. Any answer would suffice. Rual turned to Barrie and asked, "Whatever happened to the artifact we found at the Feber? Didn't you have it at one point?"

"Yes." Barrie reached over his body with his right hand and reached into his satchel. He pulled out the artifact, unwrapped it and placed it on the table. "And I still have it."

"Barrie, we have to get rid of it. That's what caused all our bad luck." Rual demanded, "We have to get rid of it now!"

"Do you really think this," Barrie grasped the artifact by its long slender neck, "caused all the bad things to happen?" His tone was more curious than defiant.

"It had to have. I don't know what it is, but we should've never removed it from the cave."

Barrie nodded his head in agreement, "What do we do with it?"

Just then a one armed stranger who was walking down the street stopped at their table. He was an eccentric looking man with long wavy hair and tattered clothes, "I'm sorry to interrupt you but I had to stop and ask. What is that?" He pointed at the artifact. "It's unusual and beautiful. I've never seen anything like it before."

"This is bad luck." Rual said. "You don't want to be anywhere near it."

"Let me introduce myself. My name is Lairnam. I am a man of the arts." His smile exposed his rotten teeth. "I've often found one man's bad luck is another man's good luck." Lairnam extended his only hand. "What are your names?"

"I am Rual and this is Barrie. This has brought us nothing but misfortune. We were discussing how to dispose of it."

"I'd be happy to take it from you. I could even pay you a little."

"What use would you have for it?" Rual asked the strange man.

"I think it would go well with my collection."

"Then it's yours, and I feel taking money for it would

add to the bad fortune it's created for us. You can have it for free." Rual lifted the artifact and handed it to Lairnam. "Here, have it."

"I'm grateful to you and wish you well." Lairnam held the artifact up and examined it. He turned it from side to side viewing the piece from every angle. "To honor your kind gift I will name this amazing piece of art after you. I will call it the *Rugal*."

"My name is *Rual* and I don't want it named after me."

But Lairnam had already turned and walked away.

Rual looked over at Barrie and said, "Let's go home."

***

The bearded man spent all afternoon sifting through the ashes of the fire and found nothing. The two survivors must have the artifact with them. They had traveled too far ahead and the bearded man had no idea which direction they had gone. It would be impossible to find them. Impossible to stop them from sharing the artifact.

Disappointed in his failure, the bearded man would have to be patient until the artifact reemerged. He had no choice but to return to where he came from and wait.

Chapter 31

Before the Debate – Tatalc & Lila

"You've found a solution that would stop the sun from growing? How?" It had taken Lila a few moments to digest what Tatalc had told her.

"I don't think you understood me correctly," said Tatalc. "We think we've found a solution that might save Cytheran civilization. I've never heard any mention about slowing down our sun's growth; I don't think that's even possible. Have you heard something about slowing down our sun's growth?"

"No, no, I haven't. That's why I was a little stunned. I didn't think it was possible either. But I don't understand how else we could save Cythera."

"Well, we couldn't save Cythera the planet, but we could save the citizens of Cythera." Tatalc began to explain, "Maybe not *all* of them, at least not initially, but there's a professor named Dafur who might have discovered a way to move citizens off Cythera and further away from our sun."

"Move citizens off of Cythera, to where?"

"The next planet. The one you can sometimes see in the night. Do you know which one I'm talking about?"

"I do."

Tatalc continued, "Dafur believes that if we could launch citizens off of Cythera he could direct their vessel to safely land on the other planet."

"That sounds dangerous." Lila responded.

"It is. But if it worked, and if we had enough time, we could move every citizen off of Cythera. We could save everyone."

"What was the professor's name again? I've spent a lot of time at the university. There's a chance I might know him."

"His name is Dafur. He's an engineer."

"Dafur. I think I've heard of him." Lila thought for a moment. "I have heard of him, but I don't know him. But I could find out about him. Is this why you wanted to meet with me? To see if I would help you find out more about this Dafur?" Tatalc reared back in his chair and laughed out loud. She asked, "Why are you laughing at me? I'm trying to be nice and help you."

"The thought had never crossed my mind to do a background check on Dafur. But that's what makes you so good at what you do. You take the time to find out *everything*. That's why you are the best journalist on Cythera, *and* I suppose it wouldn't hurt any to find out more about Dafur."

"But if that's not what you wanted to talk to me about, then what was it?"

"Dafur and his colleagues have asked for my help."

"*Your* help? Since when did you know anything about space travel and science and all those other technical things?" Lila was now laughing at Tatalc. "What could you possibly help them with?"

"They need a *voice*."

"Oh. Well. You are good at that. But why do they need a *voice*?"

"The science they are working with is complex and they should be focusing their time and energy on the project, not on building public consensus. They have limited financial resources and their plan would be expensive. In order to build their prototypes and test their theories they need resources and a lot of them. They're scientists, they don't feel they have the ability to articulate what they are doing in a way that the average citizen could comprehend."

"That makes sense," validated Lila. "But doesn't Wickem control which projects receive resources and which ones don't? Why don't you talk to him?"

"Who do you think told me about Dafur?"

"Of course, I should've known that. But still, if Wickem is in charge of all the projects that could help save Cythera, why do they need your help to raise awareness?"

"Father and Dekayb have reviewed numerous plans that would supposedly save us from our growing sun. I've seen my fair share too. We're convinced none of them will work except Dafur's. And as you can imagine, Father is pressured to fund some of these other ideas that have no chance of success. It's political. It seems everyone has a relative or friend with an idea and they all need resources to research it. To be successful, we'll need to dedicate all resources towards Dafur to help accelerate his project. It's really the only chance we have. If I can create consensus from the citizens, they will apply pressure on the elect to fully support Dafur. This would allow my Father to shift all resources to Dafur without having to pick a fight with every politician on Cythera."

"Are you convinced that Dafur's plan will work?"

"Yes, I've met with him and his assistant several times now. I can't absolutely tell you that their plan will work and I won't be able to until it is attempted. But based on what I've learned from them, and considering the other options available to us, I believe Dafur's plan is our best, and maybe only, option for survival."

"This is a big undertaking for you, Tatalc. It's one thing to rally a bunch of students who want to save money. It's an entirely different thing to move the masses into alignment on a controversial subject like this. As I was telling you earlier there are a lot of different opinions beginning to emerge about the Rugal and the future of Cythera. It's not going to be easy for you."

"I know and that's why I need your help."

"Okay. Tell me what you need me to do."

Chapter 32

Before the Debate – Lij's Story

When Dafur asked Lij to marry him she didn't hesitate and she answered yes. Lij had fallen deeply in love with Dafur and couldn't wait to share the news with her family.

Her family had always supported her choices. When she decided to leave her family's rural existence to pursue an education in Regiowide all of her family backed her decision. For generations Transients had found equal opportunity in large metropolitan cities such as Regiowide. Even so, Lij was the first in her family to leave their small village to pursue greater dreams.

Lij's two older brothers had been to visit her several times in Regiowide. Her parents had not been to visit her, since travel was difficult at their age. The only time she would see her parents was when she made the long journey home. Since her engagement to Dafur she had spoken to her parents several times but had not told them the news. She wanted to tell them face-to-face.

Lij had been hoping Dafur would be able to join her and had been waiting for a time he would be available. Unfortunately, Dafur was too close to discovering a suitable material for the vessel and didn't foresee a time in the near future that he would be able to accompany her. Lij knew she couldn't keep the secret from her parents much longer. She decided it was time to make the long journey back home and tell them. They would have to wait to meet Dafur.

Lij's homecomings were special. Her parents would always host a dinner and invite all their close friends and relatives. This visit would be no different, though it would be more special. Lij had told them to expect an announcement, an exciting announcement, but they would have to wait for her arrival to hear the good news.

The town she grew up in sat in a low valley. West of the valley was a thick forest where long ago a path had been cut that curved down a hill and crossed over a creek leading into the main part of town. On the east side of the valley was a swift small river that provided the needed water for the town's survival. On the north and south sides of the valley were large hills that led up to flat lands perfectly suited for farming. There was a certain indescribable charm to the small town. Because it was surrounded by hills and running water, there was not a lot of room for growth. This kept the town small and close. The citizens who called Bellcreek home preferred things this way. Many generations ago the town had been settled by Transients who were looking for a peaceful existence and safe haven to perform their rituals. Everyone living there was either born a Transient or married to one. It was a tight knit community.

Lij had decided to travel by water. When covering long distances, traveling by water was more efficient than traveling by land. There was a place in the river called *the dead end*, named because on approach it looked like the river was coming to an end. There was a high wall of land where long ago children tied ropes to swing out and fall into the water. As a child Lij had spent a lot of time playing at the *dead end*.

It wasn't a real dead end. The river didn't actually end there. Instead, the river turned to the right and to the left, and led to the landing on the eastern part of town. When Lij saw the long rope hanging from the tree she knew she was almost home.

Waiting for her at the landing were her two older brothers. As soon her raft was tied down, Lij ran off the boat and into the arms of her brothers. After they hugged, Dran, the oldest, jumped on the boat to grab Lij's things. "Lij which satchel is yours? We're in a hurry, everyone's waiting." Lij pointed to a large blue bag, Dran reached down and lifted it and pulled it over his shoulder. He jumped back off the boat, "Are you ready to go?"

It was a short ride from the landing into town and to the park that was reserved for Lij's reception. Approaching the park Lij noticed how large the crowd was. "Why are so many here?" she asked.

"Because everyone loves Lij." Hilp, the younger of her two older brothers, joked. Hilp always had a smile on his face.

Dran, who was the more serious of the two brothers, added, "Mother's been telling everyone you have an exciting announcement, that it's really good news. Everyone knows you've been working on a solution to the crisis. I think everyone assumes that's what your good news is about. That's why they're all here."

"You are here to *save us all*, right?" Hilp joked again.

Lij had trouble finding words.

"You *are* here to save us all, right?" Hilp repeated.

"Not exactly."

Chapter 33

Dekayb's Story

During Wickem's life there had only been a few women who meant as much to him as his assistant Dekayb. Unlike Wickem's first wife and the other woman he had spent time with, Dekayb was not refined in her appearance. She was attractive, but she carried herself differently than other women. She felt no need to dress fashionably or make herself up. Usually she wore her long black hair pulled back in a tight bun. And on most days she wore a conservative wardrobe befitting a professional woman.

Dekayb had always set high expectations for herself. After being educated in government policy and law, she had difficulty finding a related career. She was an excellent student, finishing near the top of her class, but was still unable to find work in her desired specialty. It was poor timing. The government was going through a period of contraction and was in the process of reducing its staff, not expanding it.

Rightsizing was rather common for Cytheran government. While working for the government was a prestigious profession, it wasn't reliable. This design was good for the citizens. When they needed a larger government they would get one, but when a larger government *was not* required, Cytheran leaders made appropriate cuts. This model enabled a broad range of efficiencies that fostered an almost perpetual state of economic and social growth.

Dekayb assumed when the tide shifted and the government began to expand again she would have the opportunity to fulfill her dream of working for an elected representative. She was right, but she never could have imagined the path that led her to her goal.

Her first professional position was with a law firm practicing estate law. While she hoped this was temporary, she still dedicated herself to her responsibilities and earned the respect of her peers and managers. She soon found herself being asked by senior partners to assist with their largest and most important clients. This is how she first met Wickem.

After the violent death of Wickem's father, he needed to settle his father's estate. He hired Dekayb's firm.

The estate was to have been a simple transaction— all of his father's wealth would be transferred over to Wickem's mother. But as his mother's health began to deteriorate, matters became more complicated. It was during these difficult times that Wickem and Dekayb began to spend time together, dissecting the family's assets to determine the appropriate course of action.

Dekayb had impressed Wickem with her intelligence and understanding of the law, but it was her compassion for his family and their trials that stood out. As they spent more time together they grew to be friends. Eventually Dekayb revealed to Wickem her true passion was not estate law, but government law.

Shortly after Wickem's mother's death he approached Dekayb and offered her a position as his personal assistant. Initially Dekayb wondered if the position met her professional expectations but Wickem assured her there was no one on his staff he valued more. Dekayb believed Wickem and accepted.

Dekayb never complained about her position as Wickem's assistant. Understanding her value, she was above questioning her worth. Outsiders may have perceived her to be nothing more than a secretary, but behind closed doors she was Wickem's closest and most trusted advisor. Her job description was simple; she did what Wickem needed and supported him in every way she could. Dekayb never regretted her decision. She felt valued by Wickem and she was able to influence decisions being made at the highest levels of Cytheran government. This was her dream and she excelled. Even small tasks were performed with enthusiasm.

One of her lesser roles was to screen Wickem's calls. Some might have considered this a menial responsibility below Dekayb's abilities, but Wickem understood the importance of his *first voice* being that of someone he trusted. Dekayb was happy to fulfill this need.

Dekayb knew who Wickem needed to talk to. When Dafur called, she knew Wickem needed to talk to him.

"Dekayb. It's Dafur. Is he available?"

Dafur's tone was high pitched and he was talking fast. Usually Dafur's voice was deep and he took time choosing his words. Dekayb guessed it was something important and hurried to connect him with Wickem, "Yes. Let me get him for you."

Dekayb walked back into Wickem's office, "It's Dafur."

Wickem picked up the receiver, "Dafur, how are the experiments going?"

Dekayb remained in his office while he talked to Dafur. Her intuition was correct; even though she could not hear what Dafur was telling Wickem she could tell by his expression it was good news. Wickem nodded his head a few times and he was smiling. Eventually Wickem looked up to Dekayb; she could tell the call was almost over. Wickem nodded his head again and told Dafur, "We can leave now."

Wickem stood up and walked towards Dekayb, "I need

to go to Dafur's lab and I want you to come with me."

Chapter 34

The Discovery

In the history of Cytheran civilization there had been numerous stories told of individuals who had great opportunities but failed. Their actions warned of the evils of life. Some of these individuals were monsters who defined what others should strive to avoid, others were simply lost souls who found themselves in situations that challenged their will power. These stories have been passed down from generation to generation providing lessons for future generations to learn from. The story of Lairnam is one of these.

* * *

Lairnam was born with significant birthright - his family was wealthy. Like most families of the early era, his family was large. Children were an asset, expected to work for their parents in an effort to build and extend the family's wealth. There was one exception. The first-born children, whether male or female, were free to pursue their own interests. Lairnam was the first-born.

From early childhood Lairnam had multiple talents and naturally excelled at everything he attempted. He was a superior athlete and an accomplished artist. But his most notable talent was as a musician. He was especially gifted at playing stringed instruments.

By his seventh cycle he was already well known by the musical elite and was considered to be the next great prodigy.

By his fourteenth cycle he was known throughout Cythera and shared the same type of fame usually only reserved for politicians, journalists and mathematicians. He was a pioneer. He was the first musician to ever obtain such stature.

But since he was the first, there had been no stories or lessons from the past for him to learn from, to insure he remained grounded. Likewise, there was no precedent for how long someone with his talents would remain relevant in the public's eye.

Around his twenty-first cycle, a new talent began to emerge - the next prodigy (there's always a *next*). Soon after, many talented musicians began gaining fame for their work. As Lairnam's popularity began to subside, he unraveled. For so long he had been the first and only shining star, but while other stars where beginning to form, his began to burn out. In a desperate act to prolong his fame, he made a deal with a group of investors.

The investors required a large up-front investment from Lairnam in order to guarantee they could reestablish his fame. Though he came from wealth, Lairnam himself was not wealthy. The substantial wealth one could earn as a popular musician would not be established for several more generations.

But Lairnam knew where he could find the needed investment. Returning to his family, he told a terrible lie that was motivated by his selfish desire to be famous again. He told his parents he needed access to the family account because he wanted to start a school that would teach music to less fortunate children. His parents agreed this was a worthy cause and allowed Lairnam access to their wealth.

When Lairnam returned to the investors with the original sum they had requested, they told him they needed more. This continued for a long time—the investors always needed more money and Lairnam always raided his family's bank account. Finally, when the family's account was near empty, Lairnam realized the investors had never intended on helping him reassert his fame. Enraged, Lairnam confronted them. Without hesitation they admitted never intending to help him. Lairnam realized he was being extorted, he realized the shame in lying to his parents and stealing from his family to fulfill his own selfish desire. Lairnam fell to the ground, begging them to go away, to leave him alone. He told them there was nothing more for him to give, all of his family's wealth was gone.

One of the men walked over to Lairnam, who was still crouched on the floor. Reaching out his hand, he asked Lairnam to stand up. As he stood, Lairnam extended his left hand. The man grabbed hold of Lairnam wrist tightly. Pulling out a long blade, he severed Lairnam's left hand.

Lairnam fell back to the ground holding his severed arm. The worst had happened; he would never play an instrument again. The last words he heard from the investors were *then I guess we no longer have a need for you.* Lairnam could not return to his family. He could never go home again.

Ashamed, Lairnam let his hair grow long, so he would never be recognized. Without his left hand he could no longer hold the strings on an instrument and play music. His only income came from the small paintings and sculptures he created and sold in the small towns he passed through on his journey to nowhere.

It was by pure luck he stumbled across the artifact in the village of Reechoed. A bald Transient man and his young companion were sitting at a table discussing how to dispose of the interestingly shaped statue. Lairnam could hear their conversation and couldn't understand why they would want to part with such a unique work of art; he had to ask about the piece. Fortunately, the Transient man and the boy were trying to get rid of the artifact and he was even luckier they gave it to him for free. Lairnam told them he was willing to pay for it, which was a lie, he had no money. All he could give the bald man was the honor of naming the work of art after him and before the bald man could change his mind, Lairnam quickly walked away. Now that Lairnam had this original piece of art that he named the Rugal, a piece of art that someone even of his natural talents could never have created, he would be able to sell it and regain at least part of his lost fortune.

That night, while sleeping alone at a small camp he had built on a hillside, Lairnam had a dream. He was in a large room standing next to a pedestal. On the pedestal was the Rugal. Behind him were numerous paintings and sculptures; many he recognized as his own works. In front of him was a line of citizens that stretched outside the opened front doors. The citizens were coming to see the Rugal and paying him for the pieces of his art on display behind him.

When he woke up from his dream he had a revelation. Maybe the Rugal could bring attention to his other works and they would become more valuable. Maybe he could build enough fortune to earn back what he had stolen from his family. Maybe he could go home.

From town to town he traveled showing off his newest piece of art. He created a fictional tale of how when his life was at its lowest point he was inspired to create the Rugal. It was a compelling tale that only increased interest in all of Lairnam's art and he began to gain notoriety again.

Soon, the vision he had seen in his dream began to materialize. Because the word of the Rugal was spreading, his other art was selling. At every stop he noticed citizens would come to see the Rugal and buy something else. He cut his hair and decided to go home.

In a short time he amassed a small fortune selling his new art. When he met his parents and his siblings at their home he accepted responsibility for all the troubles he had caused them. After presenting them with a large sum he promised he would pay back everything he had stolen. He owed them a lot more, but he was confident his renewed fame would allow him to earn the remaining debt and he would make things right with his family. Lairnam's family all welcomed him home.

His public notoriety continued to grow. Not to the point where it had been when he was a musician, but to a degree where citizens went out of their way to meet him. His life was beginning to return to normal, but normal for Lairnam was not normal for an ordinary citizen. His greed and hunger for fame simply didn't allow for it. All he had ever known or wanted was fame and adoration. After his visit home and promise to return his family's stolen wealth, he never went home again and he never returned any more of their fortune. While the Rugal helped Lairnam regain some popularity, he never again reached the level he desired.

Eventually, a new artist came along (there's always a next) whose work was more original and unique than Lairnam's. Even the interest in the Rugal faded away.

Lairnam's life ended at the opposite spectrum of where it started. His lifelong quest for popularity drove him to the point of insanity and he took his own life. Lairnam died a lonely man that no citizen cared about.

After his death the last few items he had owned were collected and offered to his family. They didn't want them. Lairnam's possessions were packaged into a box and sent to a museum. Here, they sat on a shelf in a dark room, untouched for a hundred generations. In the box were several paint brushes, a pair of boots, a blue vest and the Rugal.

Chapter 35

Before the Debate – Lij

In the center of the park where Lij's reception was taking place was a large shelter built by the first generation of Transients who had settled in the valley. It wasn't a fancy structure by Cytheran engineering standards, but it served its purpose by providing large gatherings shade from the sun.

The structure had been built in the shape of an octagon with each side of its roof pitching upward and coming together to form a chimney in the center. The chimney extended high above the top pitch of the roof giving the structure the look of an inverted funnel.

On the ground in the middle of the shelter was a round pit where a large fire was burning. Several men stood around the fire threading flightless birds onto spits, to be grilled over the open flame and served as main course for the feast. Off to the side was a long banquet table. The table was full of bowls holding various fresh fruits and vegetables. As usual, with a Transient banquet, there was more food than needed.

Comfortable conversations were taking place among different locals socializing with one another. A hum of chatter filled the air. It was the pleasant, simple sound of longtime friends having a good time.

As Lij and her brothers entered the shelter, guests continued their conversations. Even though everyone recognized Lij, no one approached her. It would have been impolite to be the first to welcome her. That honor was reserved for the banquet's hosts, Lij's parents.

Moving forward through the crowd Lij recognized the large man whose back faced her. The man's arms were flailing about and he was making an array of gestures with his hands. *I wonder what wonderful story he's telling now,* Lij thought. Her father had always been one to enjoy sharing a good story; his big stature and animated personality had always drawn listeners.

Lij weaved through the crowd, hoping to surprise her father. Many of the guests noticed her demeanor and were watching as she made her way towards the story teller.

Her father, entranced in his tale, didn't notice the crowd had quieted. By the time Lij reached her father almost everyone was watching. They all wanted to see the expression of the surprised father welcoming his beloved daughter. Then with the quickness of a striking snake Lij surprised her father with a thick hug from behind.

The near silence gave way to a loud cheer on behalf of the reunited father and daughter. "Lij!" her father turned to give his daughter a proper welcoming embrace, "You're here. It's so great to see you!" Looking over at his two sons standing behind Lij, he said, "Go find your mother so she can . . . "

"I'm right here." A soft voice came from behind Lij's father. Stretching out her arms, she welcomed Lij. The guests cheered.

Now that Lij had been greeted by her parents, other guests were free to welcome her. She circulated amongst old friends, reliving stories from her childhood and catching up on everyone's lives. The gamy smell of roasting birds was beginning to fill the air. It would soon be time to eat.

When the bell rung it was time to dine and everyone became quiet. Lij's father offered a prayer to Steffer then they all formed a line and filled their plates. Lij, her parents, her brothers, and some other close family sat at a long table perpendicular to the rows of other tables where guests sat. Every table was full, some guests even had to sit on the ground.

After most guests had finished eating, Lij's father stood up at the front table and clapped his hands. His large hands collided, creating a deep popping sound that was meant to gain the attention of the guests. Realizing their cue, all the guests began to clap. Slowly, the applause built until it was a loud rhythmic beat that shook the structure they were sitting under. Then her father raised his hands high above his head, and everyone became quiet.

"First, I want to say thank you to everyone who helped prepare this feast. It was delicious." He shouted, "Does everyone agree?" All of the guests hollered. "I would also like to thank all of you for coming today. My heart is again touched by the many friends we are blessed to have." Everyone cheered again.

He continued, "My grandfather used to tell me a story about a wealthy man that lived on a large estate. He was a good man, but he was growing old and was still without any children. He had all the possessions one could ever desire. He had riches beyond belief. He had a large amount of livestock, hundreds of servants who would answer his every call and a wonderful wife.

But his greatest desire was to have child, a son to carry on his name. One night he had a dream in which he met a wish giver. The wish giver told the man that if he would be patient and continue doing good works, he would eventually have a son.

"The next morning the man awoke with a love in his heart for a son not yet born. For the rest of his life the man waited. As he grew older he wondered if his son would ever come, but he never gave up faith on the promise the wish giver had made.

"All of you know how this story ends, but that is not my point. My point is that the man patiently waited, with all of his love, for the arrival of his son, because he knew there would be so much joy when that time came. In my case, I already have my children and I am blessed for that. But when Lij left home, I found myself in the same position as the wealthy old man, patiently waiting with all my love for the return of my sweet Lij. And today she's home and I thank you all for joining me in celebrating this joyous occasion!"

All at once everyone stood and cheered. Many had children who had also moved away, his sentiments were understood. Once the crowd quieted, Lij's father continued. "And today, Lij has come home, with a special announcement that she hasn't told me or her mother yet." He turned and looked at Lij and extended his hand to help her stand. "Lij, we want to hear what you have to tell us."

Lij stood up and kissed her father on the cheek. She turned to the guests, "Thank you again for coming and I do have a big announcement." She paused for a moment. "But it's probably not the one you are expecting and I hope you are not disappointed. I know a lot of you are wondering about the future of Cythera and were hoping I had news from Regiowide that everything would be okay. And it's true that I've been working on a possible solution to the crisis, but there are many smart citizens around Cythera working on solutions right now. I think we're getting closer, but we're not there yet, and that's not what my announcement is about."

Everyone was quiet and Lij could see the disappointment in their eyes. She was frozen in the moment. This was not her fault. She had not given anyone the idea she would be announcing anything about the Rugal crisis. They had decided this on their own. *It was not her fault.* Yet she still felt she'd somehow let them all down. She was about to announce her engagement to Dafur, but would any of them care?

It was obvious Lij was uncomfortable. The awkward silence continued until someone from the crowd spoke up in a warm and comforting voice. "Lij, it's okay. We were hopeful that's all. But I know everyone's still interested in what you came to tell us."

Lij felt better and she continued on, "Thank you. You don't know how much that means to me. Well, I guess I will say it then. I'm getting married!"

Chapter 36

Before the Debate – The Prototype

When Wickem and Dekayb arrived at Dafur's lab, Tatalc was already there. Tatalc had Lila with him. "Lila." Wickem was surprised to see her. "It's been a long time, what are you doing here?"

"It *has* been a long time Wickem." Lila turned to Dekayb and rolled her eyes, "It's been even longer since I've seen you, Dekayb."

"Hello Lila." Dekayb's response was polite but her tone was shallow. It was obvious Dekayb and Lila didn't care for each other.

"I invited her." Tatalc answered his father's question about Lila's presence.

"Why?" Wickem asked.

But before Tatalc could answer, Rigby spoke. "Good everyone's here. Let's all sit down. We have something to show you."

They walked to one of the large work tables in the back of the lab and sat down. On the other side of the table was Dafur. In front of him was a large box draped by a soft cloth.

"Where's Lij?" Tatalc asked.

"She went home to visit her parents," said Dafur.

Rigby interjected, "Why don't you tell everyone *why*? I don't think they know yet."

"Lij and I are getting married and she went home to tell her family."

"Congratulations!" Tatalc was the first to say.

"Yes, congratulations," Wickem added.

"Thanks. But I have some other news that I need to share." Dafur reached over to the box and raised the cloth to reveal a metallic cylinder. "Do you know what this is?"

"Is that what I think it is?" Wickem asked. "A prototype?"

"It is." Dafur confirmed. "Rigby, can you wheel out the

Fictioverse."

Rigby walked towards two large doors on the other side of the lab. He opened them and walked into the small storage room. After disappearing into the darkness for a few moments, he emerged pushing a large machine on wheels.

Dekayb, who was never ashamed to ask a question she didn't know the answer to, leaned over to Wickem and asked, "What's a Fictioverse?"

Wickem, who'd been to the lab several times, moved his head from side to side, "I don't know. I've never seen it before."

Lila looked over to Tatalc to see if he recognized the machine. Tatalc, who had also been to the lab several times, shrugged his shoulders indicating to Lila he didn't know what the Fictioverse was either.

Rigby positioned the large machine next to the lab table. The machine was as tall as an average man, the width and depth of the machine were equal. It had the look of two boxes sitting on top of each other. The bottom half was fully enclosed on all sides. Switches and levers covered one side panel. The top half was transparent and was built of triple paned glass with a removal lid.

Where the top half met the bottom half there was a wide circular opening that funneled into the bottom of the machine where the system mechanics were housed. The opening was perforated with hundreds of tiny holes and was cut into a vortex-grooved spiral.

"I guess you're all wondering what this is." Dafur's comment was more a statement than a question.

"Yes, I think we're all pretty curious. What does it do?" Wickem said. "I don't think of any of us have ever seen anything like it before."

"I don't think you have. We usually only bring it out at night." Dafur walked over to the machine and flipped a few switches on the console. The machine began to hum. "It uses an immense amount of energy, energy we're supposed to be conserving."

Lila raised her hand as if she were in a classroom. "I have a question. What did you call it? A *fikty-ferse*?" Like any good journalist she had a notepad and pen and was taking notes.

"A Fictioverse. *Fik-she-o-verz*." Rigby enunciated.

"Here's what the Fictioverse does." Dafur pointed to the bottom half of the machine and began to explain. "What you can't see down here is that behind these panels are a series of elemental logic controls that when activated can simulate different environments."

"For example, we could simulate extreme heat, extreme cold, humidity, pressure, really any natural environmental state you can imagine," Rigby added.

"Including deep space?" Tatalc asked.

"You're a quick learner," Dafur replied.

Pointing towards the holes in the funnel, Rigby continued, "The chamber below houses the components. When activated, the desired environmental outcome is created and forced up through these openings. Let me show you how it works."

Rigby turned around and walked over to a small sink in the back of the lab and filled a ceramic mug with water. Placing the mug of water on a tray, he put the tray inside the top section of the Fictioverse. After securing the lid he flipped a few switches to activate the machine. "There it's done."

"What's done?" asked Lila.

"I'll show you." Rigby opened the top of the machine. Using a set of long tongs, he reached inside and grabbed the mug. Removing the mug from the machine, Rigby placed it on the lab table for all to see. "Do you notice anything?" he asked.

Tatalc was the first to respond, "It's frozen solid. How'd you freeze it so fast?"

"We created an extremely cold environment." Dafur answered.

"Impressive," added Wickem.

"Now watch this." Rigby used the tongs to lift the mug of frozen water and placed it back inside the machine. After securing the lid he adjusted several of the switches on the panel. "Done."

"What did you do now?" asked Wickem.

Rigby reached inside the machine and removed the mug. He placed it on the table. Now the mug was completely empty.

"What happened to the ice?" Asked Lila, still taking notes.

"I changed the environment to extreme heat. The ice melted into water and the water evaporated." Rigby said.

Wickem reached over to touch the mug and feeling the heat resonating from the mug he pulled his hand back, "That's amazing."

"It's a powerful machine." Dafur said.

"I have a question." Dekayb's questions were usually good. "You say you can simulate *any* environmental condition. How do you simulate darkness? Do you have to cover the machine?" Lila looked up from her note taking and chuckled indicating she did not think Dekayb's question was useful. Dekayb glared back at her.

"That's a good question Dekayb." Dafur noticed the tension between Lila and Dekayb but continued "True darkness is not an environmental condition. Darkness is the absence of light. And light is nothing more than a series of particles and waves created by electromagnetic radiation. Once you suppress the amplitude of the particles and waves, light ceases to exist and you are left with pure darkness. Even though we wouldn't be able to see it, the Fictioverse can remove all the radiation that produces light so the environment within the chamber would be *lightless*. It's not something you would notice with the naked eye, but the conditions inside the machine would be the same as in complete darkness."

"That makes sense." Dekayb answered and then looked over to Lila defiantly.

"The same can be said for cold," added Rigby. "Cold is the absence of heat. To create a cold environment we simply suppress all the heat. And that's really the interesting thing about deep space. Technically deep space, with its extreme cold and darkness, is not a natural environment at all. It is really the *absence of environment*."

While Rigby had been talking Dafur had walked over to a tall cabinet. Opening the door, he found what he was looking for. At the precise moment Rigby said *absence of environment*, Dafur returned to the table. He held a metal object about the size of a small loaf of bread. "Let me show you something. Rigby, set the machine to deep space conditions and add solar energy and radiation." Rigby placed the metal object inside the machine and secured the lid. "What Rigby placed inside the machine is made from the same material we use as structural support when we build a large building."

"You mean steel?" Lila asked.

"No, not steel. I guess some still build with steel, but all the newer buildings use this. Your office building, The Diamond, was built with this. It's called Roonite and it's the strongest commercially available polymetal on Cythera. Rigby, turn it on. Now watch." Dafur instructed.

The object began to compress as if all the air was being sucked out of it and then it exploded. "We've run this same experiment with a live mouse inside the vessel. As you can imagine, it wasn't pretty." Dafur reached over to the prototype that had been sitting in a box on the table and popped open a small hatch. "Rigby, can you get me a mouse?"

Rigby walked back to the storage room and returned with a live mouse. After he placed the mouse inside the prototype vessel, he closed the hatch. Dafur positioned the prototype inside the machine. "Go ahead." Rigby turned the machine on. They watched as the machine activated. This time the vessel didn't collapse on itself. Its integrity withstood the environmental simulation. "Rigby, turn it all the way up."

"Nothing is happening."

"Precisely, and that's a good thing. Right now the machine is simulating an environment ten times more rigorous than what we expect on the mission. As you can see, the vessel is withstanding the environment. Go ahead and shut it down."

Rigby shut down the machine and opened the lid. Reaching into the machine with his tongs he removed the prototype and placed it on the table. Opening the small hatch, the mouse climbed out unharmed. "We've run this and other similar experiments multiple times and we haven't found any environment yet that can damage this polymetal."

Tatalc looked over at his father and Wickem looked back. They were convinced. "Are there any other trials you need to run?" Tatalc asked.

"No, this has passed every imaginable test and it *will work*," said Dafur.

"Congratulations." They could tell by the look on Wickem's face he was convinced the polymetal would work. "So what's next?"

"I'll be blunt." Dafur stated. "We need resources, a lot of resources. This is an expensive and time consuming process. If we're to produce a full scale vessel to launch into space we'll need government support and resources."

"Ok." Wickem said. "We're convinced. We'll start the campaign immediately. Hopefully it won't take too long to persuade the elect this is the best solution for our crisis.

"I'll lead the effort with the government and Tatalc will lead the effort with the citizens. Consensus won't be easy, but if we can have all government resources reallocated to you, how long would it take you to build the vessel?"

"If we could start soon, we could have the *first* one done around the time of the truton ceremony," answered Dafur.

"The *first*?" Wickem inquired.

"Yes, we intend to build as many vessels as possible. The more vessels, the more citizens get off of Cythera."

"Of course. I don't know why I never thought of it like that. For some reason I always thought there would be only one vessel."

***

As they all left the lab Wickem couldn't stop thinking about the fact there could be multiple vessels transporting citizens off of Cythera. How many citizens will they be able to save? Hundreds, thousands? Who will they be able to save? *Who will they be able to save?* Wickem hadn't thought about this yet either. *Who will they be able to save?* How would they decide which citizens will build the new Cythera and which citizens will be left behind to die?

Chapter 37

Before the Debate – Lij

The Transients cheered. They were all happy for Lij. The fact that she came home to share the news of her engagement announcement, made her visit more special. Her mother, who was sitting near Lij, began to cry, as did her father. The three of them embraced and were joined by Lij's two brothers. As the applause began to quiet, someone from the crowded shouted, "Who are you going to marry?"

"Yes Lij, who?" Her father whispered in her ear.

Lij turned around to face the guests. "His name is Dafur. He's an engineering professor at the university in Regiowide."

"Is he here?" Someone shouted.

"When do we get to meet him?" Someone else shouted.

"I'm sorry, but you won't get to meet him today. He wasn't able to come." Lij looked around at everyone in the crowd and could tell they were disappointed they would not be meeting her fiancé. "He's the one I've been working with on a solution to the Rugal crisis, and he was too busy to come with me this time, but he's a wonderful man and you'll meet him soon, I promise."

Again all of the guests stood up and cheered. Their happiness for Lij was genuine and she was touched by the outpouring of joy. This is why she loved coming home; everyone here was like family.

But as family does, the residents of her village would question every decision she made. It wasn't only her town that was like that. Across Cythera were many other small Transient towns like hers. Everyone questioned every decision each Transient made. It was the Transient way. The questions weren't motivated by hate or jealousy. They were motivated by concern and the need to protect one another. For generations, Transients had been the outcasts. They had no other choice but to look out for one another. They would not have survived otherwise.

"Is he one of us?" Someone from the crowd shouted.

Because of the loud cheering, Lij barely heard the question.

"IS HE ONE OF US?" This time *everyone* heard the question and *everyone* quieted and stared at Lij. *Everyone* wanted to know the answer.

Lij paused for a moment. She knew this question would eventually have been asked. "Dafur is not a Transient, but he's not an elite either. I'm not sure what class he's from. None of that matters to him." Lij worried about how *everyone* was going to respond. Needing strength, she grabbed the hand of her father. "I've never heard him insult or judge anyone. He's a good man who does good things without bias or without asking for anything in return. He's funny and I enjoy time with him.

150

He's curious about our ways, open and accepting of our traditions and values . . ."

Lij's father stepped in and interrupted her. Speaking loud enough for *everyone* to hear, "You don't need to explain your love to us. If you love him and he loves you, that's all that matters. He sounds like a wonderful man and we can't wait to meet him." Her father turned his head now speaking *directly* to the guests. "And he will be welcomed as family here. You need not worry about that!" Lij began to cry and she embraced her father. She never imagined her wedding announcement was going to be so emotional.

Afterwards, most of the guests found their way to Lij. They hugged her, congratulated her, and told her they loved her. More than anything, she wanted them to accept her decision without judgment. Eventually *everyone* did.

Lij was glad the banquet was over. She felt tired and drained. She left with her mother and father and returned to their house not far from the park. The house she'd grown up in. Her two older brothers, Dran and Hilp, also came over. This was the first time they all had been together in their childhood home in a long time.

Her mother brewed some conish and they sat around the patio and talked. It was comforting and peaceful to Lij, the kind of soft peace one always finds when they return to their childhood home. Here she could speak freely without any fears or judgment. "I think he really did like it and if he didn't, he did a good job of fooling me."

"What are you talking about?" Lij's mother asked as she walked onto the patio with their conish.

"Lij took Dafur to see *Pepper*. It was their first unofficial date." Hilp said.

"Did he like it?" Lij's mother asked as she passed around the mugs.

"That's what I was saying when you came out. If he didn't like it, he at least pretended, which was sweet of him."

"He's a smart man." Her mother said. "You're father lies to me all the time about liking things I know he doesn't like, just to make me happy."

"No I don't."

"See. He did it again."

Everyone laughed.

"Maybe you're right Mother. Dafur is a smart man, actually rather brilliant. It's one of the traits I love the most about him."

"Yes, most beautiful women are attracted to intelligence," her father said. "That's why Dran and Hilp are still unmarried."

"I'm too busy for love." Dran responded. "But I could see that being Hilp's problem."

"That's not my problem," replied Hilp.

"Then what is?" asked his mother.

"I only have enough love in my heart for one woman and that's you Mother."

"What about me?" said Lij.

"Okay, two women."

"I hope Dafur has thick skin," Dran stated. "He's going to need it in this family."

"He'll fit right in. You'll love him. I can't wait for you to meet him."

"I'm looking forward to meeting him too," her father

said. "We might have to visit Regiowide though. I imagine he won't have any breaks in his work anytime soon."

"You're probably right. And you would really come to Regiowide? You *should* come to Regiowide. All of you, you could meet Dafur and I could show you all the work we've been doing. That would be great!"

"It's been a long time since I've been to Regiowide, since before you moved there. I *would* love to see your work. Are things still going well?" Lij's mother caught herself. "I'm sorry. I know you don't want to talk about your work."

"No Mother, it's fine. I didn't want to talk about it in front of *everyone*. They were expecting answers to questions I don't know yet. But I'm happy to try to answer any questions you have?"

"I'll be honest with you. I'm not even sure what you're working on. I know you are trying to figure out a solution for the *end of Cythera*," her father said. "But I don't know any of the details. I'm not even sure if I understand why the *end of Cythera* is coming."

"I'll give you the short version," replied Lij. "Our sun is growing bigger. It's like any other living thing; it started out small and keeps growing. As it grows, it gets closer and closer to us. When it gets too close, the heat will burn off our atmosphere and Cythera will become uninhabitable."

"And we'll all die," added Dran.

"Unfortunately so."

"So then what are you and Dafur proposing we do?" her father asked.

"We move to another planet farther away from our sun."

"How are we going to do that?"

"That's what Dafur is working on. I'll spare you the details but we're close to figuring out a way to move citizens off of Cythera."

"All of us? Everyone on Cythera?" Hilp asked.

"No, that's probably impossible. But if we can move *some* citizens, they can start a new life and keep our civilization alive."

Hilp looked concerned, "How will you decide who gets to go and who stays here and dies?"

"I don't know Hilp. We haven't talked about that yet."

"I can tell you one thing," Dran interjected, "If only a certain number of citizens can go, it won't be any of us."

"Why would you say that?" Lij asked him.

"They won't send any Transients." Dran walked over and stood next to Hilp. The brothers were having the same thought. "I think we all know that if the elect have to choose between sending Transients or sending the elite, all of us Transients will be left here to die."

"Dafur would never let that happen."

"He may not have the choice."

Chapter 38

Before the Debate – Tatalc

The earliest editions of *The Daily Word* were distributed shortly after sunrise. Most small shops and diners sold the publication since it was important to have copies available for early commuters. It was an especially hot morning and the heat was taking its toll on the man delivering the early edition. He had barely started his route and he was already profusely sweating and feeling short of breath.

The third stop on his route was a small shop called Nisnocs where he always left a bundled stack of the publication next to the front door. When he bent over to place today's copies of *The Word* on the ground by the door of Nisnocs a large drop of sweat fell from his forehead and splashed on to the headline at top of the page.

The headline read **Officials Expect Record Number of Truton Applications**. The delivery man reached down and tried to wipe his sweat off of the front page. It was too late. The fibers of the paper had already absorbed his sweat, and when his large hand moved across the page it smeared the ink of the headline. He had ruined the copy and the owner of Nisnocs wouldn't be able to sell it. The delivery man thought about moving a clean copy on top of the one he had ruined but decided it wasn't worth his time, instead he turned and started his way towards the next stop on his route.

Alongside the blur of ink making up today's headline was the secondary front page article filling the right column of the page. It was titled **Opinions & Options: How to Survive the Crisis**. The article was written by *The Daily Word*'s lead journalist, Lila. She had convinced her editor that *The Word* needed to start being more proactive in addressing the Rugal crisis. She told him how she had been researching the subject and had been interviewing those involved in trying to develop solutions, which was true to a certain degree.

The article presented an articulate and clear overview of the interpretation of the Rugal and the effects those predictions would have on the citizens of Cythera. It was Lila's opinion that all citizens needed to become more educated on the topic so they could form a consensus on the best course of action. Lila concluded the article by listing several options where one could find out more about the crisis.

But it was the final sentences of her article that revealed Lila's true motive. *To learn more about this important issue please attend an upcoming event at the university where Professor Dafur of Regiowide University will give a short demonstration on how our sun is growing. Also listen to the popular leader, Tatalc, share his opinions on the subject. Seating will be limited. Reservations are recommended.*

***

When Dafur took the stage, the auditorium was only one-quarter full. Standing backstage, peeking through the side of the long red curtain, stood Lila, Wickem and Dekayb. "Maybe you've lost some of your influence," Dekayb said to Lila. "Look how small the crowd is. I'm not sure your article motivated many citizens."

Lila glared back at Dekayb.

"Dekayb." Wickem scolded Dekayb.

Lila smiled at Wickem, then heard Tatalc approaching from behind. When Lila turned to face Tatalc, Wickem looked back at Dekayb and winked.

"How's the crowd?" Tatalc asked.

Before anyone else could answer, Lila said, "About what we'd expect this early."

"Good. How's Dafur doing?"

"So far all his demonstrations have worked. He looks as confident as you would expect," answered Wickem. "Where have you been?"

"I was talking to Rigby." Tatalc moved closer to the edge of the stage where he could peek out from behind the curtain and see the audience. "It's starting to fill up."

"The place will be overflowing by the time Tatalc goes on." Lila stated.

Wickem ignored Lila's bravado and looked his son straight in the eyes. "Take whatever advice Rigby gave you. Rigby's a smart man." Tatalc acknowledged his father's advice. His advice was rarely wrong.

"I'm proud of you. Those citizens out there, they've always believed in you. I've always believed in you. Your mother would be proud." Wickem hugged his son and whispered in Tatalc's ear, "I love you."

***

On stage Dafur did not notice the crowd filling the auditorium. He was too caught up in his lecture and demonstration. Dafur had decided to keep everything simple. He had set up a large display on a table to the left of the speaker's podium. The display was a row of a different sized orbs attached to small poles. After his introduction he pointed to the largest orb on the far left. "This is our sun and its size a long time ago." He pointed to the third orb. "This is Cythera."

He reached behind the table and pulled out an orb much larger than any of the ones currently on display. Walking back to the far left of the table he replaced the original orb with the new, larger one. "Now this is the current size of our sun." Dafur adjusted the other orbs to bring them closer to the larger sun. "This danger is compounded by the fact that as our sun grows, its gravitational pull strengthens, pulling Cythera's orbit closer. The distance between our sun and Cythera is now significantly less."

Dafur walked back to the podium and continued his lecture. He explained in great detail how the growth of their sun was going to impact livable conditions on Cythera. Backstage, everyone watched as Dafur did his the best to keep the crowd engaged. By the time Dafur was concluding his lecture, the auditorium was full and citizens were starting to stand near the back of the hall.

This was a much different crowd than the one Dafur had lectured to when he first met Lij. That audience had been an academic crowd interested in the science of Dafur's studies. This crowd was filled with citizens from every race and background, ordinary citizens mostly interested in hearing Tatalc speak. Some probably didn't even know what the topic of the evening was. They were fans. But these were important citizens. They would spread Tatalc's message. These were the advocates – the perfect audience.

Dafur finished his lecture and was given a small ovation before leaving the stage. His objective had been to give a simple explanation for what was happening, laying the groundwork for Tatalc's speech. Dafur felt he accomplished that.

At the instant Dafur left the stage Tatalc went on. Everyone stood and began to cheer. Wickem stood backstage amazed at the influence his son had on citizens. Everywhere Tatalc spoke, they came out to listen. They absorbed and followed his words. Tatalc had a cult-following similar to an artist or musician, unheard of for any politician or public servant in recent history.

Wickem, wise in his understanding of how much power someone in Tatalc's position wielded, never fully understood the deep connection Tatalc had with his audience. It was incomprehensible. No matter. Tatalc had only abused his power once and paid dearly for that mistake. Since then, Tatalc had shown great respect for his *calling* and had accomplished many great things. Wickem knew tonight would be the greatest accomplishment of them all.

***

Accustomed to this type of reception, Tatalc confidently approached the podium. The room was deafening to the point Tatalc had to raise his hands and ask the audience to quiet down.

"Do you know why you are here tonight?" he asked. The crowd cheered. Tatalc continued in a loud bold voice. "No! Do you know why you are *really* here tonight?" Tatalc walked from behind the podium up to the front of the stage and pointed down to a young attendee. Tatalc stared at him and asked, "You. Why are you here tonight?"

The young man was elated Tatalc had selected him but found difficulty articulating his thoughts. "I . . . I . . . came to hear you talk. I . . . I've never seen you before."

Tatalc crouched down and leaned towards the young man. It was as if he was having a private conversation with this stranger and no one else was in the room. "Do you know why I'm here tonight?" Tatalc asked the stranger.

Dumfounded, the stranger couldn't answer. Tatalc stood up tall and spoke loudly to the entire audience. "Do you know why I'm here tonight?" They all cheered, then Tatalc raised his hands and they all silenced.

"I'm here for one reason and it's simple." In an authentic and sincere tone Tatalc said, "I need your help." The auditorium was silent. Everyone was looking back at Tatalc, spellbound. Tatalc let the silence build for a few moments then pumped his fist in the air and loudly erupted. "Are you going to help me?" Everyone jumped out of their seats and clapped and screamed.

"Hopefully, you heard what my friend Dafur had to say." Tatalc pointed to the back of the auditorium. "Those of you in the back, I saw you come in late. Shame on you, and listen closely to what I'm about to say. You can't be late next time! You can never be late again!" Tatalc often used this type of motivation. He wasn't intending to embarrass anyone, but to challenge his audience's true intentions. He had to know if they were really *in* for the cause.

"We can't afford to be late or to be casual. You heard Dafur; the countdown has started. We only have a certain amount of time left. And the scary part, the real scary part, is that we don't know how much time we have!

"Dafur has a plan and I believe in him and now I need you to believe in me!

"This won't be easy. There will be those who say none of the predictions are true. But their denial is their weakness, and the truth will be your strength! There will be those who say their solution is better. But their pride will blind them, while you clearly can see the bright glow of survival! There will those who say we should spend resources elsewhere. But their greed will reveal their intentions. You carry the currency of truth, which is more valuable than any possession! There will be those that say there is no hope." Tatalc paused and nodded his head back and forth. "No hope? Hope is desire and if they have no hope to live, they have no desire to live!"

Tatalc pointed to an individual in the crowd, "But you have hope, right? You have hope that we can save this civilization, our civilization?" He pointed to another citizen. "You have desire, right? You have the desire to live, the desire to fight unto the end? I have hope! I have desire! So for those who say there is no hope, you tell them they are wrong! There is hope, they only have to desire it!"

Tatalc paused as the crowd reacted with a loud cheer. "So the question is what do we do now? How do we take our desire for survival and the solution Dafur has created and turn it into a reality? A reality that will give ALL OF US our best chance at survival!

"Here is what I need you to do for me. Actually, don't do it for me. Do it for yourself, for Cythera! When you leave here tonight tell the story, the whole story, the true story, to as many citizens as you can. Contact your political representatives and tell the elect the story! We need the support of the citizens and the government for Dafur to gain the resources needed to accomplish this objective. We cannot do this without you! You need to decide right now if you have the desire for truth and the desire for survival, and if you do, when you leave here tonight do what needs to be done. Turn your hopes and desires into your strength!"

Tatalc raised his left arm high in the air and opened his hand towards the sky. "Carry in this hand your strength." He raised his right arm high above his head and opened his right hand. "And in this hand carry the truth. And we will succeed!"

Chapter 39

The Revelation

Even though he was not being paid, the student was

glad that he had won the internship at the museum. It would be hard work. Work the curators didn't want to do. But this had been his plan all along.

The museum was in a period of transition. Over the last several generations Cytheran society had progressed. Society no longer put as much weight on birthright and birth class. Transients and other non-elite groups were more accepted into society. It had been a progressive era for all of Cytheran culture. The inclusion of diverse imaginations and creativity had spawned a renaissance in everything from fashion to architecture.

Located in an older part of Regiowide, the museum was being revitalized. Buildings in the area worth keeping were renovated, buildings not worth keeping were destroyed, and new buildings were built in their place. The museum was worth keeping.

As a part of the museum remodeling effort, many students were hired as interns to help with the project. Tasked with inventorying the museum archives, the student was pleased with his assignment. It was a tedious task but it was the one he wanted to do. The one he had to do.

The museum's archives had been untouched for so long, the curators had lost track of the many collections the museum owned. It was time for one of those archives to be found. The student didn't know where it was. He only knew it was there somewhere.

Every morning he came and sorted through crates categorizing different types of art and artists. There were paintings, sculptures and other art forms he would identify and log into a record book. Occasionally, one of the curators checked on him, but for the most part he was left alone to do his work, and to search for the Rugal.

He had learned the Rugal had been credited to the famous musician Lairnam. Lairnam had experienced several episodes of fame during his life but was remembered as much for his insanity as he was his talent. After taking his own life, Lairnam's few remaining possessions were sent to the museum and had been there ever since.

The student knew the Rugal was small enough to fit into a storage crate. Therefore it would not be easy to find. There were over a thousand unlabeled storage crates in the museum archives. He was willing to be patient. The Rugal had long been forgotten. He was the only one who knew the Rugal existed and for what purpose it served. Eventually he would find it, he was sure of that, but this was only the first part of his task. The more difficult challenge would be to decide how to use the Rugal once it was found.

Coming in early and staying late, the student rarely spoke to anyone else. He barely eased up from his work, bringing his lunch with him, he was diligent and thorough, because he couldn't risk losing his internship while he was this close to finding the Rugal.

Then, it appeared. The crate was small and unlabeled, as he had expected it would be. At the top of the opened crate, he discovered a pair of boots and a pile of old brushes lying across a blue vest. He could tell something was under the vest. Reaching into the crate he lifted the vest and there it was, *his* Rugal. He grasped it by its long neck and lifted the Rugal in the air; he held it in front of his bearded face and smiled. After spending a few moments admiring the piece and recalling the many lives the Rugal had saved, he placed it in his satchel and started to walk out of the museum.

Chapter 40

Before the Debate – Lij

Lij was cleaning her apartment. She always considered herself to be neat, but between time at the lab, time at school, and time with Dafur she was never home and a mess had built up. Her family would be arriving in Regiowide soon and this would be the first time her parents visited *her* home - the first time since she left home *they were coming to see her*.

There are always a lot of firsts when a child leaves home. The first evening of anxiety for the parents who will no longer hear their child come in at night. The first time the child gets scared and has no one to comfort her. The first time the child welcomes family into the new home she has established on her own.

Lij didn't need her apartment to look perfect, but she wanted it clean. Her mother had always taught her the importance of keeping a clean home. More than anything, Lij didn't want to disappoint her mother. She also wanted both parents to have confidence she had been doing fine living on her own in the big city.

Her two older brothers, Dran and Hilp, were coming too. Lij wasn't worried about what they would think of the upkeep of her apartment; she was worried about what they would think of Dafur.

Lij was sitting at the small desk in the corner of her kitchen when the bell rang. They were here. She shoveled a stack of papers into a desk drawer, *out of sight, out of mind,* she thought to herself. She jumped up from her chair and ran out to meet her family.

"Mother, Father, I'm so glad to see you. Hurry, come in out of the heat." Lij greeted her parents with a big hug. She turned to her brothers and also gave them a big hug. "How was your trip? I hope you didn't have any issues?"

"Everything was fine dear." Her mother answered. "The train was a little bumpy, but it didn't keep your father from sleeping the whole time."

"You missed a lot of pretty rurals Dad." Hilp said.

"I've seen plenty of rurals. I'm sure I didn't miss anything I haven't seen before."

"Why didn't you take the rivers?" Lij asked. "It's a much faster trip over water."

"A lot has changed since you were home," replied Dran.

"But it wasn't that long ago."

"I know. It's happened fast. The rivers have been drying up. We've had to close our docks."

Hilp added, "Some of the farmers are starting to lose their crops. And I've heard a few reports of wild fires not too far from town."

"But there's been other droughts," her father added. "We'll be ok. You don't need to worry about it Lij."

Lij knew her father was underestimating the recent changes in Cythera's climate but she decided now was not that time to challenge his statement. Instead, she led them up the steps and into her apartment. "Everyone follow me. I'll give you the grand tour. It will be quick." Following Lij were her mother, then her father. Her brothers were behind, carrying everyone's satchels.

"Do you have to go up these stairs every time you come

home?" Her father wondered out loud. "Now I know why you spend all your time at Dafur's."

"It's good exercise. It helps build your lower body frame," Lij responded. Walking through the front door of her apartment and into the main living room she announced, "Here we are, welcome to my home."

Looking around, her mother said, "It's nice Lij, I'm proud you keep a clean home. That says a lot about someone." Lij's cleaning had paid off.

"You can set your stuff down there." Lij pointed towards the corner. "This is the main living room, I'll sleep on the sofa." Lij led them to the back of the apartment. "Back here is the kitchen. I don't think there'll be enough room for all of us to be in here at once." She turned down the hallway. "The room on the left is my bedroom. Mother and Father you can sleep in my bed, everything's clean." She pointed to a room on the right. "Here's my office. The couch folds out." She looked at Dran and Hilp. "I think you can both fit if you snuggle up tightly."

"Dran can have it. I can't sleep anywhere near his sour feet," said Hilp. "I brought a pack. I can sleep on the floor somewhere."

"At the end of the hallway is the bathroom. Sorry I only have the one." They all walked back into the main living room. "Well, that's it. Like I said, it would be a quick tour."

"I think it's perfect. It fits you." Her mother validated.

"I guess you'll be moving out when you and Dafur marry?" Her father asked.

"Yes. He owns a home near the school. We'll live there."

"Speaking of Dafur, when do we get to meet him?" Dran asked.

"I thought I'd let you rest from your trip for a little while and then we'll meet him for dinner."

"I don't need any rest," her father said.

"Of course you don't. You slept the whole way here," said her mother.

"We made reservations at a diner that serves some of the best strafultap in Regiowide." Lij said. "I figured since it's out of season at home you'd want some while in town."

"Sounds good to me, I can always eat strafultap. I . . ."

"Hello! Hello! Lij are you up there?" Dafur's voice came from the bottom of the steps.

"Dafur?" Lij went to the top of her staircase and saw Dafur coming up the stairs. "What are you doing here? I thought we were going to meet later?"

"I thought I'd surprise you and be here when your family arrived." Climbing the stairs Dafur walked into her apartment where he saw Lij's parents and brothers. "Oh, I guess you've already arrived." Approaching her father first, Dafur extended his hand. "Hi, I'm Dafur." After the introductions they all sat down on the couches and chairs in Lij's main living room.

Feeling he owed Lij's family an apology for missing Lij's reception, Dafur said, "I want to tell you how sorry I am that I couldn't attend the banquet. Lij has told me a lot about Bellcreek; I hope to be able to visit soon. From what Lij has told me it sounds like a wonderful place."

"Have you spent a lot of time outside the city?" Lij's mother asked.

"Yes, I've spent time outside Regiowide, but it was usually in other large cities. I haven't spent a lot of time in the rurals."

"What city do you claim as home?" Dran was curious.

"Regiowide is definitely my home. I've spent the most time here."

"Were you born here?" Hilp asked.

"No, I wasn't born here."

Dran added, "Where were you born?"

"I would tell you but I'm sure you've never heard of the place. It's on the other side of Cythera."

"Is your family still there or do you have family here in Regiowide?" Lij's father asked.

"All of Dafur's family has moved on." Lij answered for him.

"What brought you to the university? I assume that's why you moved here?" Hilp asked.

"Correct, that's why I moved to Regiowide. But that's a long story and not an interesting one."

"Can you cook?" Lij's mother asked.

"What kind of question is that Mother? Enough questions everyone, Dafur didn't come here to be interrogated," Lij said.

"Actually, I do need to get back to the lab. But I wanted to stop by and say, 'Hi'. And we're all having dinner later, right?"

"That's the plan." Dran stated.

"Lij has promised us fresh strafultap." Her father added.

"I can't wait." Dafur stood up and started walking out of the apartment. "I'm glad you made it safely and I'm looking forward to spending more time with you tonight." Pausing, he smiled and looked at Lij's mother, "And yes, I can cook." Dafur kissed Lij goodbye and walked down the apartment steps and out the door.

Lij was eager to hear her parent's first impressions of Dafur. "So what did you think?"

Her mother answered first. "He seems like a nice man."

Awaiting their response, Lij turned to her father and brothers.

"A nice man," her father stated.

"He was nice, but sort of vague." Dran added.

"Vague?" Lij asked.

"I noticed that too." Hilp said.

"I'm not sure what you mean by vague?"

"The way he answered the questions about his past - he wouldn't give any specifics." Dran said.

"I didn't notice." Lij said. "He was probably nervous because you were asking him so many questions. Why were you asking him so many questions anyway?"

"That's what you do when you meet somebody for the first time," said her father. "You ask them questions so you get to know them."

"It seemed like a lot of questions for someone you just met." Lij replied.

"No. They were pretty simple questions. He just didn't answer them."

"Dran, why are you always looking for something? You don't need to be so eager to learn every little fact about someone in the first few moments you meet them."

"Do you know where he was born or why he came to the university? Has he ever told you?" Dran asked Lij.

Lij thought about it for a moment. "Well, no, I don't

think he has. But I don't know if I've ever really asked. He had a life before me and to love him, I must respect his past, and his privacy."

"Well let's hope there's nothing in that *private past* we, or I guess you, should be worried about."

"I think you are overreacting. Wait until you get to know him more. There's nothing mysterious about the man."

Chapter 41

Before the Debate – Wickem & The Chief of State

Momentum was building.

After Tatalc gave his speech asking for the help of his followers, the word of Dafur's plan quickly spread. More and more citizens were becoming engaged in supporting the cause.

Tatalc left Regiowide and began traveling to other large cities around Cythera. Joining him, Lila documented his rallies in regularly published articles in *The Daily Word*. Her articles were read by millions of citizens around Cythera.

Dafur, Rigby and Lij had perfected their prototype for the vessel and were finalizing the interior design compartments that would house the travelers and provide life support during the voyage. They still had not figured out how to launch the vessel, but they knew once it was off Cythera they could guide it to the next planet and safely land.

Even with their progress, they knew it would be impossible to execute their full plan without the appropriate resources from the government. While Tatalc could motivate the citizens, only one man could get them the resources they needed to save civilization. Fortunately, that man was Wickem. Momentum was definitely building.

***

Wickem's instinctive wisdom had always been his guide. Knowing timing is everything, he knew an average idea at the right time was better than a great idea at the wrong time, and he knew a great idea at the right time could save Cythera. Now was the *time* for his great idea.

Sitting at his desk Wickem reviewed the facts and arguments he would soon present to the elect. All of Cythera's senior government officials would be at the meeting, including The Chief of State. As leader of the Federal Safety Commission Wickem made presentations to this group on many occasions, but this one would be different. To his advantage he knew these officials well. He was one of them.

"Are you about ready?"

Wickem lifted his head and looked up at Dekayb. "Let's go." Wickem and Dekayb walked out of his office and down the hallway. At the end of the hallway there were two sets of doors. Wickem turned towards the doors on the left, which led outside.

Dekayb stretched her arm across Wickem's chest, and said, "Why are we going that way? It's too hot outside." She pointed to the doors on the right, which opened to a skyway connected to the government offices, "We always take the skyway."

"I know. But today we're walking outside." Wickem walked through the doors and into the outside heat. Dekayb followed.

It was a short walk from Wickem's office to the

government building where their meeting was taking place. As soon as they were outside in the brutal sun, Wickem felt the first bead of sweat form on the back of his neck. By the time the first bead was half way down his back, several other beads of sweat had formed and were racing each other down to his waist.

His forehead began to sweat. Unlike the individual beads that formed on his neck, the sweat on his head collected as a thin damp pool along his hairline. Even though he knew it would only make him hotter, he couldn't resist the temptation to reach up with his hand and push the sweat back into his gray hair. After each push, the dryness he created would only last a fraction of a moment before fresh sweat repooled.

Under his arms the thick sweat was mixing with bacteria and beginning to emit his unpleasant scent. With nowhere to go, the swampy mix collected and bled through the fibers of his shirt. Between his legs, where his thighs chafed together with every step, new salty sweat burned his freshly rubbed flesh. By the time Wickem reached the government offices he was covered in sweat from head to toe. So was Dekayb.

Wickem and Dekayb entered the chambers and sat down at a large table in the center of the room. All of the important members of senior government were already present including The Chief of State. Everyone noticed how Wickem and Dekayb were sweating.

"Were the skywalks closed?" One of the officials asked.

"We could've sent a carriage for you so you wouldn't have had to walk outside." Another official added.

Without answering their questions, Wickem asked, "Does anyone know how long it takes to walk from my office to here?"

The officials all looked around at one another then one said, "I don't know. It can't take too long."

"It doesn't," affirmed Wickem. "And what's our usual climate right now?"

No one answered.

"When was the last time any of you walked outside for more than a few moments?"

Still no one answered.

Wickem nodded at Dekayb. She opened her satchel and began passing around a set of documents to all of the officials. Wickem continued, "I know most of you have seen this data in some form or another and I know you all realize we have a problem, the *Rugal crisis* we call it. But are you paying attention to how fast the climate is changing?"

By now all the officials had their copies of the documents in front of them. On the front page was a picture of them all from a previous meeting.

"Look at the picture on the front page." Wickem asked, "Does anyone know when that was taken?"

No one answered.

"That was taken around this same time last cycle." Wickem stood up and pointed to his body. "Look at me. I was only outside for a few moments. Look at the picture. We all have vests on!"

"Wickem," The Chief of State said, "I'm not sure I understand where you're going with this. We know there's a crisis. We're doing everything we can. You're doing everything you can. We have citizens all over Cythera working on a solution."

"Therein lies the problem. We have too many citizens

working on this. Our resources are spread too thin and we're running out of time!" Wickem sat back down and asked, "How many of you at this table are currently sponsoring and funding a crisis solution project right now? Please, raise your hands."

Everyone raised a hand.

"Do any of your project teams have a realistic solution yet?" Wickem paused for an answer he knew would not come, "Dekayb and I have reviewed every project currently receiving government aid and there's only one that will work. We've already reallocated 100% of the Federal Safety Commissions resources to this one solution, and I'm asking you all to do the same with your resources."

"One of my project teams is close to a solution. I can't cut their funding." An official yelled.

"You mean the Aguaroute project?" Wickem remained poised. "Building canals to spread out our waters in an effort to keep Cythera cool?"

"Yes. It's a great idea and could sustain us for a long time."

"All our water would be evaporated before they're a quarter way through the terraforming." Wickem deflated the possibility of that idea.

Every official took their turn defending their projects. Some were decent in concept but impossible to implement, others could provide short term results but no long term solution. Wickem's facts came easy to him; he knew the details of their projects better than they did. He was easily able to explain how *none* of their projects would solve the Rugal crisis.

The Chief of State spoke up, "Wickem, you've more than made your point. I don't know about everyone else at the table but I regularly receive letters from citizens who've read about your solution or have heard your son speak. Let me be frank with you, we all know your son has this *power* over citizens. His influence is unmatched, but that doesn't mean he is right or yours is the only way. If we all of sudden halted every project but yours and turned all of our resources over to you, what type of message would that send?"

"It would send the message that we have a solution and we are doing everything we can to save the citizens of Cythera!" Wickem fired back.

"Your support is growing. We realize this, but not every citizen has bought into Tatalc's propaganda. Some will oppose this narrow strategy *even if* your plan would work."

"Why do you say *even if* our plan would work? We've proven the plan will work. We need more resources to make it a reality." Wickem glared at The Chief of State. "Or are you telling me you don't think our plan will work?"

"It doesn't matter if your plan will work or not. What matters is that citizens *think* it will work! Because if they don't think it will work, or when the charms of Tatalc have worn off, the citizens will turn on us and we will be the ones blamed for all their problems."

"You are such an ignorant coward!" It was unlike Wickem to be so insulting, especially with the most powerful citizen on Cythera. He'd been given no choice. "I don't know what's worse. That you are turning this crisis into a campaign strategy or that you're too stupid to realize there will be no more campaigns," Wickem slammed his fist on the table, "Cythera is going to die!"

Everyone was quiet. The uncomfortable truth had begun to sink in. All of them, including The Chief of State, were coming to the realization that politics no longer mattered, the constituents who were offered resources for their loyalties no longer mattered, elections no longer mattered, and their careers no longer mattered. The only thing that mattered was survival.

"You can have my resources," said the Commissioner of Energy Consumption, "I will shut down all projects except the minimum required to maintain my office's responsibilities. All other resources I have I will commit to you and your team."

"I'll do the same." Said the Minister of Economics.

"I will too."

"And I as well."

Around the table every senior member of the Cytheran government committed all of their available resources to Wickem. Wickem had achieved what he came here to do. They now had the resources needed to build the full scale solution to the Rugal crisis and move citizens to the next planet.

Chapter 42

Before the Debate – Tatalc & Lila

Tatalc and Lila were on their way back to Regiowide when they heard the news about the government's decision. They had been visiting major cities throughout Cythera in an effort to build support for their cause; the response to their rallies had been overwhelming. At every stop, citizens attended in larger numbers than the stop before. Some came to hear the message, some came to hear Tatalc, but they were all given the same instructions. Tatalc's message was simple— become informed, tell others, and tell the elect.

Upon receiving the news, Tatalc leaned over to Lila, "Now the real work begins." Tatalc was thrilled to hear the news but he'd been confident all along. He always felt it would only be a matter of time before citizens pressured the government to align all resources to Dafur. Once citizens applied pressure to the elect, Tatalc knew his father's influence would do the rest.

Tatalc realized they would be successful after the first speech he gave in Regiowide when he followed Dafur on stage. Lila had warned him that a lot of citizens were beginning to doubt the prophecy of the Rugal. But it wasn't doubt Tatalc saw in the audience's eyes that night. It was fear. The type of fear so embedded in one's conscience that it can only manifest itself through denial and doubt. Tatalc knew all along if he could claw through the denial and doubt and reach their fears he could turn their fear into the most powerful asset, the most powerful motivator. Fear drives resolve, and resolve drives action, Wickem had taught him that.

Lila looked up from her notepad. She had been in the process of completing her final edit on her next article when the message arrived. Lila turned to Tatalc and joked, "Real work? Maybe I'm starting to get too old for this because I consider following you all over Cythera to be a lot of *real work*!"

"I thought you liked spending time with me." Tatalc teased Lila. "You can't call it work when you have good company."

"That sounds like something Wickem would say, and if that's the case, Wickem hasn't worked a moment in his life since Dekayb showed up."

"No need to be mean. You can't hold a grudge forever."

"You're right, she probably saved me more heartache

than she caused." Lila held up her notebook. "Enough about her, she bores me anyway. What do you think, should I put the good news at the front of my story or build up to it?"

"By the time your article is published it won't be breaking news. You're not going to surprise any readers. I'd lead with the *good news* and use it to build publicity for the next event."

"Great idea, if you ever lose your voice you would make a great editor. By the way, we need to move the event to a different venue."

"Why? I like the idea of returning to the university auditorium where we started. I feel like we would've come full circle from our first night with Dafur. Dafur is still going to present his latest findings though, right?"

"As far as I know, he is. But the university auditorium is not large enough to hold the expected crowd and that was *before* the government announced they will be giving us exclusive support."

"Where will we have it then?" Tatalc asked.

"At the Muy," answered Lila.

"The Muy? I thought that was only used for truton ceremonies and other official government business?"

"Tatalc, everything has changed. We have the full support of the elect. Now *this* is official government business."

Chapter 43

Before the Debate – Lij

When Lij's parents and brothers came to visit Regiowide they had only intended to stay a short time. It was supposed to be a quick visit, allowing Lij's mother to contribute to her daughter's wedding plans. The first night they arranged to have dinner with Dafur. This is when everything changed.

When Lij and her family arrived at the dinner, Dafur was already there. Noticing them entering the dining hall, Dafur stood to greet them. He pulled a chair out for Lij's mother. Turning to her father Dafur said, "Would you like to sit there?" Dafur pointed to the chair beside the empty chair next to where Lij's mother was sitting.

"And where will you sit, Dafur?" Lij's father asked before sitting down.

"Between the two of you of course," answered Dafur.

Lij's mother looked over to Lij, "You've been teaching him, I'm proud of you."

Lij looked back to her mother, "I didn't tell him *anything*. I promise."

Everyone looked at Dafur.

"She didn't tell me anything." Dafur grinned back at Lij's mother. "I've been studying your culture in my spare time, the little I have."

Lij's father was impressed.

"If I understand the tradition," Dafur explained, "When someone wants to be accepted into a Transient family, they ask to sit between the father and mother. Do I have that right?"

"You do have it right," Lij's mother affirmed, "but typically this occurs at the formal family dinner the night before the wedding."

"I know." Dafur said.

Hilp and Dran turned to each other, they were brothers and often knew what the other was thinking. Hilp spoke first, "Are you saying what I think you're saying?" He directed the question to Dafur but then looked over at his little sister Lij. "Lij, what's going on?"

Lij tried her best but she couldn't keep the secret any longer. "We're getting married tomorrow!" she shouted. She looked over at Dafur expecting him to be disappointed that she had revealed their secret too soon, but he wasn't. "We were going to surprise you after dinner, but I couldn't hold it in any longer."

Dafur and Lij had made the decision two nights ago when they were talking about the stress the long trip to Regiowide would have on her aging parents. It made no sense to have them come all this way to Regiowide then return home, only to have to travel back later for the wedding.

They were not planning a large formal wedding. Invited guests were mostly their colleagues from the university and Lij's parents and brothers. The site was a garden in a public park near Lake Regiowide.

When the thought of moving up the wedding occurred, Lij and Dafur called the park to see if their site would be available. It was. They also called several of the invited guests from the university and all but one would be able to attend. It all made such perfect sense.

There was *one other important reason* it made sense to

move up the wedding; the most important reason of all. "Tomorrow?" Her father said, "Tomorrow. I thought the wedding was going to be later." He seemed more confused than angry. "Why would you move it up?"

"And I didn't bring my appropriate Transient garments. Your wedding should be traditional." Her mother interrupted, "Lij, you should have told us."

"I'm sorry mother. You were already on your way to Regiowide when we decided; it was the other night. And the wedding will be informal. You won't need your traditional garments."

"Lij, you never answered my question," her father interrupted, "Why are you moving it up? Is something wrong?"

"No Father. Nothing's wrong at all. Everything is perfectly fine."

"I'm not sure I understand then."

Lij didn't want to offend her parents by telling them they were too old to be repeatedly traveling long distances. She told them the *other* reason, the more important one. "To be honest, we don't know how much time we have." Lij pushed her chair back and stood up.

She walked around the table and stood behind Dafur and placed her hands on his shoulders. To her left was her father and to her right was her mother. Her two older brothers were sitting across the table. "The one thing we do know is we won't have a full life together."

Lij paused and again looked over at her father and then her mother. Small tears began to form in the corner of her eyes and slowly rolled down her cheek. "We won't get to grow old together like you have. We won't have time to have children. Even if we did, we'll never see them grow up. Why wait? We love each other and in the little time we have left, the little time we all have left, we want to be together as husband and wife."

Lij took her hands off of Dafur's shoulders and reached over and wrapped them around the neck of her father giving him an affectionate and childlike hug. "That's why we are moving the wedding up, Father. It's not that we don't want to wait, it's that we *can't* wait. I hope you understand."

Fighting back his own tears, her father said, "We do. We understand." He leaned his head back and his daughter gave him a soft kiss on his forehead and then returned to her seat. It had been an emotional moment and everyone was quiet. Then their server arrived.

"Good evening and welcome to . . ." When the server approached the table he realized he had interrupted a *moment*. "I apologize, I can come back."

"No. No. You're fine," Dafur smiled at the server, "I know what I want. I'll have the strafultap. I think that's what everyone wants, right?" Dafur looked around at everyone else at the table and they all nodded their heads in agreement.

"Strafultap for everyone then," the waiter confirmed and then turned around and walked back towards the kitchen.

"A wedding tomorrow," Lij's mother said, "Is everything ready? What can I do to help?"

"Everything's ready. It's going to be small but we'll have some food and entertainment for everyone after the ceremony. You won't have to do anything Mother. You can relax and have fun," said Lij.

"There is one thing left to do," Dafur said. "A small formality."

Lij looked perplexed. She didn't know what Dafur was

talking about.

Dafur looked across the table at Lij's brothers, "Dran, Hilp, I'd be honored if you would stand with me tomorrow?"

Dran and Hilp looked at each other, again knowing what the other was thinking. "We'd be happy to." Hilp said.

"Great," exclaimed Dafur.

"Dafur, can I ask you a question about something Lij said earlier?" Dran asked.

"Sure, you can ask me anything, we're almost family now."

"Lij said you moved the wedding because there's not much time left until Cythera dies. If you are the one building a ship, or vessel, or whatever you call it to move citizens off Cythera, wouldn't you and Lij be on it? Wouldn't we all be on it? Since we *are* almost family now?"

"To be honest Dran, I haven't put too much thought into who would go. It probably won't be my decision anyway."

"But you'd think whoever makes that decision would let you go since you're the one that came up with the solution," added Hilp.

"Even if that were the case, I wouldn't go with the first group. I'll need to stay back to help build and launch more ships so we can move as many citizens as possible off Cythera."

Lij's father spoke up, "How many ships do you plan on building?"

"We don't know yet. It depends on how much time and resources we'll have."

"But it sounds to me like you're willing to put yourself in a position to stay on Cythera," Lij's father paused for a moment, "which means you're *willing* to die?"

"If that's what happens, yes. I'm willing to die," Dafur answered. "This isn't about me surviving; this is about our civilization surviving. In the big scheme of things, my death would be a small sacrifice and one I'm willing to make."

"Very noble of you," complemented Lij's father.

"Hypothetically speaking, who do you think should go?" Dran asked.

"Hypothetically? I think we should have citizens from every class and ethnic group. I would hope our civilization would be able to continue as a whole."

"Including Transients?"

"Of course, Transients are citizens too."

"Not everyone feels that way, especially the elite."

"Do you really think they wouldn't send any Transients?" Dafur asked Dran. "Relations are so much better now, it's not like it was generations ago."

"From your perspective it probably appears that way. But the undertones still exist. The elite and those with birth right are nice to us, but they have no real choice. It would be frowned upon to still treat us as animals, like in the past. But the reality is that the feelings are still there, just not on the surface. And when push comes to shove, there will still be a lot of citizens who think the new civilization would be better without Transients."

"I hope that's not the case, and if given the opportunity, I'd definitely speak out against a plan like that."

"Dafur," Dran looked straight into Dafur's eyes, "I will hold you to that. I won't let Transients be forgotten."

Chapter 44

The Revelation

"Stop!"

The voice came from behind him.

"Stop! Wait, I've been looking for you and I need to talk to you."

The student had spent many mornings in the basement of the museum looking for the Rugal and now he was only a few short steps from being outside with the artifact. When he heard the voice, he knew it would only cause suspicion if he kept walking, so he turned and answered, "Yes." He recognized Emot, who was a junior curator from the museum's artifacts department and one of the few employees that ever visited the student in the museum's basement. Emot's face was smooth and childlike, almost the complete opposite of the student's bearded, gruff face.

"Where are you going? I've been looking for you?" Emot asked the bearded student.

"I'm going to get something to eat." It was the first thought that entered his mind.

"Huh, I always thought you brought your lunch." Emot commented, "I've never seen you leave for lunch."

"I ran out of deli last night and didn't have time to go shopping."

"Let me join you then. I'll buy. There's something important I need to talk to you about."

This was not the easy escape the student had planned

on. Having no real choice, he accepted Emot's invitation. And after lunch he would come back, work the afternoon, and leave the museum at his normal time in the evening. Then he would disappear with the Rugal.

"Sure. Where do you want to go?"

"Wherever you were planning to go will be fine with me." Emot said.

"How does Echoes sound? I've heard they have a tasty honey stew."

"Sounds good to me."

They walked out the door of the museum and turned right.

"Why do you have your satchel? It looks kind of heavy to be carrying around everywhere." Emot asked the student.

Stopping at the corner they waited for a safe time to cross the street. When it was clear they crossed. Once they were safely on the other side of the street, the student answered Emot's question. "I have an appointment after work tonight and I'll need to change." The student reached down with his arm and patted his satchel. He could feel the Rugal and the lunch he had packed but pretended the bump was his other set of clothes. "I didn't want to leave my stuff in the museum. There's no where for me to lock it up."

"Hopefully it's not a job interview."

They walked into the front door of Echoes and found a table.

"A job interview? No, it's not a job interview." The student opened the menu and began to look at it, "It's a meeting with my academic counselor to discuss what courses to enroll in next term. I can get pretty dirty looking through the old artifacts so I thought a clean set of clothes might be a good idea."

"Good, we would hate to lose you. Matter of fact, that's what I needed to talk to you about."

Just then the server came up and took their order. They both ordered the honey stew.

"What *is what* that you need to talk to me about?"

"A job interview." Emot said. "We have a position opening up in our department. It's entry level and flexible, you could still go to school. You're the first one we thought of."

"Why me? I'm only an unpaid intern sorting through old art."

"Exactly. But isn't that the whole point of taking an unpaid internship, to have the chance to earn a permanent place? I know it's not been challenging work, but you've done well with what we've asked you to do."

"Thanks." He appreciated the compliment. "What would I be doing?" The student was not really interested in the job opportunity. After today, he would never step foot in the museum again. But for the sake of masking his true intentions, he entertained Emot's conversation.

"You would be helping me with a special project I've been assigned."

"Special project?"

"We're putting together a display of ancient revelation art. You probably don't know this but we have *actually* been reading your reports. We never realized how much revelation art we had until you started sorting through it all. Have you studied ancient revelation art yet? It's kind of a new trend."

"No, I'm not familiar with it."

"There've been a few articles written about it and our head curator has started writing a book on the subject. Which, if you want my opinion, is probably why we are putting together the display. Oh good, our food is here."

Their server put the honey stew down in front of them and asked if they needed anything else. They didn't.

"As I was saying," Emot continued, "The concept behind ancient revelation art is that there are secret messages hidden in the art of our ancestors. To be honest, I'm not sure I believe it, but it doesn't matter what I believe. If the public will pay to see it that's all I really care about it."

The young student was in mid-bite when what Emot was explaining sunk in. He tried to swallow and almost choked on a piece of meat. He took a bite of bread to push the meat down his throat, and then he was able to catch his breath.

"Are you alright?" Emot asked.

"Yeah, I'm fine. I should have chewed that chunk of meat more," answered the student. "Ancient revelation art. It sounds interesting, but I'm still a little unsure of what would be expected of me."

"Simply put, we'll need to determine what pieces of art you've found that would be classified as ancient revelation art. It has to be art with some type of secret that we could derive and build a story around. The nice thing is all the artists are long dead so we can pretty much make up whatever story we want. But they have to be good stories. They have to be believable."

"Is it possible that some of the stories and revelations could be true?"

"That would be even better. What do you think, are you at all interested?"

The student had his Rugal but he didn't know what he was going to do with it. He didn't know who to trust to decode it. He didn't know if he trusted Emot, but this could be an opportunity to expose citizens to the important message the Rugal told.

"I'm glad you stopped me before I left the museum and I'm glad we had lunch. I think I'm interested in this opportunity. Actually I'm very interested in it."

"Great. I'll talk to my supervisor when we get back. Depending on how fast we can negotiate your pay and benefits we could move you over to our department fairly soon."

They finished their meal and walked back to the museum. When they arrived back at the museum the student returned to the basement where he had been working.

He reached into his satchel and pulled out the Rugal. Holding it in his hand he looked at it closely, confident he was making the right decision. Sitting the Rugal down, he picked up his inventory journal and wrote. Item 1 from artist Lairnam - Rugal - hold for ancient revelation display.

Chapter 45

Before the Debate – Frodd & The True Cytherans

Dafur and Tatalc hadn't been able to spend as much time together preparing for the event at the Muy as they would have liked. The event was originally going to be held at the university auditorium. But after the support Tatalc had built and the government announcing support of Dafur's plan, the event grew in both size and importance. This would be the first public event in which they could articulate their message as being a universally supported plan for the survival of Cythera. This shifted the priority of their presentation from soliciting support, to building the foundation necessary to execute their plan for survival.

Dafur, who had been busy entertaining Lij's family, didn't hear about the government's decision until his wedding, when Rigby shared the good news. As happy as Dafur was, he made the decision to keep his commitment to take Lij out of Regiowide to celebrate a short honeymoon. When they returned from their honeymoon, Dafur would only have a short time until the event at the Muy.

The program would be similar to the first event Dafur and Tatalc held together. Dafur would go on stage first to explain and demonstrate the science behind their plan. Then Tatalc would follow with instructions for how everyone should prepare for what was coming next.

Dafur hadn't spoken publically on the topic since the first event, and a lot had changed. The algorithms sequencing solar flare activity were complete and he and Rigby had mapped over four-hundred variable routes the vessels might follow to safely arrive on the next planet.

Prototypes for the vessel had been built and tested, and the construction designs for the full-scale vessels were complete. Now that the appropriate resources were available, Dafur was only waiting for Wickem to approve the start of construction on the first vessel.

The only issue still unresolved was how to launch the vessels off of Cythera. In fairness, Dafur and Rigby were not focusing much time on the matter. But now that the project had been approved, they would have the money and the time to find a solution. Expecting some citizens might be critical of the fact that they had not figured out how to launch the vessels, Dafur was prepared to answer any questions. Of the three components of successful execution – launch, travel, and land – he believed launching was the least complex. He knew he could defend this point if necessary.

Dafur had also been occupied with another significant change. Lij's speech during dinner the night before their wedding, about everyone having only a limited amount of time, had touched Lij's mother in an unexpected way; Lij's family had decided to move to Regiowide to spend more time with Lij and Dafur. With their village in the rurals experiencing a severe drought, and the unknown time left, Lij's family felt this was the best decision.

There were other benefits to being in Regiowide. Lij's family would be at the epicenter of society and could keep a close watch on the progress towards a solution to the crisis. Also, her brothers wanted to ensure inclusion of Transients in Cythera's plan for survival. This would have been difficult to do from the rurals.

Lij was in the process of moving in with Dafur. For now Lij's mother, father and brothers had moved into her cramped apartment. Because of all these factors, Dafur and Tatalc were only able to meet once to prepare for the event at the Muy. But it was not their lack of preparation that caused the event to get out of control; they could not have planned for the unexpected.

***

Dafur's presentation had gone as expected. All his demonstrations worked perfectly. And unlike the first event, where most came late and showed marginal interest in Dafur's lecture, this time the arena was full when Dafur took the stage.

Throughout Dafur's speech the crowd seemed engaged and interested in his science. Each one of them must have imagined themselves on one of the vessels traveling through space to the new planet.

Tatalc took the stage under a thunderous welcoming applause. As Tatalc spoke, the crowd focused on every word that left his mouth. In unison, the audience leaned forward and when Tatalc emphasized a point in the way only an accomplished orator could, his audience would explode with cheers.

Part way through his speech Tatalc knew something was different. *He was different.* Through his countless experiences he had never had this feeling. He felt almost possessed, as if he were guided by a spirit other than his own.

His words smoothly rolled off his tongue, without thinking, without looking at his notes, his words poured from his mind to his mouth, touching his audience. Tatalc actually felt like he could see his words *touch* his audience. If there was ever time, when Tatalc needed to be at his best, tonight was the night, and tonight his words could have moved a mountain.

Nearing the end of his speech his exhaustion began to set in. The amazing energy he had projected was nearly spent, and he needed one more push. One more crescendo in his masterpiece.

Tatalc looked into his soul and saw Cythera dying. He knew right then that almost every one in the building was going to die, only a few of them really had the chance to be selected to travel to the next planet. But they cheered him on anyway, because each hoped to be one of the few chosen to rebuild their civilization.

Tatalc thought of the one citizen in the building who

could be the first to step foot on the new planet. *Where were they? Who were they? What do I need to tell them at this moment?* In the background of Tatalc's mind, while he still spoke about everyone's roles and responsibilities, the words for that one individual, the one who would be first to step foot on their new home, came to him . . . that's when he noticed the crowd of citizens coming down the aisle towards the stage.

The man that led them was tall, taller than everyone in the group that followed him. He was undoubtedly their leader. The group was moving fast, but not out of control. Tatalc continued to focus on his words, but his audience was beginning to take notice of the disturbance, and Tatalc was losing the attention of his crowd. He did not know who the tall man was or what he wanted.

The tall man and his followers continued walking down the aisle towards the front of the stage. With every step forward, more and more of the audience turned their attention away from Tatalc and towards the tall man. Even Tatalc could no longer ignore the distraction. He had to acknowledge the man.

"My friend, I'm glad you and yours are enthusiastic about the cause. There'll be plenty of work for everyone. I'd be happy to meet you after the . . ."

"We're not here to do your work, Tatalc!" The man's voice was loud, bold and clear. He didn't yell but his words carried.

Tatalc looked at the tall man but said nothing. To his right Tatalc could see security guards gathering backstage. He held his hand up with his palm facing towards the guards, signaling them to hold their ground and to not come on stage.

"We are the True Cytherans and we are here to expose

your lies!" The tall man attempted to say something else but he couldn't be heard over the loud jeers that were filling the arena.

Trying to silence the crowd, Tatalc raised his arms above his head. This was not the first time someone had interrupted one of his speeches and he was not intimidated or afraid of the tall man. When the crowd finally quieted Tatalc asked, "What's your name?"

"My name is Frodd and I'm the leader of the True Cytherans."

Again the crowd began to jeer, Tatalc raised his arms. "Everyone stay quiet. Let me talk to him." Tatalc looked at the tall man. "Tell me Frodd, I'm a little confused, I thought we were all true Cytherans?"

"No! You are the liars, the frauds. You are everything but the truth."

"I'm not sure I understand." Tatalc was telling the truth, he really wasn't sure what Frodd was talking about.

"This whole thing. This whole crisis. It's all a lie made up by citizens in power like you *and* like your father."

Tatalc tried to reason with him, "Frodd, you're not making sense. Why would anyone make up a story about Cythera coming to an end?"

"Citizens with power have always wanted to control the citizens without power. It's been that way forever. And now you think you've come up with the perfect plan to take advantage of us without anyone fighting back. But we're here to tell everyone that it's a lie! It's *all* a lie!"

"Frodd, that's your name right?" Tatalc didn't give him a chance to answer, "I'm not sure where you've been getting your information, but nothing we've said is false."

Frodd puffed his chest out and exclaimed, "Everything you've been preaching is based off a silly looking antique and some false prophecy. You tell us Cythera is warming and we're going to die. You convince the government to grant you every available resource. This is nothing more than a hoax to give more power to the powerful and to make the rich even richer. You don't care about us. You only care about yourself. You are not a True Cytheran. You are a liar! WE are the True Cytherans!"

Tatalc was unphased, "It's unfortunate you and your friends feel that way. It took a lot of courage for you to come here in front of this audience and call me a liar. But do you call me a liar because of what I say or because of who I am? I don't think you even know the difference between what's a lie and what's the truth! I'm sorry you don't believe me but the reality is you're not going to believe anything I ever say because I'm not like you, so to you I'll always be wrong."

Tatalc approached the front of the stage and was nearly on top of Frodd. "Yet you boldly proclaim this is all a lie so I can grow my power and wealth to create even more separation between citizens like me and citizens like you? It's not I that wants to separate from you my friend, it is you that wants to separate from me. I think you've taken up enough of our time this evening and it's time for you and your friends to leave."

Frodd refused to back down, "Why do you want us to leave? Are you afraid your audience has listened to our truths and will turn their backs on you?"

"No Frodd, I'm afraid if you don't leave soon this audience won't let you leave peacefully." The crowd cheered. If Tatalc wanted his audience to, they would've torn Frodd to pieces.

"I'll leave, Tatalc, but this won't be the last you hear of

the True Cytherans!" After making his final proclamation, Frodd turned and led his followers back up the aisle and out of the arena. A chorus of jeers continued while they made their exit. Tatalc didn't ask his audience to be quiet this time.

When they were finally gone and the audience settled down Tatalc knew it was time to conclude the event. He could not return to the cadence and influence he had established before the distraction, and he knew it was unlikely he would be able to bring the audience all the way back. Now was the time to end the evening, but he would leave them with one last thought.

"If I'm a liar, that would make all of you . . ." Tatalc gazed across the audience, "If I'm a liar, it would make every one of you fools. Are you fools? I don't think you are fools, and I am not a liar! I don't know who that man was, but he will not be the last one to try and convince you that you're wasting your time. There will always be doubters. Don't let them discourage you. They are blinded by their own fear and they refuse to acknowledge it. They will say anything to avoid facing their fears. You've faced your fears! You're doing something about it! You are strong! And your strength will allow us to survive!"

Tatalc ended the speech by raising his closed fists high above his head and opening his palms to the audience. The crowd returned Tatalc's salute by cheering and chanting his name. "Tatalc! Tatalc!! Tatalc!!!" As Tatalc walked off stage he thought about what had happened during his speech, the distraction was unexpected but likely did little to sway any followers, he wondered who this Frodd character was, he would need to talk to Lila.

Chapter 46

Before the Debate – The Chief of State

Part of the agreement Wickem had made with the government was that The Chief of State would be allowed full access to the project. It was important to The Chief that he could answer questions and defend the project if necessary. Originally, Dafur was concerned The Chief would be meddlesome and in the way. Wickem assured Dafur The Chief was not interested in the details; once he had enough information to protect himself from embarrassment, he would keep his distance.

Timing for their first meeting was unfortunate. The story of the True Cytherans interrupting Dafur and Tatalc's event had become a front-page story in *The Word*. Lila, who didn't write the article, did everything she could to convince her editor to move the story off the front page, but he wouldn't budge. It was too big of a story.

Like Tatalc, neither Dafur nor Wickem considered the True Cytherans any more than a disgruntled club attempting to attract publicity. But they knew The Chief wouldn't see it that way. He lacked the courage to stand up to opposition. The Chief was notorious for trading his leverage to avoid conflict.

Arriving at the government office together, Tatalc, Dafur and Wickem entered the small meeting room. Already seated at the head of the table was The Chief. In his hands he held a crumpled version of *The Word*. The version with the headline reading: **How '*True*' are the True Cytherans?**

"Who is this True Cytheran group?" The Chief directed

his question towards Wickem. Wickem was the only one The Chief knew well. He had known Tatalc since he was a child but had not spent much time with him and this was the first time he met Dafur.

"We don't know," Wickem said. "We never heard of them until they showed up at the event."

"We're working on a profile of their leader. We should have something soon." Tatalc added.

"How could you have let something like this happen? The article says they walked right up to the stage. You didn't have anyone there to stop them?" It was a rhetorical question. "And then you gave him a voice. Tatalc, why didn't you ignore them?" The Chief was not at the event and was quoting from the article. It was his only point of reference.

"I think you're overreacting." Wickem was calm in his response.

"I'm not overreacting Wickem, this is . . . " The Chief held up the paper and waved it front of them, "something we have to prevent. We can't have citizens questioning our decisions!"

"It's only one small group. The worse thing we can do is give them undeserved attention," advised Wickem. "I'm not saying it's as easy as ignoring them and they'll go away, but if we make a big deal out of this, all we'll do is add fuel to their cause."

"But it's not only *one small group*." The Chief reached into the portfolio he always carried and pulled out a large stack of papers. He threw them down on the table and the sound made a loud thump. "We only recently made the decision to solely support you and I've already received many letters opposing the decision. And it's not only the True Cytherans who are against your plan!"

"We knew there would be some opposition." Tatalc stated.

"I realize that," confirmed The Chief, "But factions have formed. All with their own agenda." The Chief started flipping through the stack of letters he had thrown down on the table. He was looking for something specific. "Here, this is an example." He pulled out one of the letters and pushed it towards Wickem. "I have received a few from this group."

Wickem picked up the letter and scanned it then passed it on to Tatalc and Dafur.

"That one is from a group called The Devoted. I think I have about five letters from them."

"What's their cause?" Dafur asked.

"They're a strange group." The Chief answered. "They believe in the Rugal prophecy but they don't think we should do anything about it."

"You mean they want to die?" Tatalc questioned.

"Yes. They want to die." The Chief flipped through the stack of letters in front of him and found another letter from The Devoted. "Here's another one from them. What's the word they use?" The Chief read through the letter. "Destiny, that's it, *destiny*. They say it's our destiny to be burned up by our sun. Something about the natural order of things, mother planet, you know the type."

"What are they threatening to do?" Tatalc asked The Chief.

"Nothing yet, but I'm sure it's only a matter of time. There are other factions too." The Chief flipped through more of the letters. After finding the one he was looking for he pulled it out and passed it to Tatalc. "This group might be considered a legitimate threat."

Tatalc scanned over the letter, "The Forgotten. I wouldn't worry too much about them."

"Who are The Forgotten?" Dafur asked.

"The Forgotten are the Transients. They also believe in the Rugal prophecy and they support the mission to move citizens to the next planet. They're worried we won't let any Transients go to the next planet. They're worried we will use this as an opportunity to finally rid ourselves of their kind." The Chief answered. "Which might not be a bad idea."

"Be careful with your words," Wickem advised, "Dafur recently married a Transient."

"You did?" The Chief didn't seem to care if he offended Dafur but apologized anyway, "I'm sorry. I didn't mean to insult you."

Dafur wasn't offended. He wasn't one to look for offense in every word another citizen spoke. "Can I see the letter?"

Tatalc handed the letter from The Forgotten to Dafur. As he read through it he began to recognize a familiar tone in the words. When he reached the end he saw it was signed *Dran, Leader of The Forgotten*.

"I know who wrote this." Dafur stated.

"Of course. We all do, he signed the bottom. He's sent over twelve letters and boldly signs all of them," responded The Chief.

"No I *really* know him." Dafur stressed. "Dran is my wife's brother."

"Lij's brother?" Tatalc asked. "What does he want?"

"He wants what The Chief said he wants. He's told me before." Dafur said, "He wants to make sure Transients are included."

"Not every citizen will get what they want," said Wickem. "We will only have a limited amount of space. There might be some groups we have to leave behind. We might not have the choice."

"I'm sure we can find room for them," Dafur replied. "I think we should do everything we can to send as many diverse citizens from all the classes and races. This is the only way to assure the *complete* survival of our civilization."

Wickem looked back at Dafur, "I'm not sure I agree with you Dafur. If we only have limited space shouldn't we send citizens who have the highest probability of restoring our civilization on the new planet?"

"Not at the sacrifice of part of our identity." Dafur defended. He was passionate about the topic. "All citizens will need to do is repopulate, any citizen can do that."

"We can't send random citizens. We need to hand select the ones with the best chance and the best skills to rebuild civilization, regardless of their lineage. I'm not saying we would deliberately ignore any group, I'm simply saying it should be a non factor."

"But if we only send the best, and certain classes and races are left behind, the new Cythera won't be a true representation of our current civilization. Sir," Dafur looked over to The Chief, "who do *you* think should go?"

All three of them, Dafur, Wickem and Tatalc, looked back at The Chief.

"I don't know." The Chief said. His response surprised no one. Even Dafur who had just met the man knew he was indecisive and would not make any decision that might cause conflict. "But I do know we should not decide this right now, in this room, with only the four of us."

The Chief leaned back in his chair. He did this often when difficult decisions were presented to him. He thought the gesture established his authority, but it had the opposite effect. It illustrated him *moving away* from an issue, not confronting it head on like a leader in his position should. "This is a decision that should involve the League of Representatives. I think you both make valid arguments and you both should have the opportunity to present your views. Let's take the issue in front of the elect and let you debate your points."

"A debate?" Dafur didn't like the idea. He had never been a great speaker and Wickem was a seasoned politician.

"Yes. A debate."

Chapter 47

The Revelation

The curators at the museum decided on seventeen pieces, each telling their own story. Some of the stories were fabricated but they were *good* stories, ones citizens would be interested in and pay to see.

Emot was surprised by how well the student was able to conceive believable stories based on the ancient art they selected. He expected the head curator would also be pleased.

The head curator of the Regiowide Art Museum was establishing himself as the authority on ancient revelation art. His book on the subject was in final draft and its publishing would coincide with the opening of the museum exhibit. Success of his new book relied on the success of the exhibit.

All the displays were staged in the primary exhibit hall, the largest hall in the museum. The student was busy finalizing the arrangement of a painting called the *Shadow of Ancestors* when Emot and the head curator walked in. It was an important moment. This is when the head curator would be granting final approval on the exhibit.

"I really like this one." The head curator stood next to a ceramic statue called *The Ripening*. He read the story accompanying the piece "That makes sense. I knew it before I read it. The imagery is so alive. Feast and famine, balancing the scales. It's all here. Excellent work with this display."

He moved on to the next piece and then the next piece. When he arrived at the podium on which an odd shaped artifact with a long neck and an orb rested, the head curator extended his hand. After grabbing the artifact, he held it in front of his face, he twisted and turned it in order to view the artifact from every angle. Sitting it back on the podium he looked at the *story* accompanying the piece and read it out loud.

"*The Rugal*, artist: Lairnam, an early era artisan. *The Rugal* illustrates a time in the distant future when complex forces threaten the existence of all living on Cythera. The orb, representing our sun, shines down in a long broadening ray, represented by the neck of the piece, onto Cythera, represented by the base. If lifted and turned upside down, one notices the base is hollow, like an empty cup, representing the future emptiness and darkness our sun will cause Cythera."

After he finished reading the synopsis, the head curator reached out and took hold of the piece again. He turned it upside down and placed his finger inside the carved out base.

He began to rub his finger around the inside of the carved out section. It wasn't smooth like he suspected.

"I'm not sure I like this one." The head curator looked at the student. "Did you write the story on this piece?"

The student responded, "I did. What don't you like about it?"

"It's morbid. Citizens don't want to hear Cythera will come to an end. Let's take this piece out of the exhibit. Replace it with something more *positive*."

"But what if the prophecy is true?" The student replied. "Isn't that the whole point of the exhibit and ancient revelation art? Don't we want art that reveals the truth, even if it might not be what we want to hear?"

"Don't argue with him," Emot ordered, "replace it."

"Wait." The head curator still had his finger in the concave. He lifted the Rugal up and looked into the opening. "These markings in here," he pulled the piece closer to his eyes and moved it around, "they almost look like symbols of some kind. Some of them even repeat."

Handing the piece back to the student he said, "See if you can decipher something from these symbols and take an image of them to post next to the piece. I trust you'll make it interesting. You can stay with the *end of time* theme, but don't make the story *too* dramatic. Yes. Let's keep this piece in the exhibit. It's already growing on me."

Chapter 48

The Debate

The debate was originally scheduled to take place at a small government office, but as word of the debate spread citizens demanded they be allowed to witness the event. In an attempt to appease the public The Chief moved the event to a larger venue, The Muy.

Unlike Tatalc and Dafur's rally where a stage was positioned at one end, the stage for the debate was centered in the floor of the arena. Circular in shape, the stage had tables and chairs placed all around the edge. This is where the elect would sit.

In the middle of the circular stage was a small section higher above the primary stage. Another table and two chairs were on the smaller stage. This is where Dafur and Wickem would sit. There was a small lever in the middle of their table that would allow Dafur or Wickem to rotate their smaller stage towards any representative posing a question.

The Chief began the event by reminding the audience they were to be silent during the debate. Any outburst would lead to immediate ejection from the arena. He then led them in *The Call*, a patriotic chant that was often delivered during the launch of an official event.

The Devoted sat together in one section. Frodd and the True Cytherans sat in another section. Dran and The Forgotten sat in another section. There were also supporters of smaller factions in attendance. All told, approximately a quarter of the audience that filled the arena came from factions. The rest of the audience were supporters of the plan to send travelers to the next planet who were only interested in hearing the answer to the question being debated. Who gets to live?

***

It was obvious Dafur was not as comfortable with the debate format as Wickem and he was relieved when the first question was not directed towards him.

"Wickem," a representative from the rural region of Ampato asked the first question. "I'll get right to my point. Now that you have access to every resource you need, how many vessels can you build and how many citizens can be moved off of Cythera?"

As usual Wickem was prepared to answer any question posed to him. He and Dekayb had spent a great deal of time reviewing every piece of data they had collected since they were introduced to Dafur's solution. Wickem would not lose the debate because of lack of preparation; that was a given.

"Each vessel will support life for thirty two Cytherans," Wickem answered. "Once full production begins it will take around a telth to build a vessel from start to finish."

"When could we expect the full production cycle to begin?"

"After we launch the first vessel and we know it has safely landed we would begin production on the next vessels," answered Wickem.

"You would wait until the first vessel lands?" The representative from Ampato didn't like Wickem's answer. "It seems to me you would be wasting time. Why wouldn't you start production right away on the additional vessels?"

"We need to make sure the first one works. It's true

that in the amount of time it will take the vessel to travel to the new planet we could probably build several more vessels. But if there are any problems with the first vessel we would need to reset our production lines. We would have wasted resources on vessels we couldn't use. It's simply not worth the risk to build additional vessels until we know the first vessel will arrive safely."

"I'm not sure I agree with you." The Ampatoian turned his attention to Dafur. "Dafur, would you like to rebut?"

Dafur had assumed the debate would be focused solely on the issue of who to send; he had not prepared for the questions being asked about the vessels. Saying the first thing that came to his mind. "The first one will work," his words came out much calmer than he thought they would, "Yes, the first one will work. I think we should go ahead and start building the next vessels as soon as we can."

"Dafur, I have a question for you," a different representative asked, "How can you be so confident that your vessel will land safely when you don't even know how you plan to launch your vessel?"

While he was not expecting to be asked this question during the debate, Dafur had been expecting this question at some point and was prepared with an answer, "Launching is actually a simple process. All we have to do is create enough force to defeat the strength of gravity and gravity weakens as you move away from the surface of the planet. The vessels are designed to support life in space, outside of our atmosphere, therefore they will be more than capable of supporting life as they exit our atmosphere."

"But you haven't solved this problem yet have you?"

"No, we have not, and we likely won't finalize any

solutions until the first vessel is built and we can accurately measure the energy needed for the vessel's mass to defeat gravity."

"I have a question for you both," the voice came from behind Dafur and Wickem. Using the lever on their table, Wickem rotated their stage around to the representative who was speaking. "How will you know if the first vessel survives its landing?"

Dafur and Wickem looked at each other to see who would answer. Dafur responded, "Each vessel is equipped with a call back button the passengers would press when they safely land. The call back button sends a signal back letting us know they reached their destination."

"But it's only a signal. You won't be able to talk with the travelers?"

"That is correct."

The questions continued. For the most part the audience behaved and remained silent, at least to the point that no citizens were ejected from the arena. Dafur was surprised by the variety of questions including topics ranging from what the travelers would eat to how they would perform their continence. Occasionally, Dafur would be slow to answer. His nerves were showing.

Wickem, on the other hand, had prepared for every possible question and found his answers easy to access. If they were being judged solely on their ability to debate, it wasn't a close competition. Wickem was clearly the more experienced debater.

After a while it became obvious the representatives were asking questions to simply ask questions. Some representatives tried to sound more intelligent than they were, some representatives tried to intimidate Dafur and Wickem, and some representatives overly complimented them. This was typical behavior when the elect came together.

Finally, a representative asked the most important question of all. The question every citizen had come to hear answered, "Each of you explain who you think should be sent to the next planet and why?"

Dafur *was* prepared for this question and responded first. "My position is that we don't view this from an individual perspective. It's not important which *individuals* go. What is important is that we send a complete representation of Cythera. We need to select individuals from every class and race so the new Cythera would be repopulated to mirror our existing culture."

"I understand the concept and your principles Dafur, but still at some point we would have to select individuals. How would we do that?"

"We would group citizens based on their class and have a random drawing."

"A lottery?"

"Yes, a lottery."

"I'm concerned about the randomness of your plan," said an anxious representative from the other side of the stage.

Dafur used the lever to turn the center stage towards the speaker. Both Dafur and Wickem were getting annoyed with the constant spinning and turning of their stage. "What specifically concerns you?" Dafur asked.

"What happens if you randomly draw the name of a citizen and they're not fit for travel? Maybe they're past the age of procreation or have early symptoms of the black?"

"There will be requirements a citizen would need to meet in order to be eligible for the lottery. Certain levels of health and citizenship will have to be met. For example sufficient trutons, a high replication factor and other similar conditions."

"Then it is not a *random drawing*."

"No, it's still a random drawing. But one's eligibility to be in the drawing is not random."

The anxious representative continued, "My other concern is about procreation. I have two issues here. First, if you randomly select males and females how do you know they will want to mate with one another? And then assuming they do, aren't you concerned such a small population would be forced to inbreed in order to protect their class and race?" Dafur began to answer but the representative kept talking. "Let me finish. My point is that your plan is built around maintaining the identities of the different Cytheran ethnic groups, but with such a small number of citizens left to rebuild society, won't the classes and races all eventually mix therefore completely defeating the purpose of your original intent?"

Dafur understood the representatives concerns, "I agree that a scenario like this could materialize. The goal of preserving all cultures may not necessarily have a biological solution. It's the traditions, the histories that need to carry on. We already have blended families now. I myself am married to a Transient. In a different time and place, if we would have the time to raise children, our children would be mixed. But they would still be taught and carry on the traditions of both my wife's and my heritage."

"What about citizens not wanting to procreate with each other, the first part of my question?"

"If we draw a citizen who is married we would allow their spouse to go. If we draw an unmarried citizen we will match them with another unmarried citizen from their ethnic group." Dafur was uncomfortable committing to solutions without having the opportunity to weigh the variables, but he had no choice. He couldn't flutter.

The representative nodded his head in approval of Dafur's response. Another representative turned the questioning to Wickem, "I feel we have a good understanding of Dafur's plan. Wickem, what's yours?"

Wickem confidently leaned forward in his chair, "Dafur's plan and mine are not that different. I too want to send a diverse representation of Cythera, but only to the extent we are sending citizens with the highest probability of success. Dafur's plan includes minimum requirements, and I couldn't agree more. Therefore the only real difference in our plans is that Dafur wants to randomly chose from a pool of eligible citizens while I think the select should be hand picked."

"And how would we go about *hand picking*?"

"We would allow citizens to apply to be a traveler. My office, with help from other government offices, would select the best suited for this remarkable opportunity."

"What type of citizens would you be looking for?"

"The brightest, the strongest, and the most influential. The ones with the best chance of rebuilding Cythera civilization on the new planet."

"Could you be more specific? Can you give us an example of an individual you would send?"

Wickem thought about this for a moment. He had already been thinking of several citizens that would be great candidates, but the one name that stood out most in his mind was Tatalc.

"Tatalc, my son, is a perfect candidate. His leadership and influence is unmatched. He would be able to navigate," as Wickem was finishing his sentence he noticed the representatives were all quizzically looking at each other. The citizens in the audience, who until this point had been mostly quiet, were now murmuring to one another, ". . . any challenge the travelers might encounter."

Wickem wasn't sure what he had said to cause this reaction. Maybe everyone suddenly realized Wickem was right and they were pleased to hear Tatalc would be one of the chosen. Wickem tried to hide the small smile sneaking into the corners of his mouth. He confidently awaited the next question. The elect were still whispering to one another when Wickem finally asked, "What's your next question?"

The elect looked around and silently nodded to one another indicating they all agreed with whatever secret they had passed around. "We don't have any more questions for either of you. I believe we have enough information to take this to a vote. Let's recess, and when we return we will give you our decision."

Chapter 49

The Revelation

Of course, the student could decipher the symbols inside the Rugal. But he had to choose the right time to reveal the Rugal's message and how he would go about convincing Emot and the head curator the message was true. He knew that if he translated the message himself, others would doubt and challenge the work of a student. He needed to find a way for Emot and the head curator to be involved in the translation.

The student sat at the desk in the small office he had been given after his promotion. He held the Rugal and pondered his next move. Emot walked in and sat down across from him.

"Have you made any progress developing a story behind the symbols yet?"

"A little," he said. The student handed the Rugal to Emot. "There's definitely a pattern. Do you see it?"

"Sort of, I guess."

"It's easier to see if you look at this." The student handed Emot a piece of paper where he had transcribed the symbols. This was the first time Emot had really taken a good look at the symbols.

"I see it now. Some of this is similar to Letric."

"What's Letric?" The student pretended not to know.

"It's an ancient language that's been dead for generations. It's thought to be one of the earliest, if not the first Cytheran written language." Emot continued studying the piece of paper with the symbols written on it. Without looking up he asked, "I'm curious, what made you think of the back story for the piece?"

"What do you mean?"

"The description you placed with the exhibit. You know how the orb is the sun, the neck is the sun's rays, the empty base meaning death to all. How did you come up with that?"

"I don't know. I guess I made it up."

"Really? That's interesting. You were pretty passionate

213

about *revealing the truth* when we were with the head curator in the exhibit hall. You didn't back down from him, which most do."

"Well, yes I think we should look for the truth when we can."

"I don't believe you." It was a calm accusation.

"You don't believe I think we should look for the truth?" The student was perplexed.

"No, not that. I don't believe you made the story up and I don't believe you've only made a little progress decoding the symbols." Emot sat the paper down on the desk. "You've known all along what these symbols mean." Emot was becoming stern. He was suspicious.

"That's crazy." The student tried to act like he didn't know what Emot was talking about. "What makes you think that?"

"I'm an authority on the Letric language. As soon as you handed me the paper I was able to read it. There are some distinctions in the characters, but its close enough to be translated."

Emot stood up from his chair and placed both hands on the desk. He leaned forward to where his face was only a few inches away from the student's face. "I guess I find it odd that you were extremely passionate about a story you *made up* that happens to be exactly in line with the translation of a language you supposedly *don't understand!*"

Emot sat back down in his chair and said, "But what really puzzles me is why you would lie about it. There's something not right here. I don't think you're another average student. There's more to your story isn't there? So tell me who you really are."

The student was in shock. Emot's confrontation was unexpected. He had no idea Emot understood Letric. But regardless, Emot did and the student now had someone other then himself to reveal the prophecy. It might not have happened the way he would have wanted, but the result was the same; the message of the Rugal was now revealed.

"So what happens next?" The student asked Emot.

"You're going to wait here and I'm going to go get the head curator and you *will* answer our questions, all of our questions." Emot stood up again and started walking out of the room. Before leaving he turned around, "Don't go anywhere. I'll be right back."

It only took a few moments for Emot to find the head curator and return to the student's office. On the walk, Emot explained to the head curator what had happened. When they reached the student's office and opened the door the office was empty. On the desk was the Rugal.

"What was I thinking?" Emot was angry with himself. "I should've never left him alone." He walked to the desk and pointed at the Rugal. "At least he didn't take this."

Emot grabbed the piece of paper with the symbols transcribed on it and handed it to the head curator. He noticed another piece of a paper. A handwritten note.

He picked up the note and started to read it out loud. *'I can't answer your questions. You wouldn't understand. All I can tell you is the prophecy is true and you must share it with all of the children.'*

"*All of the children?*" The head curator said. "What does *that* mean?"

"I have no idea," replied Emot.

The head curator handed the piece of paper with the symbols transcribed on it back to Emot. "Translate this for me."

Emot held the paper up to his face, "It's going to be somewhat broken but I'll translate it word for word," then he started to read it out loud. "Ancestors – living from – *I don't know this symbol* – are we. Universe – story – unfolds. *Here's the symbol again, I think it's where they are from* – planet – first – sun. Twelve – planets – will burn. Growing – sun – swallowing – *the place they are from, again*. Time – runs – fast. Survive – travel – next – planet – only – life – hope."

"Is this some type of warning?" The head curator asked Emot.

"Whoever wrote this is trying to tell the story of our universe," said Emot.

"But they mention twelve planets and we only have nine."

"I think I know why." Emot continued, "The writer says their planet was the first one next to our sun. But when our sun started growing the only way to survive was to move out to the next planet from the sun. I'm guessing their planet was destroyed by the sun and doesn't exist any more."

"That would mean three planets don't exist anymore?"

"Correct."

***

As one of the inventors of the study of ancient revelation art, the head curator had found the piece that would help promote his new science. He would end up rewriting his book on ancient revelation art to focus on the Rugal. The theories he stated were so well received that the government became involved. Over the next several generations scientists, philosophers and mathematicians worked diligently to prove, or in some cases try to disprove the Rugal prophecy.

At times society struggled to accept their fate and Cytheran civilization began to ignore the warning. Yet all evidences validated the Rugal's prophecy. Cythera's climate began to noticeably change. Something had to be done. A strong powerful leader was needed to influence civilization and begin planning the course for their survival. Wickem would be that leader.

***

Time did indeed run fast, at least it seemed that way to the student. It *always* had seemed that way.

After he escaped the museum, the student left Regiowide and traveled to the Feber and back to his home where he rested and waited for the right time to emerge again.

***

Time did indeed run fast, the bearded student thought to himself, remembering when he had inscribed those words on the Rugal. Then he saw the elect start to walk back on to the circular stage and take their seats at their tables.

Chapter 50

The Debate Ruling

Once all the elect were seated and the crowd inside the Muy quieted down, the Chief of State stood up. He opened his portfolio holding the prewritten speech and began to speak.

"Hopefully, many generations from now, citizens will be peacefully living in harmony on the new planet. Most of us will never see Cythera's new home; most of us will never breathe the air on the new Cythera. We can only wonder what it will be like once the new Cythera is repopulated. Even if our citizens survive, will our values survive? Will our culture survive? Will our history survive? Will the new Cythera, the future Cythera, be anything like the near utopian Cythera we all take for granted? What *is* our goal for the new Cythera? This is the question we've been trying to answer and we hope the answer will lead us to the right decision about whom we should send. Wickem stated there was not much difference between his plan and Dafur's and we agree. But Wickem wants to *hand pick*, those were his exact words, which citizens should go, essentially *hand picking* who should live and who should die. Wickem has proven his wisdom on many occasions, but we believe Wickem has begun to let his selfishness overtake wisdom. Not only does Wickem want to be able to *hand pick* who lives and dies; he wants to *hand pick* his first born son! And in this case his nepotism is matched only by his ignorance and denial. We think we know why he would want to send his son, to have the chance to carry on his bloodline. To keep his family intact so they can lead in the new world like they have led on Cythera. But, and I don't mean this in offensive manner, we all know his son will not procreate. He has always been public about his interests. Therefore, even if his son were to travel to the new Cythera, Wickem's bloodline would die with Tatalc. Wickem's proposal is illogical and it has forced us to question his motivation. We will probably never know the real motivation for Wickem's decision, and we don't need to; his actions and his judgment in this matter tell us everything we need to know. Therefore we have made the decision to support Dafur's plan.

Fully. Including producing multiple vessels as soon as possible. We have been disappointed by your judgment Wickem, but one wrong decision, even one as significant as this one, does not erase all the good you have contributed to Cythera during your lifetime. If you are willing to accept our decision, we will allow you to continue as Chairman of the Federal Safety Commission and continue with your responsibilities regarding this cause. That decision will be yours. The elect have agreed that starting tomorrow we will begin working with the appropriate divisions of government to identify and classify all citizens based on class and race. We will then filter the eligible citizens based on qualifications similar to the ones Dafur mentioned. If a citizen is chosen and decides not to go, or is unable to go for any reason, they may gift their seat to a citizen of their choice. All other qualifications and rules for the lottery will be agreed upon by the elect. We expect this to take some time. The public will be kept informed of the process. If we are able to complete this task in a timely manner, the lottery would take place immediately following the next truton ceremony to be held here at the Muy. In closing, remember, our only hope is that many generations from now citizens will be peacefully living in harmony on the new planet, and they will remember this night and celebrate the wise decision we have made. Thank you."

The Chief closed his portfolio and walked off stage.

Chapter 51

After the Debate – Wickem

The next morning Wickem woke up disappointed and angry. Disappointed because he had lost the debate to Dafur, and angry at The Chief, who had used the debate as an opportunity to humiliate him. Now, he struggled to find the energy to get out of bed. Every decision he had ever made, he was now questioning. He questioned everything about himself. How could this have happened? He even questioned his own appearance as he stopped and looked at himself in a mirror on the way to his balcony.

Most of all, he was angry at The Chief of State. If all had been left to The Chief, they would not have a plan for survival. Early on, The Chief opposed an aggressive strategy to confront the issue because of his concerns about disrupting his constituents. Wickem *had* to bully The Chief; he had no choice. Wickem knew The Chief well enough to expect retaliation at some point, but for The Chief to do what he did and insult Wickem in front of all those citizens at the debate was unforgivable, and something Wickem would never forget.

What The Chief said was simply not true. Wickem was not naïve and he was not in denial. Wickem wanted Tatalc to go for all the right reasons - his leadership, his ability to solve problems, his goodness. It was Tatalc's influence, not his seed, Wickem wanted to preserve.

With all this weighing heavily on his mind, he would have to let himself look past the defeat to the fact there was still hope for Cythera's survival. It wasn't the plan he proposed, but it was still a plan. His loyalties and the responsibility he felt for the citizens of Cythera remained unchanged. Plus, there still could be a way to figure out how to include Tatalc. Wickem had to remain involved, and he would stay on as Chairman of the Federal Safety Commission.

***

One benefit of Wickem's public shaming was that citizens and politicians kept their distance from him. He knew this would eventually pass and the requests for his time would return to normal. He tried not to let this bother him. He would enjoy the peace that being ostracized created.

He was at his office catching up on work when the call came in. Usually Dekayb would filter his calls, but Wickem had been lonely and wanting to have a conversation with someone, anyone. He was more talkative than normal.

The call was from a stranger, a truton clerk named Tienneis. The stranger had called to discuss the truton application Wickem had submitted for Dekayb.

Wickem was enjoying the man's demeanor and found him pleasant to converse with. It was also nice to discuss Dekayb and her history of important contributions to his work. Then the subject of Wickem's debate with Dafur came up. Instead of becoming angry and not wanting to talk about it, Wickem engaged himself in the dialogue.

Wickem wasn't sure if it was because Tienneis was a stranger or that Tienneis didn't know much about the debate, but Wickem was finding a soft peace in explaining the situation to Tienneis. It felt therapeutic.

***

Tienneis' excitement came through in his tone, "Have you c-considered a *Thunderwell*?"

"A Thunderwell?" Wickem didn't know what that was, "I'm sorry. I'm not familiar with a Thunderwell. I don't believe I've ever heard Dafur mention it either."

Tienneis explained, "You would need a d-deep well, or shaft. It c-could b-be man made or natural as long as it is c-cl-closed in. You would seal the t-top and affix your p-pr-projectile, or in your c-case your v-vessel to the t-top. Then you would c-cr-create p-pr-pressure within the well. When the reaction from the p-pr-pressure builds up, it will p-produce enough energy to launch your v-vessel into space."

Wickem was intrigued, "Have you ever seen a Thunderwell work?"

"I've actually b-built one b-before, well, at least on a small scale."

"I don't mean to sound rude," Wickem was being sincere, "but aren't you only a truton clerk?"

"No offense t-taken. My father was a physicist and I've study physics myself. When I was a child we would go out t-to the rurals and launch t-toy rockets using natural Thunderwells. It's just a matter of having enough p-pressure to m-match the m-mass of the object."

"And you think something like this would work to launch a vessel into space?"

"It c-could. If you'd like, I'd b-be happy to meet with you and D-Dafur and show you how it w-works."

Wickem thought about this for a moment. This could be the breakthrough they'd been looking for, the missing piece that could save Cythera. He needed to learn more. "Yes. I definitely want to see how it works."

"I'd b-be happy to show you. Let me know when you and D-Dafur want to see how a Thunderwell works. And one m-more thing, I would m-make reservations for the t-tr-truton ceremony. I think you'll want t-to b-be at The Muy when D-Dekayb receives her t-tr-trutons."

Wickem was pleased Dekayb would receive her trutons but he was more interested in Tienneis' idea to launch the vessels. A *Thunderwell*, he thought. This could be the solution to their problem on how to launch the vessels off of Cythera, and he would have been the one who found it. Then another thought crossed through Wickem's mind. A thought contradicting everything Wickem stood for. He knew it was the right thought at the right time. He needed to speak to Tatalc.

Chapter 52

After the Debate – Frodd

With each revolution the shores of Lake Regiowide receded. It was not only Lake Regiowide; fresh water had started evaporating at an alarming rate all over Cythera. Making matters worse was the increasing demand for fresh water.

Until recently Cythera held an abundance of fresh water, to the degree where many common items such as carriages and coolers relied on hydraulic mechanics. Water had always been a key element on Cythera, but with the deadly heat evaporating Cythera's fresh water, the supply was not meeting the demand.

***

On the southern shore of Lake Regiowide, Frodd, the founder of the True Cytherans, walked with his top officer and best friend, Pesi. Pesi was a squatty fellow who made up for his small stature by talking *big*.

"I think *they* are pumping the water out of the lake and storing it somewhere else. *They* are hoarding it. I would almost guarantee it."

"It wouldn't surprise me one bit," Frodd responded.

"Nothing *they* do would surprise me," Pesi said.

***

Frodd had to bend his neck down to talk to Pesi. Frodd was at least a head taller than Pesi if not more. They had been friends since childhood. Both had come from elite families. Both had turned their backs on their birthright, to oppose everything they didn't like about Cythera's society. They felt the rich were too rich and the poor were too poor; and the government used it's power to manipulate the citizens. Someone had to stand up against the government, someone had to protect those who could not protect themselves. Frodd and Pesi had self appointed themselves society's saviors.

***

Pesi walked down to the edge of Lake Regiowide and knelt down on the soft sand. Picking up a flat rock he skipped it across the surface of the lake, "A cycle ago I would have been waist deep standing here."

"Knee deep for me." Frodd smiled. He couldn't resist the easy opening Pesi left him. Frodd loved Pesi like a brother and never hesitated to poke fun at his shortcomings.

Pesi was more intent on discussing recent events and the horrors of the establishment, "I can't believe how many citizens believe *their* lies. Everything *they* are saying about Cythera warming can be explained if citizens would listen to the facts."

"I know Pesi." Frodd confirmed. "No one ever wants to listen. I think citizens like being told what to think. It protects them from having to think for themselves."

"And *they* always find a way to find profit for *themselves* and *their* friends. It's funny how it all works out that way."

"Did you see who *they* picked to build the vessels?" Frodd knew Pesi was aware, everyone was aware of what contractor would be building the vessels. It had already been published. "No surprise there. Three members of the Contractor's Leadership Council are in the League of Representatives. The rich win again."

"I can't believe more citizens aren't talking about this." Pesi said. "No one has the courage to stand up to *them*."

Frodd agreed, "And *they* are not going to build any vessels. It's all a cover up for something else, but I can't figure out what it is. All I know is the rich will get richer, the powerful will become more powerful and it will all happen at the expense of those of us unwilling to conform to *their* agendas."

Pesi threw another rock across the surface of Lake Regiowide. "I wish there was a way we could get citizens to listen to us and to stop ignoring our truths."

Frodd paused for a moment. "There is."

"There is what?"

"There is a way to get citizens to listen to us."

"How?" Pesi asked.

"How do you get the attention of someone who won't listen to you?" Frodd smiled, "You make a noise so loud *they* can't ignore it."

Chapter 53

After the Debate – Tatalc & Lila

Lila was sticky and hot when she walked into her

apartment. Earlier in the morning the city of Regiowide had unexpectedly announced they were shutting down the coolers in the underground trams to conserve fresh water.

Lila normally didn't ride the trams. She usually took a carriage to her office at *The Diamond*. But today she had left her office early to meet with some old friends. She wanted to be discreet.

When she walked into her apartment she went straight to her dressing room and began peeling the swampy hair off the back of her neck; she used a band to secure it in a tail. Lifting her hair with one hand, she fanned the back of her neck with the other hand. She was about to start unlatching her necklace when she heard a knock at her door. "Coming." She yelled.

Lila hurried across her large living room and opened the front door to her apartment. "Tatalc. What are you doing here?"

"I need to talk to you. I hope this is a good time."

"It is. Come in." Tatalc walked into Lila's apartment and shut the door behind him. "Your timing couldn't be better. I just got home."

"I know. I've been sitting across the street in the park waiting for you."

"You must be burning up. Let me get you a cold drink."

"You look like you could use one too." Tatalc said as Lila walked into her kitchen.

"You're right." Lila yelled from her kitchen, "I don't know what I was thinking. It was too hot outside to wait for a carriage, and I didn't know they were shutting down the coolers in the trams. Of course by the time I was on the tram it was too late." She returned to the living room with two tall cold drinks.

"And there are so many stops between my office and here. I felt like I was never going to get off of that tram."

"I feel for you." Tatalc took a drink. "I never liked the trams when they were cooled. I can't imagine what they were like today."

Lila sat down next to Tatalc. "What do you need to talk to me about? It has to be important if you were willing to sit out in the heat and wait for me." Lila could tell Tatalc was conflicted.

"You know I've always trusted you Lila, right?"

"Of course, and I trust you."

"And you've advised me many times throughout my life."

"Yes, I've always cherished our relationship."

"And you know I love my father."

Lila put her hand on Tatalc's shoulder. "Tatalc, I'm the closest thing to a mother you've ever had. Tell me what's on your mind."

"He was wrong."

"Who was wrong?"

"Father. He was wrong about who we should send to the next planet." Tatalc was finding it difficult to admit he disagreed with his father. "I *agree* with the decision that we should have a lottery. I agree with Dafur. We can't pick only the most influential citizens. It's not fair. And besides that's too much responsibility for any man, including Father."

"I figured you were upset because The Chief brought you up during his response."

"I'm more upset with Father for naming me as the one to send. I don't agree with *that* at all. And The Chief didn't say anything citizens don't already know."

Reassuring Tatalc, Lila said, "I've known Wickem since before you were born and I know he loves you and he would never do anything to cause you harm or embarrassment."

"I realize it wasn't intentional and I know it was coming from the right place." Tatalc paused for another drink, "But that's not the real issue any way."

"Then what is?"

"How do I tell Father he was wrong? I don't want to disappoint him."

"Maybe you won't have to."

"I can't avoid him."

"I don't mean that, Tatalc. What I mean is the decision has been made. The elect are proceeding with Dafur's plan."

"And it's the best plan." Tatalc affirmed.

"I'm sure Wickem is upset, but Wickem will fall in line. He might be wounded, but he's still loyal. I don't know why it would even come up."

"I'm not so sure about that."

"About what?" Lila asked.

"That Father will fall in line."

"Why wouldn't he? He's faced challenges before. And in the end he always puts Cythera first."

"We've talked twice today, Father and I."

"What did you talk about?"

"To be honest, I was a little confused by the conversations. Father didn't seem like himself. He was restless, like a child gets, and that's not like him. He said he met a man, a man I need to meet. A man who can solve all our problems. A man named Tienneis, a truton clerk of all things."

"What problem is the clerk supposed to solve?"

"I don't know. I asked Father what he meant and he told me to be patient and wait until our meeting."

"Are you going to meet with them?"

"I don't really have a choice, do I?"

"And you have no idea what the meeting is about?"

"No, I don't. All I know is when I talked to Father this morning he was a little depressed but he was still himself. Then he talks to this Tienneis fellow and he's all giddy and acting strange. I don't know what to make of it all."

Lila stretched over to a nearby table and opened a drawer. She reached inside and pulled out a notepad and a pencil, "*Now* I know why you're here." Lila smirked, "How do you spell it?"

"T – I – E – N – N – E – I - S."

"And you said he's a truton clerk, right?"

Tatalc nodded his head.

"Do you know which building?"

"Father said he called from The Vault."

"And when is your meeting?"

"Tomorrow night."

"Meet me for lunch tomorrow and I'll tell you everything you need to know."

"Thanks Lila. You're always a good listener."

Lila smiled at Tatalc. It always tickled her that Tatalc would never directly ask her to do something some might consider *sneaky*. He wouldn't even acknowledge that it was taking place. It was his way of keeping his conscience clean, she supposed.

Or maybe it was his way of protecting his secrets. Tatalc liked to pretend he didn't have any secrets. He had been this way since his scandal. Tatalc felt he was open and honest about everything. Lila knew this wasn't true. Everyone had secrets they wanted to protect.

Maybe, eventually, Tatalc would open up to her. She hoped. And if he did, she would protect his secrets. She would have to. Because Lila knew it might not be too long before Tatalc would need to protect hers.

Tatalc stood up and started to walk out of Lila's apartment, "By the way. I don't think I've ever seen you wear that necklace before. Is it new?" Lila didn't answer. "It's unique. I like it."

Lila placed her hand on her chest and touched the large round medallion that she had forgotten to take off. She smiled at Tatalc, "This old necklace. I'm glad you like it."

Tatalc walked out of her apartment and shut the door behind him.

Chapter 54

After the Debate – Dafur & The Forgotten

Rigby was rarely frustrated with Dafur. Rigby had worked hard to put himself in a position to choose any professor he wanted to work with, and he had selected Dafur.

There was no doubt Dafur was intellectually powerful, but so were other professors. Dafur was an expert in the area of study Rigby was interested in, but so were other professors.

Dafur's intellectual power and expertise were not the reasons Rigby wanted to work with Dafur. Rigby chose Dafur because he was extremely dedicated to his work. His work always came first, and this is what Rigby needed.

Rigby *was* happy when Dafur met Lij. He would have never stood in the way of love and he felt Dafur deserved an opportunity to love again. It was convenient that Lij could help them with their work. She did add value and Dafur had a partner to share his life with who would not distract him from his work on the project. As far as Rigby was concerned it was a good proposition for all.

It wasn't Dafur's relationship with Lij that was frustrating Rigby. It was Dafur's relationship with Lij's family, particularly Lij's brother Dran. In the short time they had known each other, Dafur and Dran were becoming close friends. Dran even helped Dafur prepare for the debate. Rigby felt that Dafur never should have involved himself in the politics of the mission; in fact, Dafur only became involved in the politics because of pressure from Dran and The Forgotten.

Rigby believed Dafur was a good man with good intentions and Dafur only wanted to help his new family. But, Rigby found it inexcusable when Dafur informed Rigby he couldn't attend the first meeting with the new contractors. Dafur told Rigby the meeting with the contractors was only a formality, an introduction. He thought it would be a good chance for Rigby to establish a relationship with the builders of the vessels. Under different circumstances, Rigby would have been fine going by himself, but he could not accept that Dafur was cancelling because Dran *had* to meet with Dafur *today*. Dafur was losing his focus.

***

Rigby tried not show his frustration, but Dafur knew Rigby too well. As he was leaving the lab to meet Dran, Dafur felt something was wrong. "You seem a little upset Rigby," Dafur said as he was walking out the door, "You're not worried about meeting them by yourself are you?"

"No, I'm fine."

"Well you should be. Most of the good ideas were yours. I couldn't have done any of this without you. And don't worry. I'll make sure everyone knows how much you've contributed to the effort."

"I appreciate that." Rigby said it as sincerely as he could. He didn't really care about recognition. What Rigby wanted, what he needed, was for Dafur to stop wasting time with Lij's brother and focus on the survival of Cythera.

Dafur walked out of the lab and Rigby followed, both of them heading in different directions, and towards different priorities.

***

Dafur didn't have to travel far for his meeting with Dran. He did have to go outside and flag a carriage, but the ride was short and he did not suffer the heat for long. It was a short ride to an old warehouse where Dran had established operations for The Forgotten. Dran was waiting for him when he arrived.

"Dafur, I'm glad you were able to meet me on short notice," welcomed Dran. Dran put his arm around Dafur and walked him into the building and through the large warehouse. "I hope I didn't pull you away from something important?"

"Nothing too important," said Dafur.

Inside the warehouse were several rows of long tables.

Citizens were seated at the tables sorting through boxes of paperwork. No one looked up as Dran and Dafur walked by. They were busy. Dran led Dafur to a small office in the back of the warehouse. He asked Dafur to take a seat and he closed the door.

"What is this place?" Dafur asked.

"This is headquarters for our movement." Dran puffed his chest; he was proud of the little club he had built.

"The Forgotten?" Dafur seemed confused. "I'm not sure I understand. I guess I figured, once the lottery plan was accepted, there was no longer a need for your faction?"

"Oh no Dafur, the lottery was only the beginning."

Dafur was really confused now. He pointed out to the warehouse, "What are those citizens doing?"

"I'll explain in a little while, but we need to talk about something else first."

"Ok."

Dran leaned back in his rickety chair, "Do you love my sister?"

"Of course I do. You know that."

"Would you die for her?"

"I would."

"But you're willing to die anyway, for strangers. You told us that the first night we met."

"That could happen, yes."

Dran leaned forward across the desk; he wanted Dafur's full attention. "Dafur, you're a smart man. A logical man, right?"

"Some might say that."

"Then let me know if this logic adds up. You say you're

willing to die for Lij," Dran hesitated before continuing with the question, "If you're willing to die for her, you would surely be willing to make other sacrifices, maybe do other things to save Lij's life. I'm being logical, right?"

"Logical? I don't even know what you're talking about."

"The Transients eligibility for the lottery has opened a lot of possibilities for us. Possibilities that would help Transients in the new world. You're one of *us* now, right? And if you're willing to make one type of sacrifice for any citizen, wouldn't you be willing to make an even larger sacrifice for your new family? Are you willing to help us?"

"Dran, I'm not sure what you're asking and if it's anything close to what I'm thinking . . . I . . . I honestly can't believe it." Dafur stood from his chair and paced around the small office. "I challenged one of the most powerful men on Cythera to assure that everyone, including Transients, would be included." Dafur lifted his hand and pointed at Dran. "I stood up for you! Not because of you and not because of Lij, but because it was the right thing to do. And now you are asking me to . . . to . . . I don't even know what you're asking me to do. But I'm not going to do anything that would give one citizen an unfair advantage over another in the lottery. Not even my wife!"

"Dafur, wait." Dafur had turned and was starting to walk out of the office. Dran reached out and grabbed Dafur by the arm. "We do thank you for what you did, for standing up for us. Right now it's easy to be noble. It's easy to say you're willing to die for the good of civilization. But the time will come when the reality of death is whispering in your ear and you'll realize you don't want to die. I know you want to live a long life with Lij on the new Cythera."

Dafur shook off Dran's grasp and started to walk out of

the small office in the back of the warehouse. "You know nothing about me."

"If you don't wait too long I'll have a place for you," Dran pleaded. "Dafur, don't wait too long!"

As Dafur left he was in disbelief. It seemed like Dran wanted him to rig the lottery. He had been so naïve to trust Dran. He had only wanted a family. A wife, brothers, parents - relationships he had not had in such a long time. His trust had been violated; he was hurt. He stormed through the warehouse with his head down, past all the busy workers sorting through papers, then he abruptly stopped and lifted his head, his eyes grew wide and his stomach soured as the thought hit him. Was *Lij in on it?*

Chapter 55

After the Debate – Wickem & Tienneis

Maybe Tatalc had overreacted. His father seemed fine as they left to meet Tienneis, Wickem was acting like his normal self again.

The background file Lila composed on Tienneis was rather dull. Tienneis had been an average student studying to become a physics professor, but after an embarrassing presentation where the other students mocked his speech impediment, he left the program. Tienneis had no significant affiliations; neither did his family. He was simply a government clerk, who had little recreation outside of work. Tatalc wondered why his father had become enamored with the man.

The only riddle was that Wickem, during his afternoon

of lunacy, told Tatalc that Tienneis could solve all of their problems. Was he referring to the end of Cythera?

"Why are we meeting with him?" Tatalc asked his father as they rode towards their destination.

"I'd like to thank him for approving my truton application for Dekayb." Wickem answered.

Tatalc knew his father was not telling him the whole story. "Then why did you want me to come?"

When they arrived at the diner Wickem was the first to exit the carriage. "He's interesting. I think you'll like him. And to be forthright, we started talking about the mission and he had some ideas. You've spent more time with Dafur and Rigby; I wanted to bring you along to see if he's making sense."

"Why didn't you ask Dafur to come?"

"If Tienneis is crazy I didn't want to embarrass myself in front of Dafur again. I think I've embarrassed myself in front of Dafur enough lately."

Remembering the end of the debate, Tatalc nodded in acknowledgement.

"Plus, you understand the science behind the project more than I do. If you think his ideas are good then we'll take them to Dafur *or* Rigby."

Wickem and Tatalc entered the diner. Tienneis had told Wickem he would arrive early and secure a table. They looked around the dining room for someone sitting alone. In the corner they spotted a man in a silver vest that matched his stringy silver hair. Tatalc recognized him from the file Lila had created but he couldn't reveal his prior knowledge of Tienneis. He followed his father towards the man.

"Are you Tienneis?" Wickem had only talked to Tienneis

on the phone and did not know what he looked like.

The man stood up and extended his hand. "Of c-course, you are Wickem and you are T-Tatalc. I've seen p-pictures of you b-both b-before. I should have recognized you when you walked in. P-pl-please. P-please have a seat."

Before they had a chance to pull in their chairs the server arrived, "What will you have tonight?"

"How's the strafultap here?" Wickem asked.

"Usually I would recommend it. But my apologies. We are out."

"Out of strafultap?" Tatalc said. "You can always get strafultap in Regiowide. Even when it's out of season."

"I know, and you're not the first customer to complain tonight. I do apologize, but our imports didn't arrive this morning. The shipping lanes have become too shallow for the freighters to come in to Regiowide. The only strafultap you'll find in Regiowide right now would be yesterday's supply, which . . . ." the server held his hand up to his nose, "wouldn't be fresh. We do have a delicious dark stew our chef has prepared. It's not a hot stew."

They all agreed the stew would be fine. They also ordered three ice waters. When the server returned with their drinks he sat down three glasses of water without ice. Wickem held up his glass towards the server, "I believe we asked for ice water."

"Once again, I apologize," the server was being overly polite, "we've had to shut down our ice coolers to save water for our food coolers. I hope you understand." Trying to avoid another apology the server walked away.

"Wow." Tienneis stated. "No strafultap b-because of the

237

shipping lanes and no ice b-because they are c-conserving water. Are things g-getting that b-bad?"

"Things are getting worse, no one can deny it. We had to shut down the coolant systems on the public transportation routes yesterday." Wickem said. "It's only a precaution right now, while we reassess supply and demand."

"I saw a man d-die from the heat." Wickem and Tatalc both seemed shocked because the comment was so unexpected. Tienneis continued, "He d-died right in front of me on the street. It was heat stroke, even though the m-medics t-tried to d-deny it." Tienneis realized his lack of social skills had once again created an awkward moment and he attempted to recover the conversation. "You came about the Thunderwell." Tienneis looked at Wickem, "You want me to explain the Thunderwell to T-Tatalc. That's why we are here t-tonight."

"Correct," said Wickem. "But first I wanted to thank you for approving Dekayb's trutons." Wickem wanted to make sure to slip that in somewhere. "But since you've brought it up, why don't you tell us more about the Thunderwell?"

Tatalc had no idea what they were talking about, "What's a Thunderwell?"

"It's the solution to our problems!" Wickem exclaimed.

That tone— there it was, again, in Wickem's voice. It was the same tone his father had in his voice yesterday when Tatalc questioned his father's sanity.

"From what I understand," Tienneis said, "you d-don't know how you are g-going to launch your v-vessels off of Cythera? B-But if you were able to launch the v-vessels you've figured out how to surf solar flares and safely land them on the next p-pl-planet and this would save Cytheran civilization." Tienneis took a breath, "I've b-been researching your p-pr-

project and have a much b-better understanding of the objectives now."

"Good, I'm glad you've been putting more thought into the project. Tatalc knows a lot more about the science than I do." Wickem said. "Tell him how a Thunderwell works."

The server arrived with their stew and refilled their waters. Tienneis was so busy talking that he didn't bother to taste the stew. "It's actually a p-pr-pretty simple c-concept, I'm c-confident it would work. All you need is a natural v-vertical t-tunnel, a c-cave that has formed straight d-down into a well." Tienneis used his hands to demonstrate how the vertical tunnel needed to be *straight down*. "You would c-cap the well with a launch p-pl-platform and affix the v-vessel. Then you would p-pr-pressurize the well. When the p-pr-pressure b-builds up it will p-pr-produce the needed energy to launch the v-vessel into space."

Tatalc was intrigued. He had never heard Dafur or Rigby talk about a Thunderwell. The truth was he had *only* heard them talk about how easy it would be to launch the vessel but had never once heard them discuss an actual solution. "I think I understand. But could you show me? I'm sure you could run some trials in Dafur's lab." Tatalc asked.

"I would b-be happy to." Tienneis answered.

"Wait." Wickem interrupted. "I don't know if we want to do this in Dafur's lab. Is there somewhere else we could test it?"

"I'm sure we c-could find a p-pl-place where we c-could run a t-test with a similar sized object." Tienneis seemed confident. "B-but we would need help. The three of us c-couldn't d-do the t-test by ourselves."

"Tell me what you need and I'll get it for you," Wickem

replied.

"Why wouldn't we test the experiment at Dafur's lab first?" Tatalc questioned his father.

"We don't want him to know."

"Why?"

"Because if we can figure this out without Dafur knowing, then we will have a way to send *you*."

Chapter 56

After the Debate – Dafur

Lately Dafur had been noticeably quiet. Since his conversation with Dran, he had been spending most of his time either at the lab or the facility where the vessels were being built. Lij joined him when she could.

Rigby had been sensing tension between the newlyweds. He assumed the elation of the wedding had worn off and they were adjusting to their new lives together, as happens with newlyweds.

Rigby was not the type to invite himself into another citizen's private life. He and Dafur were close friends. If Dafur wanted to confide in Rigby, Rigby would be there for him. But if Dafur didn't want to share, Rigby would not intrude.

Dafur and Rigby did not speak to each other on their way to the facility where the vessels were being built. At the facility they would finally see all of their ideas and concepts come together with the unveiling of the frame for the first vessel. A lot of work still needed to be done to prepare the vessel for travel but it was beginning to take shape. It was becoming a reality.

As Dafur and Rigby walked into the enormous hangar where the construction was taking place, a short stout man in a white jumpsuit ran up to them. "Here take these and put them on." He handed them both a set of tinted glasses. "You're right in time for the key arc weld. Come with me, let's get a better view."

Dafur and Rigby followed the short man to the side of the building and up a steep flight of stairs. They walked down a long narrow catwalk that stretched the depth of the hangar. At the end of the catwalk, their only option was to turn left and continue until it stepped up to a large platform near the ceiling of the hangar. From the platform they had a perfect view.

On the floor of the hangar they could see two large frames. The symmetrical pieces would soon be joined together to form the skeleton of the vessel.

"As you both know," the short man said, "Once the arc weld sets, we'll move this over to a different hanger for the next phase of the construction process. Then we'll clean up the mess in here and start working on frame number two." After digging his fist into his pocket the man pulled out his hand and opened it up, "Here put these in your ears. This is going to be loud."

Dafur and Rigby each grabbed a set of plugs and inserted them in their ears. The short man looked at both of them and gave a thumbs-up then reached over to a switch on the platform and flipped it on and off several times. On both sides of the hangar a bright orange light blinked on and off, on and off.

Then they felt it. The entire platform began to shake. Rigby and Dafur grabbed hold of the rail. The short man didn't react. He knew what to expect.

From the right side, a gigantic arm crane, powerful enough to knock down an entire city building, started to move. Its singular arm had two hinged joints to allow for agile movement. At the end of the arm was another joint and a series of fingers.

Even with their earplugs in, the sound of the crane was deafening. The sound only became louder when a similar crane on the left side of the hanger was activated. Edging over the pieces of frame, the two cranes lowered and picked up the frames.

The cranes lifted and turned the vessels inward, and then pushed them together to form the compete frame of the vessel. Both Dafur and Rigby were transfixed by the power of the machinery, until they both felt a nudge. They looked at the short man who was tapping his tinted glasses. Suddenly the hangar went dark.

A bright blue and orange light appeared in the middle of the hangar. Its incandescence cast dim light on the outline of the vessel's pieces and the crane fingers.

Starting at the tail, the flame slowly moved along the joint where the two pieces were being held together. When it reached the apex near the front of the vessel it dipped down out of their sight. The glow underneath the vessel was their only indication the welding was still taking place.

The flame came into sight again and moved up the bottom of the tail and stopped at the exact point it had started. The flame went out and the hangar was completely dark again.

A brief moment later the lights started coming back on. Dafur removed his earplugs but the short man reached out and grabbed his arm. Dafur read his lips. He said, "Not yet."

The large door at the front of the hangar began to open. Neither Dafur nor Rigby had ever seen this door open before, they had always entered through a smaller door. The opening was huge and everyone felt the deadly heat roll into the hanger.

The two cranes still held their sides of the vessel. In sync they started to lift the vessel higher into the air. Through the large opening at the front of the hanger a wide platform skid appeared and was moved into place underneath the suspended vessel. The vessel was lowered onto the platform.

After the cranes returned to their positions on the side of the hanger, the short man nudged Dafur and Rigby. He proceeded to remove his earplugs and glasses. They did the same.

The short man had a big smile on his face, "Pretty exciting, huh?"

"It's incredible," Dafur said. "To think, that *thing* down there will soon be carrying citizens to another planet."

"Yeah, it's mind boggling," added the short man. "I don't really understand how you're going to get it there. And I guess it really doesn't matter, but I hope my name is drawn because I would sure like a ride on it. Anything you can do about that?"

"I wish I could. If anyone deserves to go, it would be the ones that built it."

Dafur's comment seemed odd to Rigby. He had never heard Dafur say anything about who really deserved to travel to the next planet except that it should be a fair, random selection.

"Why is the hangar door closing," asked Rigby. "Don't you need to move the frame to another hangar?"

The short man replied, "The weld is too fragile right

now. It'll cure here overnight and we'll move it tomorrow."

"How long until it's done?"

"Probably another telth. We'll have this one and five more ready before the lottery at the truton ceremony."

"Great work," Dafur said. "You're exceeding all of our expectations."

The short man led them off the platform, back across the catwalk and down the stairs. They followed him to the smaller door of the hanger, the one they normally used. "Next time you come we should be arc welding vessel number two, and vessel number one will be well on its way towards completion."

Dafur shook the short man's hand. "Thanks again, we'll see you then."

Dafur and Rigby walked out of the hanger and into their carriage for the ride back to the lab. "It's really amazing when you think about it Rigby. All of the hard work we've done, to see it becoming a reality. To think we're really the ones who will be saving Cytheran civilization." Dafur paused for a moment. "I bet you didn't think this was going to happen when you walked in my door the first time to interview for my assistant?"

"Not in my wildest dreams sir."

"We've come along way my friend, a long way. I'll miss you when this is all over."

"I'll miss you too, sir."

They sat in silence for most of the ride, then Dafur blurted out, "Listen Rigby, if I've been a little distant I want you to know it has nothing to do with you. There's been . . . well . . . I'll just come out and tell you. I know I can trust you."

"Of course you can, sir."

"Do you remember the first time you came to the facility? When I backed out to go meet with Dran."

"I remember."

"I'm not sure what he's up to, but it's something sinister. He has a warehouse full of citizens sorting through government documents and he said the lottery was only the beginning of their cause."

"Only the beginning?" Rigby asked.

"Yes. And I left right after he implied I should help them find a way to rig the lottery so that the Transients would be chosen."

"You'd never do anything dishonest."

"I'm glad you feel that way and I hope you're right. But obviously Dran manipulated me, or at least tried to manipulate me. The crazy thing is I would've defended the inclusion of Transients anyway because it was the right thing to do."

"And you're worried that Lij lied about loving you so she could get you to help her brother's cause?"

"You're perceptive Rigby. It's hard not to think she was in on it."

"For what it's worth I don't think she was. But the only way to know for sure is to ask her."

"I know. I'm still waiting for the right time."

"She won't disappoint you, and as far as Dran is concerned I wouldn't worry about him. He seems to be a man of many words but little action."

"I'm not so sure. He's seemed to have gained a lot of exposure for The Forgotten, more than I would have ever imagined him capable of. And he's planning something big, but I don't know what it is yet. Do you know what else he told me?"

"What?"

"He told me if I ever changed my mind and decided I wanted to *live*, to let him know and he would include Lij and I."

"Include you in *what?* He has no control over the lottery."

"I have no idea. But it has made me think about something."

"And what would that be?" Rigby asked.

"Am I really willing to die?"

Chapter 57

After the Debate – Rose

"My father has lost his mind." Tatalc stormed into Lila's apartment. His face was dirty like he had been walking through a sandstorm.

"Tatalc. What are you doing here? You should've told me you were coming."

"I'm sorry to barge in on you, but I had to talk to you." Tatalc sat down on the sofa in the main living area.

"I'm not sure this is the best time. I'm expecting . . ."

"You won't believe what he's planning." Tatalc was not in the mood to listen to Lila; he needed someone to *listen* to him. Lila tried to think of another reason to tell Tatalc now was not a good time. She was having trouble thinking of one he would believe.

"It's much worse than I thought Lila. Father is going to conspire against the government!"

Lila wasn't sure she heard Tatalc correctly. Her mind was elsewhere. "He's going to do what?"

"He's conspiring against the government. The government our family has helped build for generations. The government he's a part of."

"I'm not following you." Tatalc now had her full attention. "What is Wickem going to do?"

"Remember Tienneis? The truton clerk I told you about?"

Lila recalled from his background check that he was rather boring. "I remember a lot about him. More than I'd ever care to know about a truton clerk."

Tatalc was too upset to appreciate Lila's wit. "Apparently Tienneis is more than your average truton clerk. He's some type of amateur physicist, or something like that. He claimed he knew of a way to launch the vessels."

"And Wickem believed him?"

"Yes. And I believe him now too. I saw it work." Tatalc pointed towards his face. "That's why I'm so dirty. We were out in the rurals watching him demonstrate the Thunderwell. Father already has a team secretly working with Tienneis."

"*What* are they working on? And what's a Thunderwell?"

"That's how we can launch the vessels, using a Thunderwell. It's a pressurized cavern that when it explodes it projects the vessel into space."

"Then why are you upset? Haven't you been looking for a way to launch the vessels?"

"Yes. But that's not the problem." Tatalc started to say something else but was interrupted by a knocking at Lila's door.

"Are you expecting someone?" Tatalc asked.

"Yes, I am. I was trying to tell you that when you came in."

Tatalc stood up from Lila's sofa, "I'm sorry, I wasn't listening to you. I can come back. But we need to talk soon."

"Hold on." Lila walked over to the door and opened it.

In walked Rose. She had short brown hair caressing the nape of her neck, large bright eyes and skin that was fresh like a child's. Tatalc could not take his eyes off of her.

Lila led her into the living room, "Tatalc this is Rose, she's a dear friend of mine. She's stopping by to pick something up."

Tatalc struggled to find the words needed to properly introduce himself. His stomach was fluttering. He had never had this type of reaction to a woman before, never.

He extended his hand, "I'm . . . I'm Tatalc." He said.

"I know who you are." Her voice was smoky but pleasant. "It's nice to meet you."

Their hands touched as they greeted each other. She was warm, Tatalc could feel her energy. Tatalc knew the polite action would be to excuse himself but he couldn't take his eyes off Rose. He didn't want to leave. Rose walked past him and went to Lila, and they embraced.

"Do you have it?" Rose asked Lila.

"It's in my room. I'll go get it." Lila walked back towards her bedroom leaving Rose and Tatalc alone.

Tatalc felt awkward being alone with Rose, "How do you know Lila?" was the only thing he could think to say.

"I've known her for a long time. I'm surprised this is the first time we've met. She talks about you often."

"Hopefully she says nice things about me?"

Rose smiled. "She calls you the *son she should have had,* if that gives you any indication."

Tatalc was hypnotized. He stared, and he knew he was staring, but he couldn't help it. Rose's eyes began to dart around the room. She put her hand on her chest and twirled the chain of her necklace.

Tatalc righted himself, "I'm sorry I'm staring at you. But your necklace . . . is that Lila's? I saw her wearing one like it."

Rose touched the medallion hanging around her neck. "This? No it's a . . ."

"I found it Rose," Lila came back into the room. "Sorry it took me so long. I forgot where I hid . . . put it." Lila handed Rose a small box.

"Thanks, and everything else is ready." Rose delicately placed the small box in her satchel. "I guess I'll be going. It was a pleasure meeting you Tatalc."

"Yes it was a pleasure meeting you too. Maybe we'll see each other again soon." Tatalc replied.

"Maybe." Rose turned to walk out of the apartment. "Lila, I'll see you tonight, right?"

"Yes, I'll be there." Lila answered. Rose closed the door behind her and was gone.

"I guess it's true." Lila said.

"What's true?" said Tatalc, who was still staring at the door as if Rose were going to reappear.

"Cythera *is* coming to an end."

"Huh?"

"The mighty Tatalc has been smitten by a woman.

249

Cythera must be coming to an end!"

"You think you're so funny."

"I think I'm right."

"She was nice, but not for me, they never are *for me*." Tatalc began to walk to the door. His encounter with Rose made him forget why he had come to Lila's in the first place.

"Where are you going? Aren't you going to finish telling me about Tienneis and this Thunderwell? So you've found a way to launch the vessels?"

"Oh yes, the Thunderwell. And yes we've found a way to launch the vessels."

"And if I recall you were about to tell me why this is a *problem*."

Tatalc returned to Lila's sofa. "As of right now only a few of us know about the Thunderwell: me, Father, Tienneis, and some of Father's men who helped with the test. And now you."

"So you haven't told Dafur? Why haven't you told Dafur?"

"I'm going to, soon. But Father has one condition."

"What condition?"

"He only wants me to tell Dafur if Dafur is willing to give us something."

"What does Wickem want?"

"The designs to the vessel and the instructions for how to pilot the vessel to the next planet."

Lila tried to think of a reason Wickem would need this information, nothing came to her. "Why does Wickem want that?"

"He wants to build his own vessel."

Chapter 58

After the Debate – Tatalc

Tatalc knew what he planned to do was against his better judgment. What his father was planning bordered on treason; yet here he was preparing to meet with Rigby.

There were several reasons Tatalc decided to meet with Rigby instead of Dafur. He suspected Dafur's passion for fairness and equality might stand in the way. Rigby was more of a realist. Since the first time they had met, when Rigby visited their country estate, Tatalc and Rigby got along well. Besides that, Rigby was not involved in the politics of the mission.

Tatalc had arranged for Rigby to give him a tour of the facility where the vessels were being built. Rigby and Dafur had been back to the facility twice since the first key arc weld took place. Progress had been made and the first vessel was almost complete.

Today, there was nothing overly significant happening at the facility. A lot of work, a lot of noise, but nothing that would be considered a milestone. Rigby started the tour by showing Tatalc the welding hangar. The workers were starting a new frame for what the short man called *Number Four*.

Next, they went to the hanger where the workers were riveting on the outer skin of the vessel. The shell was made from the new polymetal that Dafur and Rigby had invented. *Number Three* was in that hangar.

Their next stop was the mechanical hangar. This was

where all the machinery that would pilot and land the vessel and all the life support systems were added. They stopped and watched a man fasten a rudder hinge to *Number Two*.

The last stop on the tour was the finishing hangar. All the remaining parts, pieces and comforts were completed here. Rigby and Tatalc inspected *number one*. Number one was almost ready.

There was one more hangar, the largest. This is where the completed vessels would be stored. Right now it was empty.

"Have you and Dafur figured out a way to launch them yet?" Tatalc asked as they walked down the ramp of vessel number one.

"No. Dafur wants to wait until this first vessel is done so we know exactly what we have to launch into space."

"You haven't thought about it at all?"

"We've thought about it a lot." Rigby trusted Tatalc and confided, "Dafur probably wouldn't want me telling you this but we've been testing launch scenarios from the beginning."

"Then why does Dafur keep telling everyone you haven't started working on it yet?"

"Because nothing has worked, not one theory has tested well in the lab." They walked out of the hanger and into the daytime heat. Tatalc began to feel the burn and hustled towards the carriage. Rigby caught up to him and continued, "Dafur is convinced we'll figure out a launch solution as soon as we have the correct mass of the vessel. That's why he tells everyone we haven't started yet. In Dafur's mind we haven't really started trying to solve the problem until the vessels are done."

"What do you think?" Tatalc asked Rigby.

"I think it could be more challenging than we realize."

Tatalc paused for a moment. He wanted to be delicate with his next statement, which would set the stage for the rest of their conversation. "Is Dafur seeking advice or is he trying to solve the problem on his own?"

"I think we'd be willing to listen to anyone with a decent idea. All of what we saw back at the facility, all of the vessels, they're worthless if we can't get them into space. I know Dafur is confident we'll come up with a solution, but time is against us. The climate on Cythera continues to turn more dangerous. Citizens are dying. The planet is dying. If we don't come up with a solution, we'll all die too."

Tatalc agreed, "I know. There were eight more deaths yesterday in Regiowide. There's no telling how many citizens around Cythera are collapsing and dying from the heat, and the water shortage is only going to get worse."

"I hope Dafur is right," said Rigby. " That once the first vessel is complete, we'll be able to solve the launch problem." It looked like Tatalc was going to say something but he didn't. "It's only a few turns until the truton ceremony and the lottery. The first five vessels should be ready by then and we'll need to launch them immediately. If we can."

Tatalc decided to ask the *real* question, "Have you ever heard of a Thunderwell?"

"No, what is it?"

"It might be a way for you to launch the vessels."

Not knowing what a Thunderwell was or where Tatalc would have heard of such a thing Rigby asked, "Who told you about it?"

"Someone my father met, you wouldn't know him."

"When was this?"

"My father met him right after the debate."

"And you're just now telling me about this," Rigby's tone was giving away his annoyance with Tatalc keeping secrets. "Why have you waited this long?"

"It's complicated."

"I'm sure if you explained a Thunderwell to me I would understand the concept."

"I wasn't talking about the Thunderwell. I was saying the reason I haven't told you is because the situation is *complicated*."

"Tatalc, everything is *complicated*. We're trying to move citizens from one planet to another through the darkness and emptiness of space. This is all *complicated*." Rigby's patience was dissipating. With so much at stake and with all they had been through together he couldn't comprehend why Tatalc had kept this from him.

Tatalc could tell Rigby was getting upset, "I've wanted to tell you Rigby, I really have. But my father didn't even tell me until I agreed to do something for him."

"And what does he want you to do?"

"My father wants a copy of the vessel design and the algorithms you'll use to flare surf to the next planet."

"Why would he want those?"

"I don't know. He wouldn't tell me."

Rigby glared. He seemed to know Tatalc was lying and it was taking every ounce of restraint for him not to lose his temper. "So if I understand you correctly, you want me to give you our designs and our algorithms and in exchange you will tell me how the Thunderwell works and how we could launch the vessels?"

"Yes."

"After everything you have done and said, after all the rallies and all the support you've built, after all the promises you made, you would withhold information that could save our civilization if I don't go along with your extortion?"

"I told you, it's complicated."

If they'd not been traveling in the back of a carriage Rigby would have walked away after such a presumptuous request, but since they were in the back of a carriage he had nowhere to go. Rigby was angry that Tatalc had stooped so low and Tatalc was ashamed that he had. After a few moments of silence Rigby asked, "How do you know the Thunderwell will work?"

"I've seen it with my own eyes. We launched an old freighter, at least three times the mass of one of the vessels."

"How do you know it made it to space?"

"We put a tracker on it and it's been in orbit for about a turn."

"I know there's more to what you are telling me Tatalc and that's ok. I suppose we're now past the point of me expecting full disclosure from you. But answer one question for me, honestly."

"I'll try."

"Is Wickem going to try to sabotage the mission? Is that why he wants the plans and the algorithms?"

"No. Absolutely not. I can promise you that."

Rigby could tell Tatalc was telling the truth. And if Tatalc knew a way to launch the vessels, Rigby had no choice, "Then I'll give you what you've asked for."

Chapter 59

After the Debate – Dafur & Lij

It was the middle of the night and Dafur was wide awake. Dafur and Lij had gone to bed a while ago. While Lij had quickly fallen asleep, Dafur had been lying in bed with his eyes open and his mind racing. This was nothing new to Dafur. Most of his recent nights had been sleepless ones. The weight of Cythera's survival was his to carry.

But his current sleep deprivation was not caused by the mission. Plans for the mission were going well. The first five vessels were complete and ready for launch. As soon as they moved the vessels from the facility, construction would begin on the next set.

Rigby had discovered a way to launch the vessels, which Dafur always knew they would. Rigby had told him he found out about Thunderwells by accident.

Rigby had been researching geological histories for climate change and found a reference to something called a Thunderwell. One thing led to another and after some testing they confirmed a Thunderwell would be the safest and most accurate means for launching the vessels.

Dafur would soon know who would be travelling to the next planet, who would rebuild Cytheran civilization. The truton ceremony and the lottery were coming up and everything was ready. It wouldn't be long until the first set of vessels launched. But as he lay awake in bed none of this mattered to Dafur.

What mattered to Dafur, what mattered more than

anything, was the woman sleeping next to him. *She is even more beautiful when she sleeps,* Dafur thought. She seemed peaceful and innocent, Lij, lying there asleep. He had always felt this way. From the first moment he saw her, when her face stood out in a sea of unknown faces and Dafur saw her glow and invited her on stage, he had loved her. From that moment to this moment now, he had loved her. How could he not? She was caring and smart, playful and strong. Anyone would fall in love with her, but why did she fall in love with him? Did she ever love him at all? The doubt, the questions, the fear of her honest answers are what kept Dafur up at night. And if she did love him as much as he loved her, how could he let that love die, let it burn to death with the rest of Cythera? How could he let their love die when he had a chance to keep it alive?

He had to know if Lij really loved him or if she was only trying to get close to him so he would help her brother. He was reaching the point where the pain of not knowing was more than the pain Lij would cause if she told him she never loved him. He had to know. Sitting up in bed Dafur could barely breathe. He had to know right now. "Lij. Lij." He whispered, "Wake up." Dafur reached over and tapped Lij's shoulder.

Lij began to wake up, "Dafur, what's wrong? It's the middle of the night."

"I'm sorry I woke you up but I have to talk to you about something right now. It can't wait any longer."

Lij sat up in bed, "What is it? What's wrong?"

"Nothing's wrong. I need to know something." Dafur reached over and held Lij's hand. "Do you love me?"

In a sleepy voice Lij said, "Of course. Why would you wake me up to ask me that?"

Dafur wasn't convinced by her answer. It was too

casual, even for the middle of the night. Lij started to sink into bed and fall back asleep.

Realizing there had to be more to the question, Lij couldn't fall back asleep. It made no sense for Dafur to wake her up in the middle of the night to ask her if she loved him. Something was bothering Dafur. She sat back up. "Really, what's wrong? Why would you ask me that?"

Dafur let it all out. It felt good to *finally* let it all out. Even if Lij told him she didn't love him, at least it was *all out*. "I know your brother tried to manipulate me. From the moment I met him he was pushing me to be stand up for the Transients. I want you to know I would have done it anyway, before I met him and even if I hadn't have met you.

"I visited him a while ago and he's planning something. I don't know what, but it's big and he's probably been planning it all along. I have to know, are you in on whatever he's planning? Did you fall in love, or pretend to fall in love with me to get closer to me, and to get me to help Dran with his plan?" Dafur squeezed both of Lij's hands and looked her in the eyes, "Please. Please be honest with me."

Lij's palms became sweaty and her hands began to shake. She let go of Dafur's hands and sat silently on the bed rubbing her moist palms against the blanket. Her lips were quivering and tears were forming in her eyes and rolling down her cheeks. Struggling to speak, she mumbled two words, "I'm sorry."

Dafur was stunned. He was frozen. His greatest fear was becoming a reality. She had never loved him. Lij had never loved Dafur.

"I'm sorry. I'm sorry." Lij cried, "But I do love you. My love is real." She reached out to hold Dafur but he leaned back.

It was a reflex. He was still too dazed to think. "Dafur." She screamed. "I do love you." Dafur could barely understand her. Lij was hysterical. "I fell in love with you the first night we spent together. I love you so much. I love you so much!"

"Then . . . then . . ." Dafur was also struggling with his words. They were both struggling to articulate their words. "Then . . . why are you sorry?"

Lij tried to slow her breathing and compose herself. Her heart sunk and her head dropped because she knew what she was about to say could cost her the love of her life.

She did her best to keep her words together. Pleading she said, "Know how much I love you; know how much I will love you forever. No matter what."

She took a deep breath, "I know what Dran is planning. But he didn't tell me until after the debate. I didn't know it when I fell in love with you: that was real. It was all real!"

Dafur felt some relief and Lij noticed, but she hadn't told him everything yet. "I can't tell you what he's doing and I can't tell you how I'm involved." Lij started to cry again, "I can't. Not now. There's so much at stake and it would put you too much at risk. I can't let you get *in the way*."

"You can tell me. If you love me, you would trust me."

"I can't Dafur. I simply can't. And that's why I'm sorry. I know you probably won't want me anymore," Lij cried.

Dafur extended both his arms and he reached out to Lij. He embraced her and held her while she emptied every tear. She was vulnerable and weakened by the emotion. As was he. They held each other. Dafur whispered in her ear, "You don't have to tell me anything more. You told me you loved me and that's all I needed to hear."

Chapter 60

The Last Truton Ceremony

The True Cytherans were going to make a statement. A loud noise no citizen could ignore.

Frodd and Pesi found it easy to sneak into the basement of The Muy. It was a good sign. No one was expecting anything. The truton ceremony was starting soon and would be followed by the lottery. They had ample time to set up their explosives. They knew innocent citizens would die and they didn't feel guilty about it. *They all think they're going to die anyway*, they joked with one another.

Before leaving his apartment Frodd had started writing a letter he would send to *The Daily Word* calling out the great lie the government was telling every citizen:

> *The Rugal was a fake; Cythera isn't coming to an end. The government only wants you to believe in the false crisis so citizens become even more reliant on the elect. By believing their lies we only give them more power. More power for themselves and more power for their friends'...*

Frodd would finish the letter afterwards while celebrating the True Cytheran's triumph.

***

This would be the last truton ceremony. In an effort to celebrate the history of truton ceremonies, the event organizers had decorated the Muy to commemorate the history of the truton system of social influence. As attendees entered the Muy they were bombarded with propaganda celebrating the truton system. Large photos of the great prophet Steffer draped the entrance. Some photos showed him writing in his journals, some showed Steffer praying. Most citizens found the pageantry to be a depressing reminder that further emphasized their impending doom and death.

Outside the Muy, The Devoted had set up booths to convert citizens to their beliefs. While The Devoted's commitment to their sun, to mother planet and to nature was appealing to some, most citizens attending the truton ceremony were not interested in conversion. They had no interest in *turning their lives over to the sun*. They wanted to get off Cythera and away from their sun. They came to the Muy, hoping to hear their names called in the lottery.

As a recipient of trutons, Dekayb was able to bypass the crowds outside and enter through a special gate. She came by herself, which was fine with her. Dekayb found solace in observing others. She was more interested in witnessing the events taking place than to participate in the ceremony.

Lila could have avoided the large crowds too. She didn't. She was covering the truton ceremony and the lottery for *The Word*. Lila wanted to immerse herself in the event. She mingled outside the Muy with The Devoted before entering through the credentialed entrance.

Wickem and Tatalc arrived together and entered through a door reserved for officials and dignitaries. This was Wickem's first public appearance since the debate, and Tatalc worried how his father might react. Tatalc questioned whether Wickem was stable enough to attend. But with Dekayb as an honored guest, Tatalc understood why his father should be there.

Dafur and Lij did not attend. They were invited as

dignitaries and would have been able to avoid the crowds. They wanted to be with each other, away from everyone and everything representing the end of Cythera. They would not waste any more of the precious time they had together.

Dafur offered to let Rigby go in his place. Rigby declined, saying he would rather have his toes skinned by sabrefish than have to sit through another long, crowded event at The Muy.

At the scheduled time the lights dimmed to darkness in The Muy. The inside of the event center was dark except for small strings of light sneaking from behind the curtains that separated the arena from the access ramps outside.

Boom! Boom! Boom! A loud drumbeat echoed throughout the arena. It started out slow and then became faster and faster. The crowd began to cheer louder and louder. Then the drumbeat stopped and the crowd quieted.

A bright spotlight appeared on the stage at the end of the floor of the arena and an elderly man wearing a white vest emerged. Taking his place under the light, he said, "I am Tong." Every citizen knew of Tong. He was one of the oldest living Cytherans and held more trutons than any other citizen alive. "It is with great honor that I have been asked to lead *The Call* at this our final truton ceremony. Please stand and join me." Tong led the crowd in the patriotic chant and exited the stage.

The commencement began with a performance telling the story of the importance of trutons and what they had come to mean over the generations. Small children, too young to have earned their first trutons, paraded around the stage. They sang and danced, unaware they would never receive trutons of their own. Their performance concluded with the promise that trutons earned in this life would be judged in the after life. Not every citizen believed this but it helped bring peace to those who did.

One by one, recipients were called on stage to receive their acknowledgements. As was customary, each recipient received applause, the intensity of which was dictated by how many friends they had in attendance. It was a slow process, but it was tradition. A tradition every citizen accepted. When Dekayb's name was called Wickem stood and cheered. She had meant so much to Wickem. He loved her.

***

In the ventilation room below the arena floor Frodd and Pesi could hear the names announced for the truton ceremony. They had both received trutons in the past and were familiar with the ceremonial process.

They had debated when would be the best time to set off their explosives. Originally they thought they would set off the explosives during *The Call* but they decided that would be defamation. They were patriots too— the real patriots.

They decided to have the bomb explode after the lottery concluded. *Let the names be announced. Let the sheep have a moment of joy and then we will kill them.* When the truton ceremony ended Frodd and Pesi would start the timer.

***

As the final recipients' names were called, the crowd became restless. It was almost time for the lottery.

By now every citizen was well versed in the rules of eligibility. Tonight they would be announcing names for the first five vessels—the ones ready to launch. Each vessel held thirty-two passengers. The lottery would fill only thirty seats per vessel. Two seats on each vessel would be reserved, one for a trained pilot and one for a trained medic. In total, one hundred and fifty seats were available.

Because of the rule regarding associated spouses, most felt only around a hundred names would be announced. One hundred random names, one hundred and sixty total passengers. These would be the first Cytherans to set foot on the new world and rebuild civilization. Everyone was glad the truton ceremony was over and the lottery was about to begin.

***

As he heard the truton ceremony end, Frodd inserted a key into the charge box. Turning the key, he started the timer on the explosives. Frodd and Pesi smiled at each other and started walking out of The Muy.

***

The Chief of State walked onto the stage. He was holding the portfolio in which he carried his speeches. Opening his portfolio, he began to read. "Tonight is the beginning of the New Cythera. If you are selected, realize the awesome responsibility you have."

No one was really listening to his words. Every citizen was eagerly waiting for the names to be announced. Waiting for *their* name to be announced.

"Earlier today under the supervision of the League of Representatives the lottery took place. We had to draw the names this way to assure all classes of Cytherans were included." He held up a large sheet of paper, "I hold in my hand the names of those who have been selected to travel to the next planet." The Chief of State began to read the names.

***

Underneath the arena Frodd and Pesi turned down a long hallway that led safely out of The Muy. They could still hear the announcements. Suddenly Pesi stopped.

"Did you hear that?" Pesi asked Frodd.

Frodd pushed Pesi along, "Did I hear what? We have to keep moving."

"They called your name."

"My name?"

"Yes. They said Frodd of Regiowide, of Fornish descent, resides at Troner complex. That has to be you."

"That *is* me." Frodd said.

"The joke's on them." Pesi turned and continued walking towards the exit.

Frodd didn't think. He reacted.

Speeding up his pace to catch up with Pesi, he grabbed him around the neck, Frodd twisted until he heard the *pop* of Pesi's neck breaking. Frodd let Pesi's body slide to the ground then started running back to the charge box. Above him, he could hear the crowds grow louder and louder with every new name being announced.

***

"And the last citizens to be selected." The Chief waved his hands in the air to try to get the crowd to quiet down. "The last citizens are a married couple from here in Regiowide. They are listed as Transients from the university complex. Congratulations Onneln and Koyo!"

Tatalc turned to his father, "I wonder if Dafur knows them?"

"Possibly."

"For a moment I thought he was going to call Dafur and Lij's name. If anyone should be allowed to go to the next planet it should be Dafur. Wouldn't you agree Father?"

Wickem didn't answer.

**

Frodd was sprinting as fast as he could. At each corner his feet would slide and he would push his arms against the walls of the corridor to maintain his balance. The loud cheers above him had quieted, he could hear The Chief saying he was about to announce the last names, Frodd was running out of time.

As Frodd entered the room with the explosives he heard the crowd cheer. The lottery was over. He ran to the charge box and pulled out the black wire. There were seven ticks left on the timer.

Frodd fell to his knees and wiped the sweat from his forehead. He had killed his best friend because deep in his heart he knew *they* were right. Cythera was going to die. But he was going to live.

Chapter 61

The Last Conversation

No one at the truton ceremony knew how close they had come to death. They probably would have preferred the quick death of an explosion compared to the slow burning death they were about to experience.

The government had begun advising citizens to avoid being outside while the sun was out. Even the nights were becoming unbearable. Not everyone listened and those who challenged the warning were becoming sick from the heat and some were dying.

The crisis was worse in the large cities like Regiowide. The rock, concrete and roonite making up the city structures were magnets for the deadly heat. Cities sucked in heat and held it. The cities seemed to never cool down.

Nights were not only becoming hot, they were becoming dangerous. To conserve energy, many cities had to shut down electricity, even at night. And since Cythera had no moon to reflect back the light of its sun, the only glow to be seen were the random flitters of burning wax.

For those with bad intentions the darkness of the night provided the cover needed to secretly accomplish their goals. Some were after food, some were after water, and some, like Rose, had much bigger plans.

When she approached the outer fence of the facility she stopped and took her time to look around. She knew guards were somewhere but she couldn't see or hear any. It was so dark she could barely see the outline of the first hangar only a few feet on the other side of the fence.

Even at the hangars, the electricity was shut down and the security sensors were not operating. Knowing this, Rose pulled out a pair of clips and cut through the fence. After each snip she paused and listened. *Did anyone hear me? Is anyone coming?* No one heard and no one came. The task was tedious, but she eventually cut a hole large enough to slide her slender frame through.

Once inside the facility, Rose's assignment was simple —burn the place to the ground and destroy the vessels. It wouldn't take much. The ground was dry and hot and there was no water near by. If she could get a good fire burning all of the hangars and their contents would be destroyed well before any water would arrive to put the fires out.

Rose reached into her satchel and pulled out a small box. She snuck around the side and to the back of the first hangar. After every couple steps, Rose stopped and reached into the box. Using her thumb and first finger she pinched out a tiny amount of the black metallic powder and sprinkled it against the hanger.

At the back of the first hanger she thought she heard a noise. She knew she heard a noise. The guards were close, but it was too dark to see more than a few feet in front of her. She had to move on.

Rose knew from the facility map she had memorized that her next target was only about thirty steps from where she stood. When she reached the hanger, she walked along the outside and sprinkled powder from the small box she was carrying. She moved quietly but quickly from hangar to hangar, sprinkling the black metallic dust.

She made sure to save enough of the powdered accelerant for the last hangar, which was the largest and most critical to her assignment. Behind the large hanger she knelt down on one knee and poured the remainder of the contents into a small pile. At the bottom of the box was a rolled up fuse. Rose took it out and unwound it. After putting the box back in her satchel, she placed one end of the fuse into the pile of metallic dust and took a deep breath.

Rose knew she would succeed now. She would burn down all the hangars used to build the vessels and the large hangar holding the five completed vessels. The Devoted would succeed in keeping citizens from leaving Cythera. Rose lit the fuse and ran.

As soon as she started to run she heard a voice, "Who's

there? Somebody's here!" She could hear a group of guards starting to gather. She could tell by their voices they were close to the hangar she was running toward.

Relying on her instinct she turned to take a different route. She could hear them running now, trying to find her. Darkness was her ally. She ran toward the last hanger, behind which the hole in the fence waited. Once she was outside the fence they would never catch her.

Then she felt the heat and from the corner of her eye she saw the blaze that was growing fast. *Around this last corner will be the hole in the fence.* She turned the corner. The fire had grown so fast and was already burning three hangers. The entire facility was lit by the light of the flames.

Where's the hole! There's no hole in the fence! Rose realized she had lost track of where she was. She wasn't at the place in the fence where she had cut the hole and there was no time to find her exit. She leapt up and grabbed hold of the fence to climb it. Behind her she could hear the guards coming. The light of the fire was growing brighter. She could see them now. And she knew if she could see them, they could see her. She had to get out.

She stretched her arm as high as she could to reach the top of the fence. As she pulled her leg up she felt the sting of pain in her lower back. With all her strength Rose tried to place her foot into the fence but it kept sliding out. The numbness was taking over her entire body. Her muscles were no longer responding to her brain's commands. Her grip loosened and she fell to the ground.

***

Lila was awake when the call came in. She had known the call would be coming in and was expecting it.

"Lila, there was a break in at the facility where the vessels are being built." It was Lila's editor. "All of the production and storage hangers have burned to the ground. There's nothing left,"

Lila tried to act surprised, "All of the vessels have been destroyed? Who would do such a thing?"

"It was someone from The Devoted. They caught her and arrested her. I think her name is Rose."

"The Devoted?"

"Yes. The Devoted. How fast can you get to the facility to start piecing together the story?"

"I can leave right now. This is all terrible and shocking news."

"It's not all bad news though. The completed vessels are intact. They weren't there. They were secretly moved to the launch sites yesterday."

***

When Lila returned from the facility, Tatalc was sitting on her front step waiting for her.

"Tatalc, what are you doing here?"

"We need to talk. Let's go inside."

"I don't have time right now," Lila tried to explain. "I don't know if you heard about the fire at the facility, but I have a deadline. I need to write the story."

"I know about the fire. I've seen the pictures." Tatalc was adamant. "Let's go inside."

Lila and Tatalc walked into her apartment and sat down on the sofa where they had shared so many secrets. But the one secret Lila never shared, Tatalc now knew. "I saw the picture, Lila. I recognized her immediately. It was Rose. Your friend who visited while I was here."

"It was Rose, Tatalc, but I have no idea what she was doing there and why she was involved in something like this."

"I don't believe you Lila." Tatalc said. "I know you're involved. You're one of The Devoted aren't you?"

"No! What makes you think that?"

"The necklace you were wearing. It was the same as hers. Is that some type of symbol for The Devoted?"

"A necklace? This is about a necklace? I think you're starting to go crazy like your father. A necklace? You can't possibly make these types of accusations based on a necklace?" Lila put her hand on Tatalc's shoulder, he shrugged it off. "Tatalc, how long have we known each other? How long have we . . ."

"What about the box?" Tatalc interrupted.

"What box?"

"I've seen a picture of the box Rose had with her at the facility. The one she carried the accelerant in. It was the same box I saw you hand her in this room!"

Lila knew she was caught. There was no longer a reason to try and hide the truth from Tatalc. She stood up and in a loud and confrontational voice said, "You don't understand Tatalc! You would never understand. We're not meant to leave Cythera. We are Cytherans! Our sun has given us life since the beginning of time and now it's going to take it away! *This* is the natural order! *This* is the way it's supposed to happen! *This* is the way Cythera dies. This is the way we all die!"

Tatalc shouted back, "But if we can move on to another planet why wouldn't we? Why wouldn't you want to keep civilization alive?"

"It's not going to work Tatalc! The launch, the flare surfing, the landing; it's all so absurd. Our sun isn't going to power the voyage! Our sun wants us to die and we need to accept it if we want to be blessed in the afterlife! Those citizens being launched into space . . . our sun will devour them too!"

"If you feel this way then why did you help me?"

"Because that's what mother's do."

"But you're not my mother. My mother died when I was a baby."

"I know. But I should have been your mother and you should have been my son. Your father loved me first! You know he loved me first!"

"You're crazy Lila!"

"No, you're crazy Tatalc! I would have told you about The Devoted. I would have loved nothing more than to have told you, to share the truth with you, but I know you would have never listened. The only one you ever listen to is Wickem. I know he's your father but he's a liar, and he's always been a liar! He's lied to Cythera like he lied to me, and you've never been anything but his puppet!"

Without saying another word Tatalc walked out of Lila's apartment.

***

This was the last conversation Tatalc and Lila ever had.

Chapter 62

The Last Breath

Before the facility was destroyed there was still hope. Hope that even if your name wasn't drawn at the first lottery, you could be picked for a future lottery. The plan was to continue building and launching vessels, but that hope was now gone. It would take time to rebuild the facility and more time to produce additional vessels. Cythera did not have time.

Each revolution seemed twice as bad as the last. Constant. Deadly. Heat. Their sun was a hungry beast gnawing away at the carcass Cythera was becoming.

Fresh water was diminishing. The drying up of important trade and transportation routes and the continuous shutting down of electrical systems were small problems compared to lack of fresh drinking water.

All over the planet more and more Cytherans were dying of heat related causes. It was becoming impossible to keep track of the tally. Even the chosen were not spared. Of the one hundred and sixty original chosen ones, forty-three had already perished.

Death was unbiased.

***

Lij sat on the edge of the bed next to her mother and wiped a damp cloth on her forehead. That's all she could really do. In a chair next to the bed was Lij's father. He was sick too but would probably last another few turns. All Lij could do was provide comfort to her mother as she neared her last breath. "It's ok, Mother, it's ok." Lij handed the cloth to Dafur who dipped it in a small dish of water. He wrung it out and handed it back to her. "It's ok, Mother." Lij wiped her head again.

Lij's mother was barely able to speak. In a dry hoarse voice she asked, "Where are the boys? I need to see my boys."

Lij assured her, "They're on their way mother. They'll be here soon."

A few moments later Dran and Hilp entered the room. Dafur and Dran ignored each other. Dafur's resentment towards Dran wasn't important. They were all there for the same reason, to be with their mother as she passed over.

Lij left the damp cloth on her mother's forehead and raised herself off the bed and went and stood next to her father. She placed her hand on his shoulder and her father grasped it. Dran and Hilp sat down on the bed with their mother, one on each side of her.

Using the last little bit of strength that remained, Lij's mother lifted her right hand up to Hilp's cheek and her left hand up to Dran's cheek. She smiled and took her last breath.

They all wept.

After a while Hilp looked over at his father, "What do you want us to do now Father?"

"You *all* need to go." For a man close to dying his voice was still powerful and strong. "Leave her where she is. I'll be joining her soon enough."

"We can't leave her here," said Lij. "She has to have a proper Transient ending."

"We'll have our proper Transient ending soon enough." Her father scoffed. "And all of you will too if you don't leave soon. There will be other citizens waiting at the launch sites to take up the seats of those who don't show up." Her father paused to cough. It was a hard dry cough. "You all have seats. You have to take them. You have to finish what we started."

"Finish what *we started*?" Dafur didn't know what Lij's father was talking about.

Lij's father looked over at Dran, "I thought you told him. He's the husband of my daughter. You better have a place for them!"

Dran answered, "I do have a place for them and I tried to tell him but he wouldn't listen. I'm still not sure if they're going."

"Lij, my dear sweet daughter, you have to go! Please tell me you are going."

"I'm going with Dafur. Wherever he goes I will stay by his side."

Lij's father looked over at Dafur. His eyes saddened and his words were heartfelt, "Dafur, take my daughter to the new Cythera. This is my dying wish."

Dafur contemplated the thought then his conscience caught up, "But we weren't chosen in the lottery and neither were Dran or Hilp." He looked at Lij, "I don't understand how we would even be able to go? We weren't *picked* for the lottery."

Dran asked Dafur, "Do you remember asking me what all those citizens were doing at the warehouse? The ones sorting through all the papers."

Dafur answered, "Yes."

"They were organizing the records of all Cytherans eligible for the lottery."

"Why?"

"So we could file claims in the event of death."

Confused, Dafur said, "I still don't understand."

"The rules of the lottery stated that if a chosen one were to die before launch they could pass their benefit on to a citizen of their choice."

Dafur figured it out, "So you falsified claims that named you as benefactor?"

"Sort of." Dran explained. "We created multiple entities, faceless organizations. We filed a claim for every citizen selected in the lottery naming one of the organizations as the benefactor if they were to die before the launch."

"And no one noticed?"

"If you were a chosen one, you didn't notice anything. They were so elated to be chosen they didn't even bother to read the articles of their contracts. Only a handful of them submitted their own claims, superseding ours."

"How did you know so many would die before the launch?"

"We only expected a few to die. We were hoping for around ten claims. But of the forty three who died, we've made over thirty claims."

Hilp added, "If you add those to the Transients who were legitimately chosen in the lottery, over half of the travelers will be Transients. It will be impossible to hold us down in the new world. Transients will be the elite on the new Cythera!"

"And this was all your idea Dran?" Dafur expected nothing less from Dran.

"No it was mine."

"She's a smart girl, Dafur." Lij's father said. "That's why you have to save her."

Dafur looked over at Lij, "But you told me you didn't know about the plan until after the debate. You lied to me, again!"

Lij ran over to Dafur, "I'm sorry. You were pushing me and I didn't know what else to say. I'm sorry I lied to you, but you know how much I love you. And I don't have to go. I will stay with you. I promise."

Dafur was angry and confused, "You won't get away with this, I won't let you!"

"Dafur," Hilp tried to reason with him, "It's too late. Boarding for the launches starts soon. Even if you told someone, no one is going to postpone the launch. No one is going to take the time to sort through all of this. What's done is done. Come with us. I beg of you, please come with us."

Dafur couldn't believe everything he had heard. All of his ideals, all of his morals had been twisted and violated by his wife. He looked at Lij, "Did you mean what you said? Do you love me enough to go where I go? To live if I live? To die if I die?"

"I meant every word. You are the love of this life and any other life I will have. I know I've hurt you and you don't know how sorry I am. But yes, I meant it. I will stay with you. This is your decision."

Dafur looked Lij in the eyes, "I don't know what to do."

Lij gave him a soft kiss and said, "Follow your heart."

"Dafur, we're sorry. We never wanted to hurt you, but this was the only way." Dran looked back at his father, then at Hilp, and then finally at Dafur, "But we need to go and you need to decide. Do you want to live or do you want to die?"

Chapter 63

The Last Vessel

The few citizens still with the strength to travel had gathered at the five launch sites spread throughout Cythera. They knew if a chosen one didn't come, there was a chance they could be selected to fill their spot. There was mild excitement and shades of hope. It didn't last long.

Site by site, each vessel filled to capacity by the citizens with the proper credentials to board. Site by site, hope was extinguished. Every citizen knew this would be the only trip to the new planet. There would be no more vessels and no more launches. There would only be more heat and death.

***

Wickem was sitting behind the desk in his office at the family's country estate reading a book. It was an old book with tattered pages and a dark red cloth covering. Tatalc walked in and sat down in a chair across from his father. Wickem didn't raise his head from the book, "Do you remember this book?" He asked..

"Should I?"

"Maybe, maybe not."

"What is it?"

Wickem closed the book, sat it down and said, "It's the *history*."

"The history of what?"

"The history of our family, our genealogies. I used to read it to you as a child. You weren't interested in it then either."

"I'm sorry Father, I don't remember."

"Have you ever been interested in our family's history?"

"Maybe a little here and there, but I prefer not to live in the past."

"Do you prefer to think about the *future*?"

"Not really. It's too unpredictable."

"Then what are you interested in Tatalc?"

"The *moment*."

"The moment?"

"Yes, the moment. The here and now."

Wickem leaned back in his chair and laughed. He pointed back at his son, "That's *it*. I've finally figured you out. All this time I've never understood what made you so special. We all spend so much time celebrating or regretting our pasts or planning and worrying about the future that most of us never learn the secret to life."

"The secret to life?"

"It's so simple, *live into the moment*." Wickem laughed again, "But you my son, you never had to learn that. It came naturally to you, that's why you are so special."

Tatalc knew his father was crazy, "The funny thing Father, is that I've never thought myself to be special. I have no idea why citizens gravitated to me. That was never my goal."

"What was your goal then?"

Tatalc thought about it and then answered, "I don't know if I ever really had a goal. I only wanted to be a good citizen, a good son and to live into every moment."

"Well you did all those things son and I'm proud of

you."

"Thank you Father. That means a lot to me."

Wickem stood up from his chair, "I guess it's time to go?"

"It is. Tienneis has everything ready. Dekayb is there too."

"Have the other vessels launched?"

"Yes, they are about to launch. We will be the last vessel."

"Who else is going with us?"

"Tienneis is bringing a lady named Konja. She's a waitress, I think. He says she's the reason he found out about all of this *and* I don't think he has anyone else. Of course Olmsted and the rest of our staff. And there'll be a few citizens you don't know."

"Who are they?"

"Two prison guards that did me a favor, and their wives. And a few others to help with our different needs. They meet your credentials. I *hand picked* them myself."

"Did you find someone suitable?"

"I did. I'm not sure she's happy I'm taking her off of Cythera. She's one of The Devoted."

"In time, she'll thank you for saving her." Wickem figured out Tatalc was *taking* the girl who had been arrested for burning down the vessel facilities. "I know I'm asking a lot from you. But you don't have to love her. Just be a good father to her children."

"You know I would do anything for you Father."

Wickem walked out from behind his desk and over to

Tatalc. He put his arm around his son and together they started to walk out of the room.

As they were about to close the door Tatalc stopped, "Don't forget your book. We don't want to leave behind our family's history."

Wickem looked back and then nodded his head, "No, let's leave it. Let's start a new family history. But can you make me one promise."

"Anything Father."

"Will you name your first born son after our eldest forefather? The *great one* who started our family."

"Sure, what was his name?"

"Adam."

Chapter 64

The Last Moment

Dran and Hilp stood on the ramp to their vessel looking back at Dafur and Lij. They didn't cry. They had already lost their mother and said goodbye to their father, their pain could not be washed away with tears.

Dafur was still angry with Lij, but she was keeping her promise. She would stay with him on Cythera.

On the way to the launch site they had all been quiet. Even though Lij would not be going with her brothers, she wanted to be with them until the end. Dafur understood.

Dafur was also coming to the understanding behind Lij's motives. Lij was only trying to protect her family. Not only her brothers, but her entire family, every Transient that deserved a better life in the new world than the life they had lived on Cythera.

To the Transients that would help build the new civilization, Lij would be their hero. The savior that pulled them up from the bottom of society and created a new opportunity for them to live as equals. They loved her, as much as Dafur loved her.

***

"Sixty-six ticks and I have to shut the door." The pilot said to Dran and Hilp. "You have sixty-six ticks to say goodbye."

Dafur and Lij were standing on the ground at the bottom of the ramp holding hands. Dafur could feel Lij's hand compressing tighter and tighter around his. He could feel the warmth and the wetness. He could feel her shake.

Hilp smiled. "Lij, don't be sad. You have Dafur. You have love. There is nothing for you to be sad about."

"Dafur," Dran begged, "Please reconsider. There's nothing left for you here."

Dafur looked over at Lij and wondered if he was making the right decision.

"It's time." The pilot said. Then the door to the vessel started to shut.

At the last moment before the door closed, Dafur screamed out, "Wait!"

***

As the crowds watched the vessels lift off from the Thunderwells, their only relief was the gust of air created by the launch, cool air. Most had forgotten what cool air felt like and it was gone too soon. They all watched as the vessels lifted higher and higher into the air and then out of sight.

Chapter 65

The Last Generation

The vessels were built with enough propulsion energy to move themselves into the right place in front of an oncoming solar flare.

It was terrifying when the first solar flare hit. The vessels felt like they were going to tear apart. But the polymetal held its strength and the vessels were projected to their next destination in empty space to await the next flare.

The first flares were the worst. But as the vessels moved farther and farther away from the sun the intensity of the flares decreased. Flares still created a forceful impact, and it was still a terrifying experience, but after the third or forth flare passengers were accustomed to the routine.

The journey was long, longer than any citizen had imagined. There were no sunrises or sunsets to help them keep time and they lost track of how long they'd been in space.

There were no windows in the vessels and the quarters were cramped. Occasionally a pilot would invite a passenger into the cockpit to look at the monitor, this was their only view of their surroundings.

For the most part, the passengers on the different vessels were getting along. At times, an individual's patience was tested, but no one broke. Some even bonded and started making their plans for the new world.

All six vessels were safely making the journey. The five

launched by the government and the one Wickem built.

No one knew what to expect when they landed. What would the land be like? Would there be abundant water? Would there be other life forms and vegetation? No one knew.

Mostly they all hoped it wouldn't be hot.

There was one common goal they all shared—they needed to repopulate. Some were lucky; they had their spouses with them. The others, the singles, would need to find a suitable match. Some matches were made aboard the vessels, and most were satisfied with their situation.

Groups on the different vessels were also beginning to take their social shape. Some groups were already developing a communal feel. Some groups had natural leaders that others were willing to follow. And one group, without a leader, was already experiencing a minor conflict between two citizens vying for power. The social structures established on the journey would shape the colonies on the new planet.

Vessel three was the first to have a clear view of their new home.

The pilot called back into the living quarters, "Frodd come here, you're going to want to see this." Frodd had already established himself as their leader.

Frodd had to lean down as he came into the cockpit, "What is it?"

"Look at the monitor. There it is. Our new home."

"It's beautiful," Frodd said. "Look at all the blue and green. Could it really have that much water? And the white . . . is that what I think it is? I've never seen it with my own eyes before."

"And look over here." The pilot adjusted the exterior

camera.

"What's that? Is it another planet?"

"I don't know."

One by one the six vessels broke through different parts of the new planet's atmosphere. The pressure and stress of the atmosphere squeezed on the vessels and seemed more intense than the first solar flare. Then one by one, each vessel safely landed.

They opened their hatches and felt the cool fresh air. They saw the tall green growths. And those landing close to water were amazed by the water's clarity and pureness.

They had arrived. Civilization was saved. This would be the last generation of Cythera. The first people on Earth.

The First

He walked through the large front doors of the museum, down the long corridor and into a small exhibit room on the left. It laid unmoved and untouched for generations. Reaching up, he grabbed the Rugal by its long slender neck. It had been too long since he had seen or felt it.

For a moment he felt guilty, like he was stealing something. Then he realized you can't steal something that is already yours and you can't steal from those that no longer exist.

He walked out of the museum and started his long walk home.

Regiowide was empty. The stench of dead bodies baking in the sun filled the air. The city was littered with the signs of a society who tried to fight to stay alive but then lost. Every city on Cythera looked, felt and smelled the same. Even the small towns and villages in the rurals were already taking the ruined shape of a dead world.

It wouldn't be long until the entire planet would be unrecognizable. The brutal sun would continue to dry and decay everything that had ever been built. Even marvels like *The Diamond* would eventually crumble and turn to dust, even the last drops of water would dry.

Eventually Cythera would become a lifeless rock floating in the emptiness of space. There would be no traces of past life or the great civilization that had once called the planet home. When the new generations would speak of Cythera they would only know her as a dead planet that was once beautiful – they would call her Venus.

THE FIRST

***

When he reached the entrance to the caves he turned around to take one more look at Cythera. It was the same view he had experienced the first time he visited the planet. His intention was never to visit Cythera so soon, but he had to because those boys had found the artifact. The civilization of that age wouldn't have understood the warning. There was too much risk. He did what he could to retrieve the artifact, but failed to get it back from the boys.

He walked into the dark cave and weaved through the network of tunnels without the help of light. He knew the path to his destination. He thought about this second visit to Cythera and the time spent in the basement of the museum looking for the Rugal. That was the name the Cytherans gave it – *The Rugal*. He had long before named the artifact after the original generation of humanity and had always called it *The First*. But labels and names were not important. He knew he had been lucky that Emot could translate the message. It made his task easier. It had been the right time to reveal the prophecy.

His most recent visit, this one, was the hardest. It was always hard to watch a civilization die, to watch the children die. This civilization was a good one, the best one yet. Cythera was the fifth planet he had watched die, but also the fifth civilization he had saved. *They've become better each time* he thought to himself. He didn't know why that was, but he was eager to see what Earth would become.

He was confident people had, by now, arrived safely on Earth to rebuild civilization. He also knew that eventually the sun would grow too large for Earth. It was only a matter of time before he would have to visit Earth and once again save the children.

287

He turned a dark corner and began to see the light bend toward him. He took several more steps and was in the large cavern. Rigby approached the glowing Feber and walked into the light.

-    *the end*

*for more information about **THE FIRST** and the author visit:*

www.micahmemorypublishing.com